NIC TATANO

I've always been a writer of some sort, having spent my career working as a reporter, anchor or producer in television news. Fiction is a lot more fun, since you don't have to deal with those pesky things known as facts.

I spent fifteen years as a television news reporter and anchor. My work has taken me from the floors of the Democratic and Republican National Conventions to Ground Zero in New York to Jay Leno's backyard. My stories have been seen on NBC, ABC and CNN. I still work as a freelance network field producer for FOX, NBC, CBS and ABC.

I grew up in the New York City metropolitan area and now live on the Gulf Coast where I will never shovel snow again. I'm happily married to a math teacher and we share our wonderful home with our tortoiseshell tabby cat, Gypsy.

Follow me on Twitter @NicTatano.

The Wing Girl

NIC TATANO

A division of HarperCollins*Publishers*
www.harpercollins.co.uk

Harper*Impulse* an imprint of
HarperCollins*Publishers Ltd*
77–85 Fulham Palace Road
Hammersmith, London W6 8JB

www.harpercollins.co.uk

A Paperback Original 2014

First published in Great Britain in ebook format as *Wing Girl* by HarperImpulse 2013

Copyright © Nic Tatano 2014

Cover Images © Shutterstock.com

Nic Tatano asserts the moral right to
be identified as the author of this work

A catalogue record for this book
is available from the British Library

ISBN: 9780007559787

This novel is entirely a work of fiction.
The names, characters and incidents portrayed in it are
the work of the author's imagination. Any resemblance to
actual persons, living or dead, events or localities is
entirely coincidental.

Automatically produced by Atomik ePublisher from Easypress

For Myra... who makes everything beautiful.

And Steve... the brother I never had.

CHAPTER ONE

"Dating you would be like dating Mike Wallace," said the dark-haired hunk, who could easily be considered for a certain magazine's Most Beautiful People issue.

Before you get the wrong idea about that comment, let me say that I do not in any way, shape or form physically resemble the legendary reporter. I'm actually a slender redhead with emerald-green eyes, classic high cheekbones with a constellation of freckles, little dimples when I smile, and a whiskey voice that sounds like it lives in a smoky bar and channels Demi Moore. Tonight it's all packaged in a brown-paper wrapper consisting of a bulky sweater and pants, while my hair is up (as it always is) in a tight bun and my eyes peer through Coke-bottle glasses. Gotta maintain the journalistic credibility. If you wanna be taken seriously as a woman in my business, you can't play the glamour card.

But as for the Mike Wallace comment, I am the city's most recognizable and feared investigative reporter who channels the *60 Minutes* icon every chance I get.

So I sorta get what the guy's saying, but then again I don't. Does he mean that he admires my work as much as that of the broadcasting legend? Or that when he kisses me he'll be thinking of an eighty-year-old guy who's dead?

So I said, "I'm not sure how to take that."

He leaned forward and I felt his knee gently brush mine, sending a subtle jolt of electricity through my body. "Oh, it's a compliment," he said with a smile. "I mean, everyone knows you're the best reporter in town."

I tried to hold back a smile but couldn't as I looked at this Greek god with the chiseled jawline sitting before me in a dark-gray windowpane suit. The rest of the bar faded to grayscale as he provided the only color in the room. His deep-blue eyes became beacons as I caught a faint whiff of Fendi cologne. A subliminal daydream whipped through my mind and I saw myself being carried to the bedroom by those broad shoulders, my legs wrapped around his slim hips.

However, given enough ointment, there's always a fly.

"But..." he said.

Oh shit, here it comes.

Again.

"I just know if I asked you out you'd probably run a background check on me and unearth any skeletons I have in my closet. And I would never be able to lie to you. I mean, no one lies to Belinda Carson and gets away with it."

Investigative reporter red flag alert. "Does that mean you lie to all the women you date?"

"I didn't say that—"

I leaned forward, eyes narrowed. "But you *have* lied to women before or you wouldn't have brought it up."

"Why do you think that?"

"Your previous statement implies that you have been less than truthful with previous girlfriends. What aren't you telling me?"

He looked to one side, flashed a crooked smile. "Geez, lady, turn it off."

"Turn off what?"

"The investigative reporter thing. What's next, hot lights and thumb screws?" He downed the rest of his drink and stood up. "Look, I don't think this is gonna work. It was nice meeting you,

Belinda." He shook his head and smiled. "Wait till I tell the guys at the office I got interrogated by the Brass Cupcake."

Yeah, that's my nickname in the Big Apple, courtesy of those clever headline writers at *The Post*. Great for journalism, a killer when trying to meet men.

The colors returned to normal in the trendy watering hole. Half the crowd leaned against the brass rail running the length of the dark oak bar, while the Tiffany lamps above the small round tables provided subdued light to the other half. My best friend Ariel Baymont slid her tall, willowy frame into the next chair and quickly noticed the previously occupied seat at our table was now empty. "What happened to the total package who was here five minutes ago?"

I exhaled, shook my head and looked down into my nearly empty glass.

"You did it again, didn't you?"

"Yeah," I muttered, then slugged down the remainder of my rum concoction.

"Trying to drown your sorrows?"

"I would, but the little bastards have learned how to swim."

She wrapped her arm around my shoulders and I leaned my head on hers. "Aw, sweetie, we're going to have to work on your bedside manner."

"You're assuming a man has been remotely close to my bed."

She pulled back and gave me a soulful look with her ice-blue eyes. "Well, all is not lost. We'll try again this weekend. Anyway, the cute guy who was hitting on me earlier wants to *go someplace where we can talk*."

"So you're taking him home."

She shrugged, then started to twirl her honey-blonde hair with one finger. "We can talk there as well as anyplace."

I raised one eyebrow. "Talk. Right."

"You know, I can see why you're such a good reporter. You really are a human lie detector."

"Yeah, I might as well change my name to Polly Graph."

"Cute. Anyway, we still on for Saturday night?"

"Thanks to my aforementioned bedside manner, my dance card is clear."

She leaned over and kissed me on the side of the head. "Great. I'll see you then. Hang in there, Wing Girl."

***

Before we go any farther, I should explain the "Wing Girl" concept and how it applies to me, since that is my current after-hours nickname.

As most women know, a good-looking guy will often cruise the bars with a "wing man" at his side, the theory being that men in pairs can separate women in mismatched pairs (one attractive, one not), using a divide and conquer tactic designed to liberate the good-looking woman from the skank. This presumes that the hot girl will not take off and leave her unattractive friend to fend for herself. The wing man swoops in like a dog after a pork chop and takes one for the team, chatting up the skank while his friend moves in on aforementioned hottie, who no longer feels obligated to keep her homely friend company and is thereby freed to engage in extracurricular activities.

It's a little different for those without a Y chromosome, and totally opposite in my case. Here's the deal. When it comes to attracting the opposite sex, I am to my friends what a puppy is to a single guy.

Ariel and my circle of friends have dubbed me "Wing Girl" because I end up taking one for the team every time. However, the strategy my friends use is backwards. Since I am a very recogniz-able member of the media, it's a case of moths, meet flame. I'm not sure if it's the fame thing or the challenge of possibly nailing the Brass Cupcake, but it works, drawing in attractive men who I naturally turn off, leaving my friends with very delectable leftovers. My friends always end up with positive results while I finish the evening without so much as a request for a phone number. My Wing Girl moniker started out as a term of endearment, something fun, but lately it's beginning to wear thin.

I don't mean to repel men like a Star Trek force field. Really, I don't. But as I approach the big three-oh, I'm beginning to wonder if I'll ever be able to drop my "prosecutor from hell" persona when I'm off the clock. And I really want to. Before that other clock, the biological one that's ticking louder every day, strikes twelve.

Because, and don't ever tell my boss this, beneath the brass lies a real cupcake looking for her perfect icing.

***

"Cupcake, you really nailed the Senator last night."

My boss, the grizzled Harry Coyne, whose face is so wrinkled it would tie up a dry cleaner for a day, smiled as I took a seat at the conference room table for the morning meeting, his daily sit-down with the dozen reporters on the dayside staff.

"Thanks," I said.

Now, before we get the PC police involved in this, let me explain a little about newsroom language. We usually call each other by last names or, in my case, nicknames. And you might think that a man calling a woman "Cupcake" in the office would violate a litany of sexual harassment laws and cause thousands of dollars of "emotional stress" to the recipient of said nickname. But since I'm cool with it and the rest of the staff knows it, it's not a big deal.

Of course, the first time Harry called me Cupcake, the human resources troll happened to be within earshot and her harassment-sniffing dogs confirmed that this improper term of endearment was, in fact, being used by men in the newsroom. I explained to her that it originated in *The Post*, we all thought it was funny (as well as dead-on appropriate), I actually liked the nickname, and considered it a compliment. The troll, a two hundred pound fire-plug, actually typed up a release form, which I had to sign saying I approved of the term and would not sue the station nor hold anyone accountable should I suddenly decide to become offended. That night after the troll went home, one of our photographers went down to her office with a chisel and added the prefix "In" to the "Human Resources" nameplate outside her door. Now she had the nickname "Inhuman Resources," which spread through the station like wildfire and stuck like superglue.

Back to the original comment, in which Harry highlighted the fact that I nailed the Senator. While this might have meant something sexual had I been a Washington, DC intern in a blue dress, the term "nailed" in the news business meant that I exposed some serious shit about a politician, in this case a New York State Senator.

And you have to understand where Harry's coming from. He broke into the business in the dinosaur age, when smoke-filled newsrooms were populated by nothing but men and the only women in the building were secretaries. When the women's movement was making inroads into the biz, the men lived by the mantra "keep the broads out of broadcasting" as they fought an unsuccessful battle. Harry is still old-school on the subject of equality in the television news industry, thinking most women are simply eye candy, but he loves me because he says I'm "one of the guys."

You beginning to see my problem?

Harry just turned sixty, and doesn't look a day over seventy-five. The shock of white hair and the closely cropped matching beard doesn't help. His gray eyes are framed by a flock of crow's feet. He's short and stocky, maybe five-six, with a bay window from too many trips to the tavern across the street for a cold one after the newscast. The trademark red suspenders harken back to a bygone era. He paced around the glassed-in conference room channeling DeNiro with that baseball bat in *The Untouchables*, whacking a ruler into his hand as he recapped the previous newscast. "Yessir, damn fine reporting." Tap, tap, tap. He stopped behind the reporter who would be this morning's victim, fortyish general assignment reporter Bob Evanson, then rested the ruler on the man's shoulder like he was knighting the guy. "She woulda done a better job on *your* piece last night."

Evanson looked over his shoulder as fear crept into his dark eyes. (Evanson, it should be noted, is a product of Catholic school and therefore has a genetic fear of rulers.) "All the facts checked out, Harry. What was wrong with it?" he asked, voice cracking.

"Oh, nothing was *wrong* with it," said Harry, continuing his parade around the room. "You didn't go for the kill shot. You had the guy and you let him off with a slap on the wrist. Softball questions." Tap, tap, tap. "Just lob the damn things over the plate like it's a beer league."

"I thought my questions were valid."

"Yeah, they were valid, but soft. The Cupcake woulda nailed his ass to the wall and lit up a cigarette afterwards on the set." (Interesting visual that would no doubt land me on the front page of *The Post*.) He stopped, then turned to face the reporter. "You know the difference between you and her, Bob?" He pointed the ruler at Bob, then me.

Evanson rolled his eyes and exhaled audibly. "No, Harry. What?"

"You're too nice. You never go for the jugular. What makes her a great reporter is that she's a bulldog with absolutely no social skills."

My head jerked back like I was hit with a blow dart.

"Ouch," said feature reporter Stan Harvey, who was sitting next to me. "That one left a mark."

Harry glanced at me with his best attempt at an apologetic look. "No offense, Cupcake."

"None taken," I said, lying through my slightly quivering lips.

And for the first time in my eight years in the business, I almost showed emotion.

Almost.

But I felt it.

CHAPTER TWO

Most interventions are surprises, hitting the target when he or she least expects it. In most cases, the focus is on someone with a drug or alcohol problem. Friends get together and confront the person, hopefully forcing that person to take action and deal with the problem.

So I was surprised when I walked into Ariel's impeccably decorated apartment on Saturday afternoon and found her and my two other closest friends sitting in a circle next to a whiteboard on an easel. It kinda stuck out amidst all the antique furniture.

"Let me guess," I said. "This is either an Amway meeting or you haven't noticed this whiteboard clashes with your decor."

"Wing Girl, we need to talk," said Ariel, patting the empty space on the dark-brown leather couch next to her.

"What the hell is going on?" I asked.

"It's an intuhvention," said Roxanne Falcone, the short but buxom raven-haired sister from Brooklyn I never had.

"I don't have a drinking problem," I said.

"No, you have a *man* problem," said Serena Dash, the tall, doe-eyed brunette lawyer who, despite average looks, manages to spend her nights looking at more ceilings than Michelangelo.

My jaw hung open. "So, what are you guys gonna do, list my bad qualities on the board?"

"No, sweetie," said Ariel. "We're taking you to charm school."

My face tightened. "Charm school? Are you implying I am without charm?"

All three looked away from me, at each other, then down at the hardwood floor.

And then I heard Harry's voice in my head. *Absolutely no social skills.*

"I've had boyfriends in the past," I said, in what I knew was a lame attempt at defending said charm.

Roxanne rolled her eyes. "Again with the college professuh."

"He was nice," I said.

"He was an illegal alien who wanted to marry you for a green card," said Ariel. "And don't even bring up that fling with the student in that career day class you taught who just wanted a job at your station."

I felt my lip quivering. Serena noticed, got up, put her arms around me and gave me a strong hug. My eyes narrowed as I bit my lower lip, trying to keep my emotions in check.

Serena pulled back and looked at me. "Let it out, Wing Girl. For once, just let it out."

"The Brass Cupcake doesn't cry," I said, standing up straight, arms folded. "There's no crying in news."

"Great, now she's channeling Tom Hanks," said Roxanne.

"You're not an investigative reporter when you're with us," said Ariel. "You're our dear friend, who we know has a huge heart. The problem is, no man can see it. It's locked away in some journalism vault by this Brass Cupcake alter ego who thinks that if she lets it out her career will dive headfirst into the shitter."

"Let it out," said Roxanne.

"There's nothing to let out!"

"We want you to be happy," said Ariel.

"I *am* happy," I said. "My career—"

"With your *life*! Ariel got up and tapped me on the head with one knuckle. "Hello! McFly! There's more to life than work."

Serena took me by one hand and led me to the couch. "Honey, if you keep going the way you're going you'll end up like one of those crazy cat ladies."

I sat down on the soft leather and let out an audible exhale. I knew they were right. I repelled men. And I did like cats an awful lot. "Fine," I said. "So what's the deal with this charm school?"

"First," said Ariel, as she moved to the white board and grabbed a magic marker, "we're going to start with what you're looking for in a man."

"Pffft. I'll settle for breathing at this point," I said.

"Be serious," said Serena.

"Give us the qualities you're looking for," said Ariel.

***

Ten minutes later we all looked at the very long list compiled on the board. Bright sunshine spilled through the large window, illuminating the room but shedding no light on my problem.

Serena furrowed her brow. "Guys, I'm not sure he exists."

"Fuhgeddaboudit," said Roxanne. "The only guys left are the Pope and Tim Tebow."

I shrugged. "So I have high standards."

"You have *unreal* standards," said Ariel. "Your problem is that you've spent your life going after politicians who are supposed to be squeaky clean, and you expect the men you date to be that way. Everyone has baggage. Some have a carry-on, others have more than a trophy wife on a European vacation."

"Fine," I said. "So I need to lower my standards."

"You don't have to lower them," said Serena, "you just have to learn to accept the fact that there is no one out there with every single quality you want."

I nodded, realizing they were right. "Okay. So I become more open minded about men. There, we're done. Let's go to dinner."

"Not so fast," said Ariel. "And not dressed like that. You're not going out in those outfits anymore."

I looked down at my clothes, a pair of red and black plaid slacks and a bulky purple sweater. "What's wrong with this?"

"It's fine if you wanna pick up a guy at Home Depot," said Roxanne.

"I always attract men," I said. "That's why you call me Wing Girl."

"The Brass Cupcake attracts men," said Serena. "Belinda needs to learn how to keep them."

"Really?" said Ariel. "Pants and flats for a Saturday night?"

"They're comfortable," I said.

"Men want heels and skirts," said Serena. "We know you've got great legs under there. We've been to the beach with you."

"And the hair," said Roxanne, rolling her eyes as she pointed at my head.

"What?" I asked.

"The bun is done," she said.

"You're blessed with that beautiful red and you tie it up in a bun of steel," said Ariel. "Meanwhile, the glasses have got to go. We need to see that green."

"I can't see without glasses."

"As a reporter you should know there's been a fabulous new invention called contact lenses," said Serena. "Maybe you've read about it."

"So you're giving me a total makeover."

"Yep," said Ariel.

"Right now?"

***

As my friends took inventory in my two bedroom closets, I wasn't sure how this makeover thing was gonna come out. I mean, I've got three women who are all very different and the combined advice might result in something out of a horror movie.

Ariel is my oldest and closest friend. She's a tall drink of water from a wealthy section of Connecticut who grew up with every privilege and ran off the trust fund reservation by actually having a career. The horror! A Madison Avenue copywriter, Ariel is clever at turning a phrase whether she has to pitch cars or feminine hygiene products. She can also weave a tapestry of words into a blanket under which a man becomes powerless.

Always impeccably dressed in classic clothes and a strand of pearls, she's the proverbial blue-eyed blonde with the high cheek-bones, a sharp nose and full lips. Add her customary four-inch heels to the five-ten frame, and you've got a girl who could prob-ably be a model if she wanted to.

Serena is an attorney from California who learned early on that male members of a jury can often be distracted by a lawyer who dresses as if she needs a bail bondsman and a public defender. Her short hemlines are legendary in New York courtrooms, as she's known for "skirting the issues" when it comes to closing arguments.

She's not a stunner by any means, but she's kinda pretty and makes the most of what she's got. In a sea of New York women obsessed with black, Serena has a closet full of red, so she always stands out. Her big, shoulder-length hair harkens back to the eighties, framing an angular face and a cute pug nose. She's got these devilish hazel eyes that always make her look like she's up to something. Probably because she is, either in the courtroom, bedroom, or both.

Serena loves the law so much she carries that "lawyer-talk" out of the courtroom and often works it into everyday conversations. (I've picked up a little myself, as I think said style of speaking sounds cool.) But despite the fact she uses her wardrobe as a weapon during trials, she's an excellent lawyer and could easily win her cases dressed in burlap.

Roxanne is my gum-snapping Sicilian friend from Brooklyn who's a hairstylist, or, as she calls it, "hairdressuh." But she's not just any salon gal; she's sought far and wide by celebrities and the wealthy, who no doubt endure her wicked accent because she's a miracle worker with scissors and a comb. She's blessed with natural wavy hair, big light-green eyes and a great rack. Beneath the Brooklyn stereotype lies a girl with an IQ of about 160 who actually has a degree from Wharton but ditched the whole corporate thing for a career with a styling brush. She makes more money with her salon than she ever could in a boardroom.

She's about five-three, making her the shortest of our group, but the one you'd want in a foxhole because Roxanne doesn't take shit from anybody. She's a tight package: tight jeans, tight skirts, tight tops, tight walk with no wasted motion. You know the type. Also has the quickest wit, and can cut a man down to size with a comment sharp enough to slice a stale bagel.

They made me get up on my kitchen step-stool like it's some pedestal and then walked around me looking at the total package.

"Let's start at the top. The hair's comin' down," said Roxanne, who reached up on her tiptoes to unleash the bun.

I leaned away. "I like my hair up."

"Men like it down," she said, grabbing my bun and struggling to pull the hairpin out of the Gordian Knot. "Geez, you could bounce quarters off this thing." My strawberry locks dropped, hitting my shoulders. Roxanne ran her fingers through it. "Gawd, it's like straw. But I can work with this. Women would kill for this color, you know."

"They can get it out of a bottle," I said.

"Yeah, but the carpet won't match the drapes," said Roxanne, with a wicked grin.

Serena had been rummaging through one of my closets. "Where the hell are your heels?"

"I don't have any," I said. "I'm five-five, that's tall enough."

"Please tell me you didn't just say that," she said. "Is it therefore your contention that you do not own one single pair?"

"Have you ever seen me in heels?"

She sat down on the floor facing me. "Now that I think about it, no. Do you even know how to walk in them?"

"I tried a pair in high school. Made my feet hurt."

"What size are you?"

"Six. Narrow."

"I'm a nine. Rox?"

"Sorry," said Roxanne. "I got pancake flippers for feet."

"Ariel?"

"Eight."

"So much for tonight." She yelled for Ariel, who was going through my other walk-in closet. "What's the dress situation?"

Ariel stuck her head out of the closet and shook her head. "Nada. No dresses or skirts. Not even a pair of shorts except for some old ones that look like they lost a battle with a spray can and a weed whacker."

"Those are my cleaning shorts," I said.

"I'm assuming you clean this room once a year, whether it needs it or not," said Ariel. "You know, a man would find this *boudoir* very inviting."

I looked around my bedroom and took in the unmade bed, pile of clothes thrown on the floor and a potato chip bag which shared the night stand with a couple of empty yogurt containers. "Fine, I'll get a cleaning service."

"A snow shovel would be quicker," said Roxanne.

"Seriously," said Serena. "You don't have a single skirt?"

"What can I say, I like pants."

"Do you even *bother* to shave your legs?" asked Ariel, ducking back into the closet.

"Of course," I said, then shrugged. "Well, not every day."

"So," said Roxanne, "besides the hair, what else is on the to-do list?"

Serena was making notes on a legal pad. "You ever try contacts?"

I nodded. "I had them in high school."

"Did you like them?"

"Yeah, but they were a pain to clean all the time, so I went back to glasses."

"Figures," said Serena, who made a check mark. "After the contacts, we need shoes and an entire new wardrobe."

"Excuse me?" I said.

"I'm starting a pile for Goodwill," yelled Ariel, still in my closet. "Geez, it looks like Hillary Clinton lives in here."

I saw one of my favorite pantsuits fly out of the closet. "Hey!"

"Shaddup and take your medicine," said Roxanne. "Meanwhile, put your hair back up."

"I thought you said men like it down?"

"They do, but I'll need half a day to fix that mess and our dinner reservations are in an hour."

I stepped off the stool. "So, I'm deemed *okay* to be seen in public with you guys this evening? I won't *embarrass* you?"

Serena got off the floor and gave me the once over. "It will have to do, but we are going to change one thing tonight."

"What's that?" I asked, folding my arms. "I've apparently got no shoes, no clothes, my hair is a toxic waste dump and I can't ditch my glasses or I'll end up going home with someone who looks like Alan Greenspan."

"That, right there. Your attitude," said Serena. "Tonight, charm school begins."

CHAPTER THREE

His eyes locked on me like a laser from across the room. Tall, well built, thick black hair and dark eyes to match. Rugged face, nice smile, dimples running the length of his cheeks. Probably about my age. Dark slacks, starched white French-cuffed shirt with gold links, red tie with a perfect dimple in the knot. Shoes shining like mirrors, something my late father always told me to notice. Looks like he stepped off a wedding cake.

Another "total package" as Ariel would say. Can't say I'd argue.

He started weaving his way through the bar traffic and headed for the chair next to me that was left purposely empty by my friends.

"Remember what we talked about, Wing Girl," said Serena.

I nodded, downed a bit of wine, and smiled as he reached the table.

He placed his hands on the back of the empty chair, obviously waiting for permission to sit. Good. Polite. Looked right at me. Big smile. "You're the girl on TV."

"*Woman* on TV," I said. Serena jabbed an elbow into my ribs. "Ow."

"Right," he said. "You did that great story the other night on the State Senator. Nice that we have people like you to keep politicians honest."

"They're all a bunch of scum. Next week—" I was interrupted by another elbow. "I mean, thank you, I appreciate the compliment."

Ariel reached one long leg under the table and pushed the empty chair out a bit. "Maybe our new friend would like to join us."

"Uh, right," I said.

"Thanks," he said, sitting down. "I'm Vincent Martino."

"Belinda Carson," I said.

"Yeah, I know." Serena, Ariel and Roxanne introduced themselves since I'd forgotten to do it, my mind too busy going over the directives they'd given me.

Serena widened her eyes as she looked at me and gave me a gentle kick under the table. *Say something. Anything.* "So, uh... I'm sorry, what did you say your name was?"

The guy smiled. "That's okay. Vincent." Roxanne rolled her eyes then threw down the rest of her drink.

"Right, Vincent." I remembered the orders I'd been given. Ask him about himself. Nothing too serious. "So, Vincent... are you married?"

"*Madonne*," said Roxanne, as the man's face tightened.

"No," said Vincent, who looked at me as if I were a space alien. "Did you think I'm some married guy out cheating on his wife?"

"Uh, no, I was... you know... just making conversation."

Serena snorted, stifling a laugh.

"That's one hell of a pick-up line," he said.

"Sorry." My pulse spiked as the checklist in my head got jumbled. My armpits grew damp. "Do you... uh... what do you do?" I smiled and exhaled. That was pretty safe.

"I work on Wall Street."

"So, you work with some shady characters."

The man shook his head and turned toward Roxanne. "Geez, Rox."

I furrowed my brow. "What's going on?"

"Vincent's my cousin," said Roxanne, cocking her head toward him. "I asked him to be our test subject tonight."

"So you weren't really going to hit on me?" I asked.

"I *did* hit on you. At least I was trying to. I would have even taken you out if we'd hit it off because Rox said you're such a great person. They weren't going to tell you it was a set-up if things went well, but..."

"So, Vincent," said Serena, who took out a legal pad and put it on the table. She clicked her pen in the air. "If you wouldn't mind giving us your first impressions for the record."

He looked at me, his eyes seemingly asking for permission. "What the hell, go ahead," I said.

"Would be nice if she remembered my name ten seconds after I told her," said Vincent, who turned to face Serena. "And asking me if I'm married? Seriously? I would have beat my feet right after that one." He turned back to me. "Listen Belinda, no offense, but Rox said you guys needed a man's point of view on your, you know, dateability."

I shrugged and looked down. "I'm not offended. I appreciate your input. Keep going. Fire away, I'm a big girl."

"You sure?"

"Hey, I take on politicians all the time. I'm not afraid of anything. Don't hold back."

"Ohhhh-kaaaay," he said, then exhaled and paused a moment. "Well, here goes. You're not approachable."

Ouch.

"People come up to me all the time."

"Because you're a celebrity," said Ariel.

"I meant you're not approachable as a potential date," said Vincent.

"Fine," I said, looking at Vincent, eyes narrowing into Brass Cupcake mode. "Tell me why I'm unapproachable."

Vincent leaned forward on his forearms. Usually they lean back when the death stare makes its first appearance. Interesting. "Well, first I call you a girl and you correct me, so I think you're some militant feminist, which I and most men hate. Then the marriage question, which was beyond weird. Along with your somewhat bizarre conversational skills, it's the overall look. The hair in a tight bun. You're sitting there on your hands, all hunched up. And the outfit."

My face tightened. "What's wrong with the outfit?"

"Rox said you're hot and you look like a librarian. The bulky sweater, baggy pants, thick glasses. Those shoes look like you're going hiking. You look like you want to be anywhere but here. There's probably a serious babe under all that but I can't be sure."

He reached across the table toward me but I pulled back and put up a hand. "Whoa!"

"Relax, would you?" he said. Serena grabbed my hand and pulled it down.

He reached toward my face and gently removed my glasses. "Wow," he said.

"What?" I asked, as my view of Vincent morphed into a Monet painting.

"You've got spectacular eyes. I mean, they're like emeralds, such a vivid green. You could do eye makeup commercials."

"If she actually wore makeup outside the studio," said Roxanne, as I snatched my glasses back from him and put them on.

"Look, Belinda. Roxanne tells me you're a beautiful girl with a big heart, but as a man looking for a date I would have no idea if any of that's true. If you weren't famous I doubt if any man would come up to you, and if anyone did he wouldn't stay long."

I bit my lower lip and felt my eyes well up. No! This wasn't happening! A man cannot make the Brass Cupcake cry! "I'd like you to leave now," I said softly.

"Hey, I'm sorry, that was a bit harsh, but you told me not to hold back—"

"Just! Go!"

Vincent put up his hands in surrender. He got up, kissed Roxanne on the side of the head. "Thanks, cuz," she said, patting him on the shoulder. He shot me an apologetic look with sad eyes, but I turned away. He headed for the door.

"So," I said, when he was out of earshot. "Whose brilliant idea was that?"

"Mea culpa," said Serena, putting her wrists out as if she were waiting to be handcuffed. "I plead no contest."

"And the rest of you were okay with it?"

"We thought it was a great idea," said Ariel.

"A great idea? Having some guy insult me like that?"

"We already know you need help," said Serena. "But we really needed a man's opinion. Rox said she knew her cousin would help out, and you two might actually hit it off."

"Vincent was just doin' what I asked. You'd like him if you took the time to know him. He's really a great guy."

"Yeah, a regular Mr Wonderful," I said. "He's just so... so..."

"Honest?" said Roxanne.

"And suppose I'd really liked him? It wasn't real."

"It might have been if you'd given him a chance," said Roxanne.

"You're a reporter," said Serena, clicking her pen again. "Did you learn anything from that interview?"

I played with my wine glass, swirled what was left before I downed the whole thing. "Yeah, you all think I'm a total loser."

Ariel wrapped one arm around my shoulder. "You're a winner, Wing Girl, and tomorrow we're going to start showing the world."

***

Most people go to church on Sunday mornings. Since sermons have bored the hell out of me since I was a little girl and I am ruled by Catholic guilt, I donate my Sunday mornings to a good cause. I figure it's better than sitting in a rock-hard pew like a member of the parish undead.

As mentioned before, I love cats. So I help out at the local cat rescue shelter every weekend for a few hours, play with my furry friends and deal with things like cat food and furballs.

Cats don't judge me, especially shelter cats. They don't have homes yet, so they appreciate any attention they can get.

And after last night, I felt the same way.

"Morning Belinda," said a cheery Diane as I opened the door to the shelter, jingling the little brass bell hanging off the top. She's the petite blonde middle-aged millionaire animal lover who runs the place, often working weekends since more kitties get adopted on those days.

"Hey, Diane. How'd the week go?"

"Pretty good. Two in, five out. Somebody even took that huge tabby."

"Great," I said, heading toward the back of the building where the kitties lived. "Jabba the Cat was eating us out of house and home."

"Oh, hey, we've got a new volunteer who started today. He's just about to leave so go introduce yourself. Name's Scott. Cute guy, Belinda." Her voice went up as she said my name, like a suggestion hanging in the air.

Like I've got a shot. I'm wearing old torn jeans, a ratty New York Giants sweatshirt with frayed cuffs, didn't sleep a lick last night and have a full set of Samsonite under my eyes.

Not that it would make any difference if I were dressed for a ball. I'm *unapproachable*, remember?

I headed down the long mauve hallway to the back and heard a man's soothing voice float around the corner.

"Oh, yeah, there it is. That's the spot. Ooooh, you like it when I rub you like that, don't you?"

Sounded like some dialogue from a porn movie, but I realized it was a man talking to a cat. If only one would talk to me that way. *"Hey, baby, come home with me and I'll make you purr..."*

I turned the corner into the shelter area and saw a man sprawled on the floor, scratching the belly of a purring Siamese who was obviously in cat nirvana. The man looked up at me and smiled.

"Hey."

"Hi. I see you've made a friend."

"Yeah, she's a sweet cat." He got up off the floor, brushed off the cat hair and extended his hand. "I'm Scott."

I shook it. "Belinda."

He didn't have what I call *the look*. The one that tells me he recognizes me from television, the one Wing Girl gets when we're out on the town. The smile looked sincere. He was maybe five-ten, slender with broad shoulders, tousled brown hair, deep-set hazel eyes. Classic anchorman's jaw with a little cleft in his chin, one day growth of stubble. Maybe thirty-five. More cute than handsome, but he had that boy-next-door thing going along with nice-fitting jeans, a button-down blue oxford and docksides with no socks. An old-money look, like many members of Ariel's family.

I smiled back. "So, you're new here."

"Yeah, I decided it was time to give something back instead of just writing a check."

"Most men don't like cats."

"My mom was a vet. She had a practice that only took cats. You could say it's in my blood. I just like their independence. And they're self-cleaning."

Cute line. Cute guy. This bears investigating.

"To a point. They don't have hands."

"Yeah, I already did the cat boxes." He shoved his hands in his pockets. "So, you been volunteering here long?"

"Every Sunday for the last four years. Ten till noon."

"I signed up for the same hours but I have a wedding to go to today, so I got here at nine and Diane sorta gave me a quick orientation. But I guess we'll be working together."

I nodded. "Guess so."

He glanced at his watch, then fished his car keys out of his pocket. "Well, I gotta run and get cleaned up. See you next week." He headed for the hallway.

"Yeah. See ya."

So much for that.

He stopped, turned and looked at me. "Hey, maybe we could go for lunch afterward."

I said, "That would be nice," before I even had a chance to think about it.

He pointed at me. "Belinda, right?"

I nodded. "Yeah."

"I'm bad with names. Just wanted to make sure. See ya."

I'm bad with names too. We had something in common.

But for some reason I wouldn't forget his.

He disappeared down the hall, obviously having no idea about the superhero known as the Brass Cupcake who prowls the streets of New York making life safe for women and children while repelling the hell out of men.

Meanwhile, I just got asked out to lunch looking like absolute shit.

Now I'm totally confused.

CHAPTER FOUR

The salon was dimly lit and quiet, as Roxanne had opened it up on Sunday afternoon just for me. (I always thought "Foxy Roxy's" was kind of a throwback name, with the term "babe" having replaced "fox" sometime back in the eighties. On the other side of the coin, I believe "skank" has serious staying power and could be eternal.) Tomorrow being Memorial Day and a day off since Harry doesn't waste me on slow news days, I was to be dragged kicking and screaming by Ariel and Serena for shoes, clothes, contacts, makeup and God only knows what else. But I was in a good mood, as a seemingly nice guy who liked cats had asked me to lunch despite the fact I was wearing the spring collection for the homeless. Still, after I related the story to Roxanne, I was confused about what had happened.

"It's a subconscious effect," said Roxanne, as she worked the thick conditioner into my hair. I caught a faint whiff of avocado, which Roxanne said made this the perfect conditioner for someone with hair that could be used by someone playing the Scarecrow in *The Wizard of Oz*.

"What the hell does that mean?" I asked, my head leaning back in a royal-blue sink. It was kind of odd looking at her from that angle, and gave me a new perspective on her terrific eyes and flawless creamy skin.

"It means that what happened last night sank in to a degree, and you were so tired you didn't have time to think about it. You were in a situation where you didn't expect to be asked out, so you didn't have your force field and death stare at your beck and call."

"I've been meaning to ask. Is the death stare really that bad?"

She stopped working the conditioner in for a moment. "Honey, when you use that thing on a man you look so possessed I think I need to call a priest."

"Hmmm." I closed my eyes as she resumed the scalp massage.

"Okay," said Roxanne, "I think that'll do it. Geez, I got sandpaper burns."

"Funny."

She turned on the faucet and began to rinse out the conditioner, as she ran the warm water and her fingers through my hair. "When's the last time you wore your hair down?"

"Eighth grade, I think."

She finished the rinse, then wrapped my head in a thick, fluffy red towel and began to dry it. She finished drying it as I sat up, ran her fingers through my hair to fluff it out, stood back and flashed a sinister smile with a gleam in her eye. I knew that look as her being "up to something."

"What?" I asked, as I looked in the gold-framed mirror behind her and saw a drowned rat.

"I've got so much to work with. You're like a blank canvas. This is gonna be fun."

"Don't do anything drastic."

She waved her hand. "Pffft. Honey, drastic is already in the rearview mirror." She led me out of the shampoo room and over to her station, where I took a seat. It wasn't the typical black-lacquer-everything you see in many salons that resembled a hangout for a coven, but rather a cheery sea foam green cubicle always accented with fragrant fresh roses. The large mirror was bordered with photos of celebrity clients.

My picture wasn't up there. Geez, I wonder why.

She draped a purple smock over me and clipped it behind my neck. Then she did something that scared me to death.

She swung the chair around so my back was to the mirror.

"Hey, I wanna see what you're doing," I said.

She shook her head. "Sorry, no backseat driving on this."

"Roxanne, if I come out of here looking like some freak on the subway... I *do* have to work on TV, you know."

She kneeled down and looked at me. "Will you please trust me? Half the movie stars in this town do. And I'm going to make you look like one of them."

***

Two hours later she shoved the comb into a pocket in her smock, stood back, crouched down, and moved her head side to side as she checked out the finished product.

"Well?" I asked.

"Shhhhh," she said, putting one finger to her mouth. She moved around behind me. I felt her fingers lightly touch the back of my head, fluff my hair a bit, then she walked around where I could see her. She looked at the top of my head, then the sides, without ever looking in my eyes. Like I was some inanimate object. She put her hands on her hips and smiled. "My work here is done."

"Well, don't keep me in suspense."

She leaned forward and swung the chair around so I faced the mirror. She stood behind me, then handed me my glasses.

I put them on and my vision cleared. I didn't recognize the woman in the mirror.

My hair shone like a beacon, with shimmering highlights amidst my strawberry red. The soft tangles lightly dusted my shoulders. I lifted my hand and touched it. It was as soft and thick as the Persian I'd petted this morning.

It had never looked so good in my life. Sorta slutty, but really good.

"You like?" asked Roxanne.

I couldn't stop staring. "It's spectacular," I said. And right then and there I knew my trusty black-rimmed glasses had to go.

She reached into my purse, pulled out my sizable collection of hairpins and shook them at me. "And if I ever see you with your hair up again, I'll stab the shit out of you with these."

***

The contact lenses were surprisingly comfortable, as there had apparently been great improvements in the past fifteen years.

But they didn't conceal the fear in my eyes as I stepped out of the changing room in my bra and panties.

"Okay, hop up," said James, the bald, green-eyed wizard known as New York's best fashion consultant from its most expensive department store. A tiny man around forty, he probably weighed less than I did.

I wrapped my arms around my waist as I stepped onto the pedestal in the middle of what had to be the largest fitting room in the city. No bathroom stall-sized cubicles here: this was at least twenty-by-twenty, complete with a beautiful cream-colored sofa, a few matching chairs and a credenza filled with champagne, a bowl of fresh fruit salad, and a large silver tray of cucumber sandwiches.

"Stand up straight, honey," he said, as he whipped out a tape measure. "Arms down."

"Just relax," said Ariel, sipping a glass of champagne. "There's no one else here. This is a private fitting room."

I shivered, but not from the temperature. James deftly swung his tape measure around my chest, waist and hips, then wrote something down on a clipboard.

"You are blessed with a perfect body, young lady," he said.

I scrunched up my face. "Huh?"

"Classic hourglass, perfect size four." He picked up my stretch pants from the chair in the changing room and looked at the label. "Why are you wearing a size seven?"

"I like things baggy. More comfortable."

He shook his head, rolled his eyes and tossed the pants into the trash, then turned back to me and patted me on the stomach. "Those toned abs are to die for." He moved behind me, slid one finger under my waistband, pulled, took a look inside and snapped my underwear.

"Hey!" I slapped away his hand. He'd better be gay.

"And such a spunky little ass under the granny panties. Goes well with the attitude."

"Thank you... I think," I said.

He ran the tape measure inside my leg, getting my inseam.

Ariel put up her hand. "Please, James, no more pants."

"You already told me. But she will need some jeans. I've got a line that will make her ass really pop."

A knock on the door startled me. I wrapped my arms around my chest and lifted one leg in front of me like a flamingo as the voice came through.

"It's Serena!"

"Come on in," said Ariel.

The door opened and I relaxed as I saw Serena's face. "So, how we doing?"

"I apparently have a spunky little ass," I said.

"Good to know," said Serena, giving me the once over.

James finished writing notes on the clipboard, picked up the phone and gave whoever was on the other end a laundry list of items I apparently needed. Then he hung up and handed me a thick terry robe with a gold crest. "Have some champagne. Your new wardrobe will be here shortly."

***

The lacquered blonde makeup artist with the ice-blue eyes had been working on me for twenty minutes, slapping stuff on my face that had never been there before. Mascara, foundation, eye shadow, you name it. Her brush danced around my cheekbones as my audience surrounded the high chair upon which I was sitting. Once again I'd been wrapped in a smock, white this time. I twisted my ankle to get another look at the bottom of my brand-new, four-inch heels. "I still don't understand why these shoes with the red soles cost so damn much."

"Because," said Serena, "they're Christian Louboutins."

"And the shoes you were wearing looked more like they belonged to Christian Bale," said Roxanne.

"Who the hell cares what color the soles are?"

"They stick out," said Ariel. "Get you more attention. And men love red."

"How is anyone gonna see the bottom of my shoes?"

"Well," said Roxanne, "if you're sitting on a chair like this one in a bar, swinging your leg a bit, that red is going to catch the eye."

"Be cheaper if I just wrote my phone number on the soles of a pair of sneakers," I said.

The young makeup girl, who in my opinion looked as though she'd put on foundation with a trowel, leaned back, smiled, and turned to my friends. "What do you think?"

"Excellent job," said Ariel.

"Yes, terrific," said Serena.

"Really spectacular," said Roxanne.

"Uh, could *I* have a look?" I asked.

"Oh, sorry," said the makeup girl, who handed me a heavy silver mirror.

The face I saw in it was a stranger, but a beautiful stranger. I looked like a magazine ad. Vincent was right about one thing. I *could* do eye makeup commercials. The pale-green eye shadow had turned me into an Egyptian goddess. "Wow," I said, looking at the makeup girl. "You're a true artist."

"You're very kind," she said.

Ariel reached into her purse and slipped the girl a fifty.

"Thank you!" she said, and pulled off my smock. "You're good to go."

"Great," I said. I hopped off the high chair and started to reach for one of the many shopping bags, but Roxanne playfully slapped it away. "We've got these."

"We're going to do a little experiment first," said Serena.

"I thought I was done. What now?"

"We're going to prove to you that you are now one of the most desirable women in New York," said Ariel. "Well, physically, anyway. Still got a lot of work to do on the attitude."

"If I look as good as you say I do, I can now get away with being a bitch, right?" I asked.

"But you're not," said Roxanne. "You are as beautiful inside as you now are outside."

I rolled my eyes. "We gonna hold hands and sing Kumbaya now?"

"Again with the attitude," said Serena, raising one finger. "But one thing at a time."

"So here's what you're going to do," said Ariel. "I'm going across the street and I want you to wait till I get there, then I want you to cross the street."

"What, I'm learning the principles of jaywalking?"

"I'm going to shoot a video with my cell phone and show you the reaction you get with your new look."

"Seriously?"

"Trust me, honey, you're gonna get a reaction," said Roxanne.

"Ohhhh... kayyyyyy."

Ariel took off and headed out the door of the department store. I started to follow, teetering in my heels that took me up to five-nine, a little wobbly as I hadn't gotten my sea legs yet. The short skirt was a bit tight, restricting my normal gait, which Ariel said reminded her of her Connecticut mailman walking uphill in a snow drift. Roxanne and Serena followed, loaded down with my haul from the day.

We reached the door and walked outside, greeted by a cool breeze and the sound of New York's heartbeat; horns and sirens. My spunky little ass felt cold, not being used to a skirt, especially one that ended several inches above the knee.

I saw Ariel across the street pointing her phone at me. "Anytime!" she yelled.

"Go get 'em, Tiger," said Roxanne.

I shrugged and shook my head. "Whatever." I had no idea what to expect but played along. Big deal, I was gonna walk across the street. Millions do it every day in Manhattan and no one notices. The light changed and the little crosswalk icon told me it was safe to go.

What happened next nearly made my jaw drop.

Because just about every man crossing in the opposite direction had his hanging open.

They gawked. They flat out stared. A young, hardbodied bike messenger heading around the corner stopped, tipped his sunglasses down for a better look, and said, "Whoa." A cabbie going the other way gave me the classic blue-collar compliment of "Hey, baby" as he honked his horn and beat his hand on the side of the car door. A utility worker ten feet off the ground in a cherry picker got distracted and sent his bucket into a telephone pole. A man twisted his neck like an owl as he crossed the street in the other direction. I heard a clang and an expletive only to turn and see he had walked into a mailbox and was hopping around on one leg.

I reached the other side of the street to find Ariel laughing hysterically as she put down her phone.

"What the hell just happened?" I asked.

"Congratulations," she said. "You're now officially a smoking hot babe."

The video rolled for the fifth time in slow motion, filling the giant flat screen in my living room.

"I love the look on the guy's face when he hits the mailbox," said Ariel, leaning back into my overstuffed beige couch while sipping a glass of red wine. She fired the remote at the screen and froze the video as the man cringed.

"I still can't believe that's me," I said. "It's like watching a stranger."

Roxanne grabbed the remote from Ariel and started the video again, this time at half speed. "Look at that hair bounce. Am I good, or what?"

"It's like there are invisible electric fans following her," said Serena. "Rox, you've outdone yourself."

"She didn't just stop traffic, she made it back up." Roxanne smiled and hit the pause button, then pointed a finger at me. "And I don't want you touching your hair tomorrow. I'll be here at seven to give you a comb-out."

"Seven?" I said. "I sleep till eight."

Roxanne shook her head. "Not any more. Beauty takes time. No more rolling out of bed and directly into a cab wearing a toothbrush as an accessory. Yeah, I've seen you do that."

"Guess I need to start going to bed earlier."

"Hopefully you'll be doing that for reasons other than sleep," said Ariel.

I looked at myself on the screen and it hit me. "Uh-oh."

"Uh-oh what?" asked Serena.

"I just thought of something. I'm not sure what the reaction will be at work."

Ariel furrowed her brow. "Seriously? You work in TV. The new look should be worth bigger ratings. They'll be thrilled."

"There's more to it than that. I realize my business is superficial but it's hard to be credible if a viewer's first impression of you has to do with how you look. That's one of the reasons I've never fixed myself up."

"The other reason is that you had no idea how to do it," said Roxanne.

"Doesn't matter. I'm gonna get some flak for this."

Ariel waved her hand. "Pfffft. They'll love it."

"You don't know Harry."

CHAPTER FIVE

Harry Coyne likes to use the phrase "back in the day" when describing the halcyon days of broadcasting. No computers but typewriters, and not the electric kind but the kind where the letter "e" got stuck fairly often. No printers but carbon paper. A huge black metal wire service machine that spit out an endless roll of copy and had to be "stripped" every twenty minutes by the low man on the totem pole. (Only because there were no women on said pole. Their poles could be found in strip clubs.) Ribbons had to be changed, film had to be developed, phones had hold buttons that flashed. And actual human beings answered them when they rang. People smoked in newsrooms and every reporter had a flask filled with something a hell of a lot stronger than Dr. Pepper stashed in his desk.

And back in the day, as Harry puts it, "A newsroom sounded like a newsroom." Watch any movie about the news business made before 1980 and you'll hear the journalism heartbeat of the past: the loud banging of the wire machine, the incessant tapping of typewriter keys, the spinning of the typewriter platen as paper was ripped out. The wire machine is now a boat anchor, replaced by digital news delivered to your laptop while reporters gently write stories on nearly silent keyboards.

I say nearly silent, because today as I arrived in the newsroom

I couldn't hear them.

Same deal as crossing the street. Everything stopped. Jaws dropped open. Hal, the kid producer, walked into a file cabinet. Audrey the newsroom secretary spilled coffee all over herself. I left surprised looks in my wake as I entered the conference room for the morning meeting, adorned in a stunning short emerald-green dress that matched my eyes, which Roxanne had worked on after my morning comb-out.

The loud conversation that usually filled the room every morning came to a screeching halt as everyone looked in my direction.

Jenna Scanlin, our thirty-something five o'clock anchor with the supermodel body broke the silence. "Oh my God! You look... fantastic!"

"Thank you," I said, sitting down in my usual spot at the far end, opposite the head of the table, newsroom "mom" to Harry's "dad."

Stan Harvey the feature guy couldn't stop staring. "Excuse me, but... who *are* you and what have you done with Belinda Carson?"

"Just thought it was time for a little change," I said, twirling a lock of my hair.

"*Little* change?" said Stan.

"I'd give you a compliment but I see Inhuman Resources lurking in the newsroom," said Bob Evanson, spotting the troll on one of her regular spy missions. "So I'll just ask if someone can turn up the air conditioning in here."

"You look amazing," said Audrey, still trying to dab coffee off her blouse.

"Thanks." I looked through the glass and saw Harry headed our way. "Nobody say anything. I wanna see if he notices."

Harry blew through the door as he always did, dropped a bunch of manila folders and a yellow legal pad in front of his chair, took a seat, banged his chipped red coffee cup on the table and spilled a bit of it. He pulled a pencil out from behind his ear and looked up. His brow creased as he noticed me, then he turned to his perky brunette assistant who sat to his left. "Audrey, you're supposed to notify me in advance when we have a guest in the morning meeting."

Audrey, who's my age, bit her lower lip, trying her best not to laugh. "She's not a guest, Harry."

People snorted, laughs were stifled. Harry slowly turned in my direction, pulled his silver reading glasses down to the tip of his nose and stared over them at me. "I'm sorry, do you work here?"

"Every weekday for the last eight years," I said. "Maybe you recognize the voice."

His eyes suddenly widened in recognition. "Cupcake?"

I smiled and nodded.

"What the *hell* happened to you?"

"Harry, you're a real charmer," said Jenna.

"In my office after the meeting," he said.

***

I followed Harry into his cluttered office and closed the door behind me. Harry moved to the window that looked out over the newsroom and twisted the Venetian blinds shut, since the entire staff had stopped working and didn't want to miss the scene about to take place. I heard a chorus of "Aw, shit" through the window. He started pacing behind his desk and shook his head. "I can't believe you did this to yourself."

"Did what, Harry?"

He started wildly gesturing in my direction. "This... this... hair, and... you're in a dress."

"Women wear dresses, Harry. Women go to the hair salon."

"But not you. You always look the same. You're—"

"One of the guys?"

"Yeah. I mean, you're a *real* reporter, not the eye-candy fembots management sticks me with."

"Are you saying I can't be credible if I look attractive?"

"People won't take you seriously."

"You're kidding, right? This is television news, Harry. Or have you forgotten we work in the world's most superficial business?"

"You just took the brass out of the cupcake."

I tapped my head. "The brass is still here, Harry. It's just been polished a bit."

Harry pulled a pack of cigarettes out of his shirt pocket, jerked it toward his head and popped one in his mouth.

"You know you can't smoke in here, Harry."

He rolled his eyes. "Shit!" He fired the cancer stick into the trash. "Back in the day we didn't have these stupid rules... aw, dammit, now I'm going to have to get new promo shot, and all your billboards will have to be replaced. Your face is on a hundred city buses and subway platforms."

"The other women in the newsroom change their hair all the time."

"You're not like them. And this is more than a change. This is like... like trading in a Yugo for a Mercedes."

A Yugo? A 1980s Russian car? I looked that bad in my "before" picture? "Is that your weird way of saying I look good?"

He shrugged and looked at the parade of Emmy awards that sat atop the battered wooden credenza behind his desk. "Let's just say it's going to be hard to sell the best-looking woman in my newsroom as the best reporter."

A huge smile grew on my face. "Thank you, Harry. Took you a while to get there, but I'll take it."

"Just tell me why you did..." He looked up and waved his hands up and down my body. "...this."

What the hell, I was determined to have some fun. I pointed to myself. "This? By *this* you mean...?"

"You know damn well what I mean!" His hands moved faster. "This! This! The hair is all... down and has curls and it's shiny and... the dress... I mean, you've got *legs* for God's sake!"

I playfully slapped the side of my face. "The horror!"

He exhaled. The man who had been like a father to me now looked at me like one for the first time. "Just tell me why."

"Why? Because I'm tired of going home alone to my empty apartment, Harry. All the Emmys and the fame and my face on the signs in the subway and the big paycheck aren't keeping me warm at night. My best friends told me I need to change, starting in a physical way. You said it yourself last week, that I have no social skills."

"I said I was sorry about that. You know I'm not the most tactful person, but I didn't mean to hurt you."

"I know. But apparently I needed some female skills as well. I need to put my best foot forward out there if I'm ever going to find someone who will love me."

"Oh, geez. Not again. Every damn woman in my newsroom."

"What?"

"I never figured you as someone who owns a biological clock. Tick-tock-tick-tock and here's my resignation." He plopped down in his beat-up brown leather swivel rocker and folded his hands in his lap. "So." Long pause. "She's gone forever?"

"If by *she* you mean the sexless woman in baggy clothes who didn't own a pair of heels and was the only girl in the newsroom who didn't kill the ozone on a daily basis, yeah, she's outta here. But I'm still the same reporter. And I'll never stop doing what I do because I love it."

He pulled a flask from his top drawer and took a sip, one of his last remaining defiant acts available in the hellish time known to Harry as *the present*. "Dammit, Cupcake, I never figured you for a *skirt*." (It should be noted that a "skirt" was the term used by men back in the day referring to women in the newsroom.) "I'm not sure this is gonna work."

"What?"

"Politicians run for cover when they know you're around. They're more frightened of you than an IRS audit. You think any man is going to avoid you looking like that?"

I couldn't help but laugh. "Harry, if it makes you feel any better, I've still got a lot of work to do on those social skills."

"Please don't."

***

My "tip line" started ringing the moment I got off the set at five minutes after five.

It's an old, battered red phone that weighs a ton and it's hooked up to an old-fashioned answering machine that uses a tape. Normally the thing only rings about three times a week. Viewers call tipping me off on stuff that they think needs to be investigated. Sometimes the tips lead to stories, more often they don't. The stuff I get on politicians is usually generated by the other party and turns out to be bogus. But over the years I've gotten some great stories out of anonymous phone calls.

I needed some new leads anyway, having put the State Senator tale to bed as the guy resigned this morning. While there were a few things I had on the back burner, nothing jumped out as a big story.

I slid into my chair, tossed my script on the desk already littered with papers, and answered the phone. "Tip line, Belinda Carson..."

"Hi, Belinda, thanks for taking my call." The voice was young and female.

I shoved some junk out of the way, revealing a coffee-stained blotter that still had a calendar for 2006, grabbed a pen and pad, poised to take notes. "That's what I'm here for. You have a tip you want to share?"

"Not really. I just wanted to say you look fantastic and I was hoping you'd share the name of your hairstylist."

My head dropped and hit the desk with an audible thud. And so it began.

The tip line got a workout for the next ninety minutes, ringing non-stop. I didn't get out of there till a quarter to seven, after fielding the following hard-hitting, investigative news tips, which would no doubt lead to Emmy award winning exclusives:

"Who does your makeup?"

"Where did you get that dress?"

"Would you like to have dinner this weekend?"

"Are your eyes really that green or are you using colored contacts?"

"What's that shade of lip gloss?"

And my favorite:

"I'm married and would never cheat on my wife, but I just wanted to call and say you're smokin' hot."

After the final call Harry walked by my desk on his way out of the newsroom.

"I noticed you were getting an awful lot of tip calls tonight."

"Uh-huh." I knew where this was going. Harry was wearing his I-told-you-so look.

"Any good leads?"

"Not one."

"See what you started?"

CHAPTER SIX

Friday night couldn't have come fast enough. I felt like my soul had been magically transferred into another body.

The old Belinda Carson, now known as "frumpy girl," had apparently died last weekend. Oh, I was still the Brass Cupcake, but I had become that rare crossover hit in the broadcasting world, an "infobabe" who actually had credibility.

Not that viewers noticed the latter any more.

At this point I was totally conflicted. I was surprised, but I had to admit I loved the attention I was getting from men. Hated that my appearance had become secondary to my reporting talent. Loved getting dressed up and fixing my hair (which also surprised the hell out of me), hated that the first comment I heard in the newsroom had to do with my outfit or hair or makeup rather than the previous night's story.

I would deal with it later, along with a bottle of wine that was chilling in the fridge with my name on it. First I needed a cab, one of the hardest things to get on a Friday night during rush hour in Manhattan.

Well, it used to be hard. I previously endured a yellow blur as taxis sped by me, often splashing me with slush in the process since I was apparently coated with invisibility spray.

Now I step one foot off the curb, raise my hand, awkwardly

stick out one well-turned ankle in a stiletto heel, and it's a lemon-colored NASCAR race to grab my fare. It felt weird, like I was in some bizarre dance class, but I'll take it.

Ten seconds after I engaged my sexual hail, a shiny cab crossed three lanes of traffic and screeched to a halt in front of me. The rumpled middle-aged man in a business suit ten feet away who'd already been at the curb when I got there rolled his eyes at me.

I opened the door and got in, then noticed the new-car smell, which is rather rare in a Big Apple taxi.

"Where to, Miss?" asked the cabbie, making eye contact by using his rear-view mirror.

"1042 East 82nd, please."

He didn't pull away, and just sat there staring at me in the mirror.

"Well?" I asked. "Is there a ride somewhere in my future?"

"I *knew* it," he said.

I furrowed my brow. "Knew what?"

I saw his eyes brighten in the mirror and then he turned to face me.

Oh shit.

"You! Vincent!"

"Oh, you remembered my name this time. I'm impressed."

"What the hell are you doing here?"

"What does it look like? Driving my cab."

"You said you worked on Wall Street."

He shrugged. "Rox told me to say that. Besides, I do pick up a fare there from time to time."

"So you're a cab driver?"

"How very perceptive of you. I can see why you went into journalism." He smiled, then gave me the once-over. "Anyway, like I said, I *knew* it."

"I'll repeat the question. Knew what?"

"That there was a serious babe under all those bad clothes."

A tap on the window interrupted us. It was the guy who'd been waiting. I rolled down the window.

"Look, if you're not going anywhere, can I have this cab?"

"No," I said, rolling up the window as Vincent took off.

"You look spectacular," he said, keeping his eyes on the traffic. "Huge improvement."

"You lied to me."

"Like I said, Rox told me to say that. Besides, you should be used to it in your line of work." He hit his horn as another car cut him off. "And you never would have talked to me if I said I was a cab driver."

"I don't judge people by their profession."

"Not what Rox told me."

My jaw tightened, then I noticed the meter wasn't running. "You forgot to start the meter."

"No charge for one of her friends."

"You'll get in trouble with your boss. They monitor those things."

"Pffft. I'm pretty tight with the boss. That's why I got the new cab. Don't worry your pretty little head about it."

"I don't want your charity."

"Well, I can see *charm school* isn't in session yet. When you get to the class on saying *thank you*, let me know."

My eyes narrowed as I stared daggers into the rear-view mirror. He looked into it, locked eyes with me for a moment, and smiled. "Don't you laugh at me!" I said. I was getting a lecture from a damn cab driver!

"Why not? You're funny."

"This is *not* funny."

"Let's see, gorgeous woman gets into my cab, I tell her she looks nice, she proceeds to bite my head off. Funny, don't you think?"

"Just drive."

"Yes, ma'am."

"And don't call me *ma'am*. I'm not old."

"Fine." Long pause. "Cupcake." The sonofabitch continued to smile at me.

I grunted and folded my arms in front of me as my blood pressure spiked. A quick look out the window told me we only had ten blocks to go.

And then the cab came to a sudden halt.

"What's going on?" I asked.

"Traffic. Maybe you've heard of it. It's a concept involving too many cars and not enough road, which dictates that two pieces of matter cannot occupy the same space at the same time."

"Wow, you got an 'A' in high school physics. Congratulations."

I was trapped in taxicab confession hell. Last week I would have jumped out and hoofed it, but ten blocks in these heels when I'm only on week one as a five-nine woman would've killed my feet.

The silence was deafening. "Wanna listen to the radio?" he finally asked.

"Anything's better than listening to you."

He didn't respond and turned on the radio. Sports talk. My pulse slowed down. I'm actually a sports junkie and listen to this station all the time.

The current caller with the Jersey accent was ripping the Mets ownership after making yet another ridiculous trade. "You tell 'em," said Vincent. "Worst trade in years."

I suddenly forgot my anger. "No shit," I muttered.

He looked at me in the mirror as traffic began to slowly move. "You follow baseball?"

I nodded.

"Football too?"

Another nod.

"Giants or Jets?"

"Giants," I said, before hitting him with the old line designed to take any Jets fan down a notch in case he was one. "There are no Jets fans, only Giants fans who can't get tickets."

"You're right about that. I've got season tickets for the Giants. Had 'em ten years. Forty-yard line. Great seats."

"Good for you."

The cab sped up and the blocks began to pass quickly. I saw my building through the windshield and opened my purse as he pulled to the curb, put the car in park, then turned around. "Nice seeing you again, Belinda." I pulled a ten-dollar bill out of my purse and handed it to him. He waved it away. "I told you, no charge."

"Consider it a tip for the sparkling conversation." I tossed the ten through the little window that separates the front seat from the back and got out of the cab on the driver's side. I headed for the front door of my apartment building.

"Hey, forget something?"

I stopped. I saw that my purse was over my shoulder and my satchel was in my hand. "No," I yelled. I didn't want to turn around, so I started walking again.

"Oh. I thought this broom was yours."

My jaw dropped while my eyes caught fire. I stopped in my tracks and spun around to face him. "*What* did you say?"

"You know, Belinda, next time your friends take you shopping, you might stop at a store that sells manners."

He sped away so fast I couldn't even get my middle finger up.

***

Several women stopped dead in their tracks and parted like the Red Sea as he walked to the corner table in our usual watering hole, which was crowded and noisier than usual. His eyes locked on mine like a heat-seeking missile. He slid his hand along the brass rail of the bar until he reached the empty chair next to me. "Can I buy you a drink?" he asked, as he arrived. The man was perhaps forty, dark-haired, about six-two, very attractive. Okay, he's beyond attractive. Looked like a marine recruiting poster in a thousand-dollar suit.

Didn't matter. I held up my wine glass, which was full. "Isn't it obvious I already have one?" Sheesh. Some guys are so dumb.

The guy's smile disappeared instantly. He shook his head and walked away. I caught the word "bitch" under his breath.

"Excuse me?" I yelled.

He put up his hand and kept walking.

"Real nice," said Roxanne. "I can see we're makin' progress on playing well with others."

"I've already got a glass of wine."

Ariel rolled her eyes. "Good God, were you raised by wolves? He was just interested in you and being polite."

"I'm sorry," I said. "But after a week of men hitting on me constantly... none of them even recognize me from TV any more. They just want to sleep with me."

"Your point being?" asked Serena.

I took a sip of my wine. "Look, before all... *this*..." I waved my hands down my body, channeling Harry. "Before all the hair and the makeup and the heels and the short skirts and the jeans that make my spunky ass pop, men used to come up to me because I was the credible girl from television news who they knew was intelligent. Now nobody even mentions it. Now I only attract men because of how I look."

"Again... wolves?" asked Ariel.

"So," said Roxanne, "you're in this pissy mood because you're suddenly hot and hordes of men are asking you out?"

"No, that's not it. Not totally. It's because I ran into your cousin an hour ago. The *cab driver*?"

"Bus-ted," said Serena.

"Fine," said Roxanne, putting up her hands in surrender. "So I told Vincent to embellish the truth a bit. Where'd you run into him?"

"I got into his taxi. You know, he's related to you so you should say something to him about the way he talks to people."

Roxanne looked puzzled as her face tightened. "Why, what'd he say?"

"He said I look spectacular and I'm a serious babe. And then we got into an argument and he said I obviously hadn't been to charm school."

"Let me get this straight... first he said you looked spectacular and were a serious babe," said Ariel.

"The nerve," said Roxanne. "I can certainly see why you were so offended."

"Let's back up a bit," said Serena, ever the lawyer, "and ask the court reporter to review the transcript. You said you got into an argument *after* he gave you two very nice compliments, referring to you as both *spectacular* and a *serious babe*. Were said compliments the cause of the verbal altercation that followed?"

I put up one hand as a stop sign. "You had to be there. And stop badgering the witness."

A waiter dropped by and slid an order of mozzarella sticks into the middle of the table. "Sorry for the delay on your dinner reservations. We should have a table for you in ten minutes. I brought you an appetizer on the house."

"Great," I said, not even looking at the guy. I reached across the table, grabbed a piece of fried cheese and shoved most of it in my mouth.

"I never noticed that before," said Serena, as she watched me eat. She then turned to Ariel. "You?"

"No. It kind of went with the total package and I guess it all blended together. I can't believe I missed it, considering my mother and all."

"Noticed what?" I asked, my words garbled a bit as I talked through the cheese. I swallowed, licked my fingers and wiped them on the tablecloth.

"Your table manners," said Serena.

I had a piece of cheese stuck in my teeth and tried to fish it out with one finger. "What about 'em?"

"The waiter didn't leave four forks as a garnish," said Roxanne. She turned to Ariel. "You know what you gotta do."

Ariel sighed and pulled out her cell phone. "I'll call my mother immediately."

CHAPTER SEVEN

Ariel's mother, Cassandra Baymont, is a best-selling author and magazine contributor. Not because she can weave words into a clever plot. Nope, her forte is non-fiction. Specifically, she's America's foremost expert on etiquette. You see where this is going?

We took a Saturday morning limo ride to the shores of Eastern Connecticut (I wanted to take the train but Mrs. Baymont would not hear of it. Besides, she's loaded.) Ariel, her mother and I were seated at a posh restaurant she owns called the *Hampton View*. You can see the Hamptons with a pair of binoculars from the tables next to a window, hence the name. The place is only open for dinner, but because Mrs. Baymont deemed this the etiquette equivalent of DEFCON ONE she brought in a few staffers to serve us a private lunch.

And, you guessed it, to teach me how to eat.

I should mention the source of my current culinary habits. My mom died when I was two, so I was raised by a single father and four older brothers. So seeing things like people vacuuming potato-chip crumbs from their sweatshirts after a long day of watching football and shooting aerosol cheese into their mouths directly from the can doesn't seem strange to me. Couple that with a career that often forces me to eat in the news car and wolf down whatever I can grab in ten minutes. The result is that Ariel said I resembled a starving man who escaped from a prison camp when I eat. She added that I had apparently never heard of the invention of the napkin, which no doubt accounted for my love of long sleeves.

So we were seated at the best table in the restaurant, next to the window overlooking the shore. Seagulls laughed and occasionally dove for minnows as the waves gently lapped the beach. Our round table was covered with a starched eggshell linen tablecloth. The cutlery was heavy Sterling silver. The place seated only about fifty people, but it felt like a museum, filled with beautiful antiques and framed prints of lighthouses. The walls were a deep red, while the twelve-foot ceiling was painted beige. The whole effect was soothing, rich and classy.

Mrs. Baymont was seated to my left. She's in her early fifties and well-preserved, an older carbon copy of Ariel. Always impeccably coiffed and dressed, I can't even imagine the woman in a tee shirt. Even though no one else was there but a waiter and a chef, she was in a lacy white blouse with her ever-present triple strand of pearls. She talked with that affected snobby lilt common to many parts of Connecticut's most wealthy towns and old money. But she's a sweet woman who would do anything for her daughter, and has always been very fond of me. Her manners are such that she's never commented on my appearance, which I realized must have made her do a slow burn every time she saw me.

"Now, dearie," she said. (She calls everyone *dearie*.) "Let's go over the place setting and the various utensils." A tall, slender middle-aged waiter in a white tux removed the large pewter plates and replaced them with bone china through which you could read a newspaper.

I raised one finger. "I have a question."

"Yes?"

"Why does the waiter always remove the plates that are on the table when you arrive?"

"Those are called charger plates, dearie."

"Because they're from San Diego?"

Mrs. Baymont frowned.

"You know. San Diego? Chargers?"

She shook her head and politely smiled. "They're decorative. The term comes from the middle English *chargeour*, but you don't really need to know that for our purposes." She pointed to the silver on the right of my plate. "Do you know why one fork is longer than the rest?"

I shrugged. "I dunno. So... you can get the food in your mouth quicker?"

Ariel snorted.

Mrs. Baymont widened her eyes and looked at me like a third-grade teacher. "No, dearie. That's your salad fork. Each fork has a purpose. One cannot eat a seven-course meal with one utensil."

I thought, why the hell not, I do it all the time, but I didn't say it. (Not surprisingly, the "spork" is not among the silverware.)

So before any food even arrived, I learned more about the history, care and feeding of forks than I cared to know. And then there was the thing about the order forks are used and that you should always move toward the plate as the meal goes on. Apparently in this part of the world it would be nothing short of a scandal if you actually ate fish with your salad fork. It was like having an air traffic controller in charge of lunch. The instruction was so detailed and went on for so long I wished she simply owned a Chinese restaurant and we could deal with sticks. I began to wonder if *spoons 101* would be as difficult.

My stomach growled audibly. Mrs. Baymont noticed. "Did you eat anything at all this morning?"

"No."

"One should never dine while starving. The result is unbecoming for a young lady. A light snack before a meal can take care of that... rumble."

I nodded as the waiter arrived and placed a steaming bowl of soup in front of each of us. I immediately grabbed my spoon but was stopped when it was inches from the bowl.

"Eh-eh-eh," said Mrs. Baymont, as she wagged her finger. "First, you're holding your spoon like a tennis racquet." She took it from me, then manipulated my hand to the proper form and placed the spoon in it. "Think of it as holding a pencil, like when you're reporting and taking notes."

Now I really *did* feel like a third grader. And a naughty one at that.

"Okay." It felt funny but I could deal with it. I started to dip the spoon into the soup.

"Eh-eh-eh." Again with the finger.

"What now?"

"Take your spoon and dip some soup into it from the back of the bowl with the side of the spoon farthest away. Your motion should be away from you, the opposite of what you normally do. This way you'll never drip any of the soup on your clothes." She demonstrated it for me, and it actually made sense. Since my shirts often look like painter's drop cloths, I figured this tip was a keeper.

I dipped my spoon into the far side of the bowl, lifted it to my mouth and took a sip of creamy lobster bisque. "Oh, that's terrific," I said. I looked to Mrs. Baymont for approval. "Did I do that right?"

"Yes, dearie. You may continue."

Two hours and countless lectures on silverware, china and crystal later, we were done. Mrs. Baymont pronounced me ready for everything from a casual lunch to a cotillion. Personally I would draw the line at hoop skirts and parasols, but it was nice to know I was now approved to eat in public.

***

I leaned back in the plush leather of the black stretch limo, fat and happy after devouring everything from bisque to salad to some incredible veal to something called "intermezzo," which I thought meant I had to sing opera during my meal but was actually a scoop of lime sorbet. We sped west back to Manhattan, the Saturday afternoon traffic pretty thin on the Connecticut Turnpike. "Ariel, that was really nice of your mother to do that," I said.

"Are you kidding? She loves doing that kind of stuff."

"Really?"

"Yep. It's her mission in life to teach the entire world to eat with the proper fork."

"It's amazing how she knew all of the things I was doing wrong. And some of them before I even did them."

"Well, there's a reason for that." Ariel pulled out her smart phone, punched a few buttons and handed it to me. "Last night at dinner when I put my phone on the table, I taped you as you were eating."

I scrunched up my face. "You're kidding, right?"

She shook her head. "I wanted mother to see what we were dealing with before we arrived, so I sent it to her when I got home."

"Oh, for God's sake—"

The video interrupted me. My jaw hung open like a trophy bass as I watched myself in a restaurant, literally shoveling food into my yap like a werewolf on a bloodlust bender, talking with my mouth full, and at one point using my sleeve as a napkin.

"Dear God, I look like that when I eat?"

"Did you ever notice you're always finished ten minutes before the rest of us? I'm surprised sparks don't come out of your knife and fork. If I was a guy and saw that I'd take you to that medieval restaurant in Atlantic City where you eat with your hands."

"Sir Lancelot's? I love that place!"

"I rest my case."

I was riveted as I saw all the "mistakes" I was making, thanks to Mrs. Baymont's instruction. "God, this is embarrassing. I can't watch any more." I handed the phone back to her. "Please delete this right now. It would get a million hits on YouTube. I can see the title. *Brass Cupcake devours everything in her path.*"

She punched a few buttons. "There. Gone forever. As are your previous eating habits." Suddenly she got a gleam in her eyes. "Speaking of which, you have a lunch date tomorrow."

***

If you had told me a week ago that I'd spend two hours getting all decked out to clean cat boxes, I would have said you were insane.

Yet here I was, after getting up at the ungodly hour of seven-thirty on a Sunday morning, finishing up my prep work for what could be a meal consisting of a hot dog from a street vendor. I felt like a teenager on a first date, eager to debut my new and improved self for a guy I've known all of two minutes. Last night I went out with the girls for a casual dinner and Ariel gave me a B+ on my new eating habits. She would have given me an A but I slurped up the last bit of soup by picking up the bowl. What the hell, I hate to waste food. Kids starving in India and all.

So I bounced into the shelter, hair all done up, eighty-dollar skinny jeans that made my spunky ass pop, tight turquoise gathered top, eyes decorated.

Diane lit up as I moved toward the counter. "Well, I was waiting to see if the new you looked as good in person as you do on my high-def flat screen."

"And?"

"Amazing. I had no idea you were a beautiful swan. That's not to imply you were an ugly duckling."

"I didn't think that's what you meant. Thank you for the compliment."

"You'll be beating them off with a stick."

"Already am, and it's not all it's cracked up to be," I said, as I headed for the back wearing a huge smile.

"By the way, he's not coming today."

I stopped dead in my tracks.

Use whatever image you want. Air coming out of a balloon, wind out of sails, man's dose of Viagra running out, whatever. My perfectly made-up face dropped. "He quit already?"

"No, he had another family thing today so he came in yesterday."

Yesterday? Shit. "Oh. Did he, uh, say anything?"

"About what?"

"Never mind. Lemme go play with my cats."

"Hey, that old Siamese you liked got adopted. Nice couple with a kid in a wheelchair that wanted a quiet cat."

My favorite cat, Pandora, wasn't there either. "Aw, I'll miss her. But glad she found a good home."

I shuffled down the hall, head down, the spring in my step gone. Most of the cats perked up as I turned the corner, and I did as well.

I crouched down and began to give some attention to each cat, getting purrs and licks in return. I was beginning to feel a little better.

And then I saw it.

A yellow sticky note with my name on it attached to the giant bin of cat food. I jumped up and grabbed it, then turned it over.

Sorry I missed you. Rain check?
-Scott

The smile I had earlier returned. I picked up a Himalayan kitten and hugged her close to my new blouse, which was immediately covered with fur. "What the hell, kitty," I said. "Go ahead and shed."

CHAPTER EIGHT

"Oh, shit. Already?"

The tip line was already wailing when I emerged from the morning meeting shortly after nine-thirty Monday morning. I would have let it ring but the ancient answering machine that had never flashed a number higher than three had apparently given up the ghost when the tape broke over the weekend. I had no idea who called, how many had called, or what they had to say, and frankly I didn't care because no one had ever called with a legit tip on the weekend. The machine flashed hieroglyphics until I mercifully unplugged the thing to put it out of its misery and tossed it in the trash. Harry placed a call to the IT geek to set up voicemail on the number. No one ever thought to do it before because it was never necessary.

But the IT guy hadn't arrived yet.

Stan Harvey occupied the neat desk opposite my pile of clutter, Harry's theory being that the hardest reporter and softest reporter should "room" together and therefore balance things out as far as newsroom camaraderie was concerned. Stan, as you might imagine, is a character with a warped sense of humor common to most feature people. Around forty, with receding sandy hair and piercing deep-set blue eyes, he's my height (well, before the heels, anyway) and thin, with that built-in mischievous look similar to

Roxanne's. Stan flashed his crooked smile at me as I arrived at my station. "Looks like your fan club is already fired up."

"I'm never gonna get any work done."

"It might help if you change your new recording with updated information each morning about your outfit, makeup and shoe preference of the day. Am I mistaken or is that shade of lipstick Desert Rose?"

"Bite me, Stan."

I started to sit down and grab the phone, but Stan reached across the desk and beat me to it. "Allow me. Operators are standing by," he said, as he answered it. "Tip line, this is Stan." He listened a moment, his smile faded. He nodded and handed the phone to me. "Sounds like a legit one."

My eyes narrowed as I knew Stan's penchant for practical jokes. He recently Saran-wrapped the toilet bowl and shoe polished the seat in the private bathroom of the Inhuman Resources troll. Believe me, you don't want to get on Stan's bad side. Thankfully, we're good friends. "It had better be," I said, as I took the phone. "Belinda Carson."

"Belinda, this is Councilman Jagger. How are you this morning?"

I rolled my eyes. The only time politicians call is to rat out people in the other party. "I'm fine, Sir. How can I help you?"

"We need to talk."

"Sir, if it's about your opponent in the upcoming election—"

"It's not," he said, just before he dropped a phrase that made my reporter's radar go up. "It's about something illegal I think is going on in my own office. And I need your help."

***

Serena called right after the Councilman, asking if I could sneak away for a few minutes before lunch to watch her cross-examine a witness. I'd covered trials she's been an attorney in before, and she's very impressive. I had no idea why she wanted me at this particular run-of-the-mill hearing, since it had no news value whatsoever. But she said she needed to demonstrate something for me. Since the old courthouse was just a block from Jagger's office and I was going to be in the neighborhood anyway, I hit her courtroom a few minutes before the judge hit the bench.

My heels echoed as I walked across the tiled white marble floor and slid into the row behind Serena. The ancient wooden bench was as comfortable as a church pew. "So, what's so important about a harassment lawsuit? You're not setting some precedent, are you?"

"Legally? No. For you? Yes. Watch and learn."

"You got the plaintiff or defendant on this one?"

"Plaintiff." She nodded toward an attractive thirtyish blonde sitting next to her. "Her former boss is a slimeball. She wouldn't give him a tumble so he fired her."

"And this is important to me... why?"

"Patience, grasshopper."

Our conversation was interrupted by the bailiff. "All rise! The honorable Jennifer Trapp presiding."

I'd been in Judge Trapp's court before, and always enjoyed covering her trials. She's a no-bullshit judge who's probably the best-looking jurist in town. A redhead in her mid-forties, she looks thirty and has a body of a twenty-year-old, along with a taste for men in that latter age range. Her photo once ended up on *Page Six* in which she was accompanied by a guy right out of college with the caption *Cougar Trapp*.

Anyway, chances are Her Honor was wearing a skirt as short as Serena's under her robes as she headed up the creaky steps and took a seat. (I noted she had those shoes with the red soles which I now refer to as *anti-Christian Bales*. Interesting.) Everyone else in the courtroom followed suit and sat down as the judge adjusted her robes and looked at Serena. Her red hair made a striking contrast against her black robe and the huge wooden seal of the state of New York hanging on the wall behind her. "Ms. Dash, you may continue your cross-examination." She turned to the man who approached the witness stand, a scrawny, chinless forty-year-old poster child for male-pattern creepiness and reminded him he was still under oath.

"Thank you, your honor," said Serena, who got up and started to strut toward the witness stand. Her tight black leather skirt was about six inches above the knee and her candy-apple red blouse low-cut enough to make any man consider (and hope for) the possibility of a wardrobe malfunction.

The seven male members of the jury were locked on her as she reached the witness. Conveniently, his eyes were at the level of her chest.

"So, Mr Harrolds, where were we?" she said. "Ah, yes, time to look at your personal life. Ever been married?"

"No," he said.

She turned her body slightly so that the judge couldn't see her lick her ruby-red lips. "Ah, single and available."

The witness gulped. "Well, yeah."

"My client is single as well." She cocked her head toward her client. "Find her attractive?"

The man looked at his own lawyer, a portly older man with a gray beard, then back to Serena. "I suppose. That's not why I hired her, though."

"I see. She had excellent references from her previous employers, did she not?"

"She did."

Serena moved back to her long wooden desk and picked up a piece of paper. "Exhibit five, your honor." The judge nodded as she held up the paper. "This is a six-month review you gave my client one month before you fired her. Would you mind reading it for the jury?"

I thought she was going to hand the paper to the man, but instead she moved very close to the witness stand and held it just below her chest in such a way that it covered everything below.

The man's eyes darted between the paper and her boobs, both

inches away. "Danielle is a... very resourceful employee who is very... thorough. She has great... attention to detail and is an asset to the company. She... uh... has great skills."

Serena then whipped the paper away from her body and fired a quick question. Now the only thing in his line of sight was her cleavage. "So, they're impressive."

The man's eyes didn't move. Beads of sweat began to form on his forehead. "Uh..."

Serena then pointed to her face. "My eyes are up here, Mr Harrolds."

Snickers filled the room. The judge bit her lip to keep from laughing.

The defense attorney stood up. "Your honor..." he said in a pleading tone.

The judge turned toward Serena. "Ms. Dash, let's stick to the questions."

"Sorry, your honor."

"Like hell you're sorry," said the judge. "But continue."

She backed up toward the desk, dropped the paper along the way and crouched down to pick it up, giving the witness an exclusive shot down her blouse. "So, my client's skills..." The witness leaned forward to get a closer look. She looked up to face him from the floor. "They're impressive."

He was riveted to her chest. "Oh yeah."

She stood up, turned and marched toward the witness. "I'm glad you find certain... skills... impressive." More snickers in the courtroom. She walked back to her desk and turned to the defendant's attorney. "Your witness."

The defense attorney stood up, took one look at his sweaty client and said, "Your honor, a brief recess?"

***

Thirty minutes later I was having lunch with Serena in a bright, airy restaurant with lots of ferns, ceiling fans and flat-screen televisions broadcasting baseball. She got an early reprieve from court when the defense attorney realized his client had sent his case headlong into the shitter and wanted to settle.

"So," I asked, taking great care to handle my fork correctly as my salad arrived. "How much was your commission on that one?"

"Can't tell you since it's an out-of-court settlement. But you knew that."

"Yeah, I did. Just thought you might slip up and I could do the math."

"You know better than to try reporter's tricks on me. Let's just say my client can buy a new car for every member of her family. And I'm picking up the check for lunch."

"Why, thank you." I gently speared some spinach leaves and slowly brought them to my mouth. I noticed she was watching closely. "I'm doing it right. Right?"

She reached over and patted my free hand. "Absolutely. I'm so proud of you, Wing Girl. Learning to feed yourself! It's like a kitten drinking from the bowl for the first time."

I smiled as I chewed, resisting the temptation for a snappy comeback with my mouth open. I swallowed, gently lifted my glass and took a sip of water. "So, mind telling me why I needed to see your flagrant manipulation of the justice system?"

"So that you'll understand the flagrant manipulation of the dating system."

"Wow, men like to look at boobs. Let me call the station so we can break into programming."

"You don't get it."

"I get it."

"No, you don't. Men are already looking at you, but you have no idea what to do with that power."

"Excuse me? Power?"

"Sweetie, you have the upper hand. And you can use it to weed out the clunkers. I used that power to win a trial back there. You can use it to thin the herd of prospective boyfriends."

"So I want a man who *doesn't* look at my boobs? Why don't I just go to a gay bar? I thought the whole idea of this makeover thing and learning to drink tea with my pinkie sticking out was to get men to pay attention to me."

"That's just part of it. Phase two of your training begins tonight."

"Phase two? What the hell is that?"

"Catch and release."

***

Councilman Jagger's massive office in the old municipal building looked like a sports museum. He's an admitted fanatic of baseball and football, so the place is crammed with autographed baseballs, footballs, helmets, gloves and jerseys. Where most politicians have photos of themselves with presidents and heads of state, Jagger has nothing but pictures of himself with athletes. He's pretty much out of wall space, as the numerous eight-by-tens have been haphazardly hung in a fashion only a man (or myself) would deem acceptable. The massive antique oak desk has a glass top, under which are so many signed trading cards you can't see the wood.

All the guy needs is a pool table and a flat screen and he's got the perfect man cave.

What makes Jagger different is that I've never had to investigate the guy. I may not agree with a lot of his politics, but he's either squeaky clean or the best I've ever seen at covering his tracks. To be honest, I don't really "like" any politicians; despite what you hear about all journalists being flaming liberals, I'm middle of the road because I've realized they're all a bunch of egomaniacs who are full of shit, regardless of their party affiliation. But at least this guy has always been pleasant and treated me like a professional on the rare occasions we've crossed paths, usually at charity fundraisers. As opposed to perp walks, during which I've run into a few other elected officials.

"Belinda, thanks for coming by," he said, as he got out from behind his desk to greet me. He's too much of a gentleman and knows I'm a serious reporter, so while he noticed the obvious change in my appearance he said nothing.

He extended his hand and I shook it. "Nice to see you, Councilman. It's been a while."

"I guess that's good considering the stories you do," he said with a slight smile. He gestured toward the old maple chair in front of his desk and I took a seat as he moved back behind his desk. Jagger was in his late fifties, tall and fit, an ex-Marine who still sported a salt and pepper crew cut. His lean, rugged face and strong chin, along with piercing steel-blue eyes made me think he could re-enlist and head right back into battle without missing a beat. His tough gravel voice went nicely with the look, and has always conveyed the straight shooter attitude he's had as a politician.

"I must say this is a first. I've never had an elected official call and ask me to investigate his own office," I said, taking a notepad out of my satchel. "As you would expect, I've been trying to figure out any political motive you might possibly have."

"Full disclosure, Belinda. You know I've never had a scandal attached to this office, and one now would hurt my re-election chances. I'd just as soon take care of this before it gets out of control. So you're right, uncovering any wrongdoing *would* be to my benefit. But what's going on is still wrong."

"You do realize if I break a story about something shady in your office it will make you look bad anyway."

"Not if you tell viewers that I tipped you off." He didn't have to say the word *deal*.

"Okay," I said. "If I turn a story I'll include that. It's the truth, after all, since you did call me."

"Fine," he said, then reached into his desk and pulled out a zip drive. "You're familiar with the change we instituted a few years ago about the pension plan for municipal workers, right?"

I nodded. "Sure. You switched all the new employees to a 401k, and the costs of the pension would eventually decline as people... you know... died off."

"Right." He handed me the zip drive. "All the books relating to the pension are on that drive, and it's up to date as of today. I didn't give you that by the way."

"Not a problem."

"Here's the curious thing, Belinda. In the last three years, the costs of the pension have remained almost the same."

I furrowed my brow. "I don't understand. I thought as people passed away—"

"One would think. But the expenditures have barely dropped at all. That makes absolutely no sense."

"Could it be management fees or something like that?"

"No, we have a fixed-fee contract with the management company. It hasn't changed since we implemented the 401k."

"Have you had your accounting people look at this?"

"No. I don't want to tip anyone off that I'm investigating this, since I have no idea who might be cooking the books. But something doesn't add up, Belinda. And I'd like you to find out what it is. Because I sure as hell can't."

I tucked the zip drive into my purse. "Well, I do love a challenge."

He stood up and walked around his desk. "I appreciate your efforts, Belinda. Oh, one more thing."

"What's that?"

"Be very discreet. If this involves the kind of money I think it involves, someone's going to be very upset if we start poking around."

CHAPTER NINE

Apparently the social skills Harry says I lack are not as easily fixable as my hair and wardrobe. When you grow up without any other women in the household, then spend your career as "one of the guys", it's only natural that you think a fly pattern is something from an NFL playbook instead of a Simplicity catalogue.

But considering my longest romantic relationship featured a man who actually left a Gas-X tablet on my pillow each night instead of a mint, I did realize I needed help in discovering the woman buried deep inside me.

The blasted whiteboard was up again in Ariel's apartment, with the heading "Catch and Release!" written in blue magic marker across the top. Roxanne, who's a decent enough artist, added a fishing pole with my name on it and a fish on the end of the line.

So here we go with round two of the intervention.

"First, Wing Girl," said Ariel, starting the meeting as she stood at the board with her hands behind her back, "we're so proud of you. You've made significant progress in beginning the exorcism of the rampant Y chromosome that has been infecting your body for so many years."

"You mean it's not gone yet?" I asked. "Are you going to give me a Silkwood shower in holy water?"

"You may have mastered the use of forks and spoons, but you've got a long way to go," said Serena.

"In other words," said Roxanne, "no more belching."

I playfully thrust out my lower lip. "Aw, c'mon. Not even when I'm home alone?"

"Nope," said Ariel. "You gotta break the habit. As for your, uh, other problem," she wrinkled her nose, "no more Mexican food on dates. I don't think I need to embellish that any further."

The image of the Gas-X tablet flashed through my mind. "Noted."

"Now, to our lesson of the evening," said Ariel, pulling a pointer from behind her back and using it to tap the top of the whiteboard.

"You're kidding me. You actually bought a pointer?" I asked.

"Seemed fun," she said. "And I figured since you went to Catholic school you'd be used to it."

After hearing that I sat on my hands, as a brief memory of being whacked with a ruler flashed through my head. (What can I say, I colored outside the lines and Sister Mary Hatchet-face got pissed off.)

Ariel pointed at the board. "Anyway, you see the term I've written here. Can you tell me what that is?"

"Well, duh, I wonder what that drawing means?" I said. "It's a style of fishing. Guys go out on a lake, drink beer, throw all the cans in the water and piss over the side of the boat, then release the trophy bass they've just caught because it is preserving the balance of nature. After that they go out into the woods and blow Bambi's brains out with a rifle because they need to *thin the herd*."

"That's a spot-on description," said Ariel. "But tonight we're talking about dating."

"Think of men in the same way as the bass," said Serena, "except you don't throw the good ones back."

"You take the good ones home and eat them," said Roxanne. Ariel and Serena shot nasty looks at her. "Oh, for God's sake. *Figuratively* speaking since we're doing the *fishing* metaphor." The other two nodded. "Though occasionally it's literal," she said, under her breath.

"Anyway" said Ariel, "a good example of how *not* to employ the catch and release program happened the other night, when that nice-looking man offered to buy you a drink. Ergo, you did not catch, therefore you did not have the opportunity to either take him home or release him."

"As I said then, I already had a drink."

Ariel then took the marker and wrote the following:

"May I buy you a drink?"

She turned back to me. "Okay, when a man asks to buy you a drink it really makes no difference if you want one or not. It's simply his way of saying..." she pointed to me.

I said nothing.

Roxanne shook her head. "Wait for it..."

The light bulb finally went on. "Oh! He wants to sleep with me!"

Serena rolled her eyes. "Dear Lord." She got up and headed to the kitchen. "I'm getting a beer."

"All men want to eventually sleep with you," said Roxanne. "But you need to find out which ones are compatible."

"Hence the term, *catch*..." Ariel cast an imaginary fishing rod at me and began to reel something in.

"And release, I get it," I said. "But am I simply to haul everything on the line into the boat?"

"Well, you don't cut the line before you've gotten the fish out of the water," said Serena, returning with her brew in a frosted mug. "Which is what you did. In the case of the guy from the other night, he was great-looking, polite, might have been your soul mate. But you'll never know since you hit him with both the death stare and a snotty comment at the same time."

"Yeah, that daily double of yours is devastatin' to a guy," said Roxanne.

"Okay, I get that part," I said. "But how about the worst case scenario? What if some total loser or a guy I find unattractive comes up and wants to buy me a drink and I'm sitting there with an empty glass?"

"If you're sure you have no interest, you politely decline," said Ariel. "A simple *no thank you* will suffice. Or the even safer, *I'm meeting someone.*"

"That's it? He'll go away after that?"

Serena nodded. "Well, usually. Most guys who get shot down don't want to prolong the agony. They know if you're not interested, or already taken, there's no point in pressing the issue and they'll move on to someone else. They're extremely fragile."

"Of course, some won't take no for an answer," said Roxanne. "That's when you bring out the death stare."

"I thought it was totally off the table."

"Nah, it has its uses," said Serena. "You could suck the soul out of a guy with that thing."

"Okay," I said. "So let's assume a guy who might be interesting offers to buy me a drink, I say yes, and he sits down. How long before I take him home or toss him back in the water?"

"Depends," said Ariel. "How long does it take you to size up someone you're interviewing?"

"Depends," I said.

"And there's your answer," said Serena.

"Wow, that's a huge amount of help," I said, as I reached for my purse. "Let me write that down."

"Here's where you usually go with your gut," said Serena. "Though in your case your women's intuition on the subject of dating suffers from serious acid reflux."

"You can thin the herd by looking for the red flags we listed during the last session," said Ariel. "Married, divorced, kids, you don't want any of that because we know you want someone with a relatively clean slate and not tied to some other woman's evil spawn. By the way, I thought of two more. If he drinks too much, that's a red flag. Smoker, outta here."

"She now has more red flags than a friggin' Russian parade," said Roxanne.

"Still, there are plenty of guys out there we would approve of," said Serena.

My eyebrows went up. "Oh, you guys get *approval?*"

"Absolutely," said Roxanne. "You're still a babe in the woods. If we left you alone you might go home with an axe murderer."

"So," I said, "let me get this straight. At least one of you will be with me at all times as I, for lack of a better term, *screen* prospective boyfriends?"

"Correct," said Ariel, who then wrote the word **CODES** on the board. "Let's move on."

"What the hell are *codes?*" I asked.

"It's a fail-safe system we've set up to protect you," said Serena. "We can't exactly sit there and tell you if we like the guy or not while he's sitting there, and that old trip-to-the-ladies-room bullshit is way too transparent. If we think a guy might be a possible boyfriend, we'll say he reminds us of someone you really like. Say, for example, your brother Will."

I nodded, as this was beginning to make sense. Will is my favorite brother, and has the qualities any woman would want. And they frequently do. "Okay, so if you think I should go forward with a guy, one of you will say he reminds you of Will."

Ariel wrote **WILL = REEL IN** on the board.

"I like this idea," I said. "A guy like my brother would be great. I'd marry Will if we weren't siblings."

Their faces tightened.

"Or if we lived in Arkansas."

"Moving on from the nuptial habits of rednecks," said Ariel.

"*Sophistication-challenged,*" I said. "Redneck is a politically incorrect term."

"Again, moving on," said Ariel. "We now need a code name to tell you to cut the guy loose. Someone you really dislike."

"Just say the guy reminds you of Vincent," I said. Roxanne gave me the wounded-doe look. I shrugged. "Sorry."

Ariel wrote **VINCENT = THROW BACK** on the board.

I raised one finger. "Question. Suppose someone starts out as a Will and turns into a Vincent as the conversation goes on?"

"One of us will pull out a cell phone and say we've gotta take the call because Vincent is on the line," said Serena. "Then we say Vincent and his friends will be meeting us shortly and we have to leave."

"Okay, all that makes sense," I said. "But suppose things are going well, the guy's a Will and we go home, and then there's a red flag and you're not there to protect me. What happens then?"

"Well, obviously you don't sleep with the guy if you see a red flag. You'll simply provide us a detailed transcript of what happened," said Serena. "After proper deliberations the jury will then decide if the man is a Will or a Vincent."

"So what you're telling me is that you guys have supreme veto power over anyone I date?"

"That's the deal," said Roxanne. "As my mother used to say, it's for your own good."

***

So Sunday rolled around, same deal. Hair, makeup, ass-pop jeans. (That's a new term I'm using.)

And after a string of Vincents last night, I was ready for a Will. Or in this case, Scott.

He was off to a good start. He obviously liked cats, and was polite enough to leave that rain check sticky note, which impressed the jury even though they hadn't met him. So I had assumed he was a guy who would actually call you if he said he would. However, I was reminded last night to keep a sharp eye out for red flags, since Wing Girl was flying solo. Roxanne seemed very worried that I'd end up with a chain-smoking, drugged-out boozing polygamist with nine kids, four wives and several identities, and I'd eventually be featured on *Dateline* as a woman scorned.

Right now I'd settle for polite.

Diane beamed as I walked through the shelter door. She lowered her voice and said, "He's heerrrrreeeee," like that little girl in the movie *Poltergeist*.

I tried to be cool but my smile betrayed me. "You playing matchmaker?"

She shrugged and looked at the ceiling, eyes filled with delight. "Let's just say I put in a good word for you. Not that you need any, looking the way you do."

"And what do I need to know about him?"

She furrowed her brow. "Seriously? If you got new contacts you should know the answer. I'd do him in a New York minute." She waved her hand as if swatting a fly. "Pfffft. Worry about his personality later. Take him home and ravish him."

"I knew you were an old-fashioned girl. So, how'd the week go?"

"Three in, four out. Though I think it's gonna be five shortly. Some guy just called to see if we were open Sundays and said he was headed right down for a cat."

"This could be a *very* good day," I said, as I headed for the back room.

I found Scott filling cat dishes with dry food, looking like the Pied Piper as a small horde of felines followed him and rubbed on his legs. "You've found the way to their hearts," I said.

"Same as men," he said. "How you doing this morning?"

"Fine. Hey, wanted to thank you for leaving the note last week. A girl appreciates that kind of stuff."

"I'd be drummed out of the male ranks if I blew off a girl who looks like you."

Was this a red flag? The obvious compliment? Classic pick-up line? Or was he just being cute?

And... cue the rose-colored glasses. "Thank you," I said. "So we're still on for lunch?"

"Absolutely. No weddings or other family obligations for the entire day." He paused a moment and rolled his eyes. "Thank God."

"How *was* that wedding, by the way?"

Big smile as he shook his head. "Oh, man, it was hard to keep from laughing. My cousin married a guy with so many body piercings he looked like the phone rang and he answered the staple gun."

I laughed. "That's funny."

"What's funnier is that they were registered at Ace Hardware."

I began to seriously relax. Scott had a sharp wit, and a smile that put me instantly at ease. He didn't strike me like the parade of losers at various bars last night, though it's probably hard to hit on a girl with your best line while surrounded by a bunch of cats in a shelter.

I heard the bell on the front door jingle. "Hey, customer. Diane said some guy was heading down to adopt this morning."

"Good, I'll get to see how the process works," he said, as I heard Diane direct the man down the hall. I hastily grabbed the community litter box and hid it in a closet, wanting to make the best impression for a prospective cat owner.

Then I heard his voice.

"Hi, I need a cat."

Oh, you're friggin' kidding me.

Not again.

Not now.

I walked out of the closet and sure enough the face matched the voice. Vincent walked toward Scott, hand out. "Hi, I'm Vincent."

"Scott." He shook hands and extended nodded toward me. "And this is—"

"Belinda," he said, with a wicked smile.

"Oh, you've been here before?" asked Scott.

"Not exactly," I said, as I folded my arms in front of me.

"We know each other," said Vincent, who was still smiling, for some warped reason known only to him.

"So, *you* want a cat?" I said, with eyes narrowed.

Vincent stuck his nose up in the air. "Yes, I *do* want a cat. What's so strange about that?"

"I just figured you were picking one up for a niece or something. Or maybe some daughter you have out there... somewhere."

"I don't have any kids. I'm not married, remember? And the cat's for me. Mine died a few months ago and I guess I'm through the mourning period."

Oh, give me a break.

He turned to Scott. "And it needs to be an indoor cat, 'cause I'm in an apartment." Vincent looked at a few kitties which were stretched out on various cat beds. "So, who wants to come home with me today?"

A tortoiseshell tabby meowed. Vincent moved toward it and began to scratch its head. It stood up and began to purr loudly, twitching its tail. "What's the story with this one?" He picked it up and cradled it.

"I'll look it up," said Scott. He moved toward the small file of index cards which held information on each cat.

"She's three years old," I said, already knowing her cat dossier. "Her owner passed away a few months ago." I moved forward quickly, my fast heel clicks on the beige linoleum floor echoing off the walls, grabbed the cat from him, held her close and stroked her soft, colorful fur, a mix of tiger stripes and golden patches. "De-clawed." I looked into the cat's eyes. "And she's fixed, so there won't be any males around."

"Sounds like your kind of cat," said Vincent, with a smirk. "Except for not having any claws."

My death stare began to brew. "What the hell do you mean by that?"

Scott began to develop a wide-eyed look of fear. "Maybe I should leave you two alone to talk—"

"No!" We both responded in stereo.

Vincent moved toward me and took the cat, who nuzzled her head against his chest. "She got a name?"

"Gypsy," I said.

He tilted the cat's head up and looked into her light-green eyes.

"Hey there, Gypsy." She licked his hand. "Seems like a gentle cat. Torbies are usually laid back."

"*You* know what a Torbie is?" I asked. I took the cat back. She started to growl as she was probably getting pissed off at being passed back and forth.

"Half tortoiseshell, half tabby. They're said to be lucky." He grabbed the cat back from me. "Some people call 'em money cats."

"Really," said Scott. "That's very interesting. I read that Siamese cats—"

"So you want the cat or not?" I started to reach for the cat again but she hissed at me and Vincent turned sideways, as if protecting her from me by putting his body between us. I put my hands on my hips.

"I'll take her," said Vincent, holding the cat so that her head rested on his shoulder. "She'll obviously be a lot happier with *me*."

"Fine!" I snapped, and started to march toward the closet. "I'll get you a carrier."

He wrinkled his nose at me. "I already brought one," he said, with a condescending tone.

"Fine!"

"So is there a fee?"

"Pay Diane up front. Forty bucks. Or more if you're feeling generous. Most people who aren't cheapskates pay more."

He took a quick look at the cat. "I think she's worth a hundred."

"Fine!"

Vincent shook his head at me, spun on a dime and headed for the door. He stopped, turned to Scott and said, "Nice meeting you, Scott." He cocked his head at me. "You might want to put out an extra saucer of milk for that one." He shot me a quick smile, then left.

"Augh!"

My hands tightened into fists as I felt my pulse pounding in my head. Scott stood there, stunned. Neither of us said anything for about a minute. Finally he broke the silence, speaking very softly. "I'm gonna take a wild stab here and guess he's... not on your Christmas card list?"

The line was so funny it broke the dam holding in my anger. I started to laugh as my hands relaxed.

"I, uh, guess you two know each other."

"Unfortunately."

"Old boyfriend?"

"Dear God, no. One of my best friends tried to fix me up with him. He's her cousin."

"Oh." Long pause. "You two don't seem very... compatible."

"Ya think?" I snapped. He backed up a bit. "Sorry, Scott, he just pushes my buttons."

"I understand. I've had a few women in my life who did the same thing. Still want to go to lunch?"

"Absolutely. Just make sure it's a place that serves liquor."

***

I leaned back and let the sun warm my face. The casual outdoor café was a perfect choice: the weather was spectacular, too nice to be indoors. The light breeze made the white tablecloths flap gently. The place was packed, our table was right next to the sidewalk, an ornate black wrought-iron fence separated us from the pedestrians. The constant foot traffic made me feel more secure since my friends weren't around to run interference for me.

Not that I felt I needed any.

Scott seemed to sense I needed to lighten up and had fired up his sense of humor big time after my altercation with Vincent: telling jokes, making me laugh, helping me focus my attention on the cats instead of myself. I still ordered a big glass of wine when we got to the restaurant and my blood pressure had taken a slow, comfortable trip down to a normal level.

Speaking of comfortable, I had that feeling about him as well.

I mentally reviewed my instructions from my mentors.

-Only lunch. If he asks you to spend the day, go to a festival, whatever, you're busy. Tell him you'd love to but you have plans.

-If he asks you out for the following weekend, be non-committal. Tell him you don't know what your schedule will be because everything changes in the news business. Ask him to call you later in the week, then see if he actually does. Men who say they'll call and do not is a red flag!

-Take mental notes for us, as we will review things with you Sunday afternoon while things are fresh in your mind.

All this was beginning to remind me of those over-protective parents who bubble-wrap their kids. But I understood they just wanted the best for me as our meals arrived. He went for bacon cheeseburger while I chose the spinach quiche. (I really wanted a burger as well, but I was now petrified of eating anything with my hands in public. And the stress from the altercation with Vincent would've made me tear into the thing like a grizzly ripping open a salmon.)

"You eat here a lot?" I asked, since he had picked the restaurant and it was my first time.

"About once a week. I live down the street. Since I work out of my house, it's a nice place to meet clients. Food's great and very reasonable."

"I guess I haven't asked you what you do for a living."

"I haven't asked you either."

Ah, good sign. He really had no idea. "You first."

"I'm an independent financial consultant. I know that sounds pretty vague, but I work with clients who need to maximize the assets of their companies. Help them cut the waste and figure out how to get more bang for the buck."

"Sort of an efficiency expert?"

He shrugged. "In a roundabout sort of way. How about you?"

"Television reporter for Channel Six." Most men were impressed by my job, and the reaction was always the same. Wide eyes, look of surprise. Wow, you're on TV.

Not this time. "Oh, that sounds interesting. I don't watch much television other than sports, so I've never seen you. Sorry."

"No big deal. Lots of people are turned off by news these days. Too much death and destruction."

"Are those the kinds of stories you do?"

"No, I'm an investigative reporter. It's kind of old fashioned, and not many stations do it any more. But I like exposing corruption, righting wrongs."

He smiled. "Well, then, you're making the world a better place. I'll have to tune in this week. What time do your stories run?"

"I'm generally live on the set for the five o'clock show, then they air the re-cut story at six."

"Well, I'll DVR the five, then. What are you working on now?"

"Just got a lead from Councilman Jagger. I can't tell you much, but there's something fishy going on with the books."

"Isn't there always with politicians?"

"True enough."

"Sounds like you have a really interesting job, Belinda."

"Yeah, I'm blessed in that I love my work. And it's something different every single day."

The conversation flowed easily, with no "dead air" as we call it in broadcasting. The topics ranged from work to cats to travel to movies. It turned out we both love science fiction, cruises, the Mets, pro football and driving with the top down through New England when the leaves change. I wished it were October instead of June, and looked forward to the breeze whipping through my hair instead of hitting the bun of steel like a wind shear.

There were no red flags. Non-smoker, only had one beer at lunch, never married (and I was wanting to assume there were no kids, but these days you never know). At one point our knees brushed under the table and I felt a definite rush of adrenaline.

I tried to keep myself from drooling over his burger as the quiche was tasty but not very filling. We split a piece of raspberry cheesecake (well, I ate most of it) as the clock approached two. I felt my pulse kick up a notch. Would he want to do something else this afternoon? Ask me out for the weekend? Simply say he'd see me next week when we could scoop litter boxes together?

I noted there was one piece of cheesecake left on the plate. He must have noticed me licking my lips, so he gently pushed the plate toward me. "Last bite's yours," he said.

"Well, if you twist my arm," I said, as I swooped in with my fork to scoop up every last bit, then had to remind myself not to shovel it in. I savored the rich cheesecake and tart berries as he tossed his napkin on the table, waved to the waitress and mouthed the word "check."

"So," he said, leaning back in his chair.

Not having any idea where he was going, I kicked back in my own chair. "So," I replied, smiling as I locked my eyes on his.

He exhaled deeply, then looked up at the sky. "This is probably a stupid question, but I suppose I have to ask it eventually." He looked at me and leaned forward. "A girl like you has gotta be attached, right?"

***

"So," said Serena, holding her ever-present yellow legal pad, "upon receipt of said invitation to a ballgame, your reply was..."

"Exactly what you told me to say. That I worked in a very fluid business and there was no way to know what night I'd be free or if I was working this weekend." I smiled as I leaned back in one of the teak Adirondack chairs on her patio. The breeze was strong on the twentieth floor of her building, but the traffic noise was negligible at that altitude. She took notes while Ariel walked across the gray slate and refilled everyone's margaritas from a tall glass pitcher. Roxanne was leaning against the patio's red-brick wall and I noticed her studying my face like never before. "What?"

"You got that starry-eyed look. Like a teenager in love for the first time. I got the fifties song playing in my head."

"I just felt a connection with this guy. We have a lot in common."

"Hmmm," said Ariel. "Let me guess, every time you said you liked something, he agreed?"

I nodded. Big smile. "Yeah. How'd you know?"

Serena shook her head as she put her pad down on an end table. "Oh, shit. It's the Celine Dion scenario."

"I was afraid she might run into that," said Ariel. "We should have gone over it with her in our previous lessons."

"What the hell are you guys talking about?" I asked.

"When a man first meets you he'll agree with everything you say, and like everything you do," said Ariel. "It's his way of getting closer to you, even if he is lying through his teeth."

"Okay," I said. "So how does Celine Dion figure into this?"

"Well," said Roxanne, "most men would rather get a hot needle through the eye than sit through one of her concerts. But if yesterday you had said that you liked Celine Dion, he would have agreed, just to make you think you have everything in common."

"So you're saying he's lying about all the things he likes?" I asked.

"Not necessarily," said Serena, "but it's likely that at least some of the things you find appealing actually make him physically ill. Was he specific about anything, like his supposed interest in sci-fi?"

"Not really. He said he loved it since he was a kid."

"So ask him a Star Trek question," said Ariel. "You've been to enough conventions to determine if he's a Trekkie or not."

"Trekk*er*. We do not approve of the term Trekkie." All three shook their heads. "And why are you guys raining on my parade? I finally meet a nice guy who's polite and cute with no red flags—"

"No *apparent* red flags," said Roxanne. "You traded in your glasses for rose-colored contacts."

"You haven't even met him yet! And you're all finding things wrong with him before we even go out!" I playfully thrust out my lower lip into a pout. "Bunch of big meanies."

Ariel walked over, crouched down and wrapped one arm around my shoulder. "We're just being careful, Wing Girl. You don't want to get hurt and then have to get Roxanne to go over to his apartment and kick his ass, do you?"

"No, I suppose not."

Serena reached over and patted my hand. "You're too precious to us. Besides, we'll find out if he's for real when we meet him Saturday night before you go out. If he gets our seal of approval, you're good to go."

"Excuse me?" I asked.

"Remember, we haven't met this guy yet," said Serena. "We still have peremptory strikes, just like when I pick a jury. Except in this case our strikes are unlimited."

"So you guys seriously want to check him out before we go out on a date?"

"Yes," they all said at once.

"And do I have any say in this at all?"

"No." Another stereo response.

"Look," said Serena, "just tell him to join us for cocktail hour before the game. We'll use the Will and Vincent codes, and then off to the game you go."

"Why don't you just come with us?" I said sarcastically, then turned to Serena. "Maybe you can borrow a polygraph from the DA's office and interrogate him about Captain Kirk."

"We're rooting for you, really," said Ariel. "And I must say I do like the choice of a baseball game for a first date. It's casual, out in the open, and it's not like he'll be expecting anything as he might after taking you to an expensive candlelight dinner."

"Yeah, what a romantic evening," said Roxanne. "A subway ride on the number seven train to Flushing. Every woman's dream."

CHAPTER TEN

So thanks to the discussion of the Celine Dion scenario that damn annoying song from *Titanic* was stuck in my head (just what I needed in the newsroom on a Monday morning), and it brought back memories of the night in the theater when I yelled "Just sink the damn boat!" about three hours into the endless movie. I got applause from all the men in the theater, in case you were wondering about the reaction.

Usually I brought my work home with me on the weekends, but since my extreme makeover was now like a second job, I resisted the temptation to check out what Councilman Jagger had given me. But now I was back on the clock and the zip drive was in my trusty laptop, which was never connected to the Internet, since I had no desire to be hacked by the competition. Or any of the other reporters in our newsroom, many of whom would steal a story in a heartbeat. Sad that we work in a business where we ask the public to trust us while we throw complete sets of cutlery at co-workers behind the scenes. And I hate to say this about my own kind, but the females of the species are the worst. Harry says "women will eat their young" for a chance at the anchor desk, and it was proven true the last time we had an opening.

Anyway, my eyes were glazed over at the seemingly endless pages of numbers on the screen when a body slid onto the corner of my desk.

Harry.

He gently placed a large Cadbury chocolate bar in front of my laptop and my eyes lit up. This was Harry's form of an apology, as he knows I'm a chocoholic and Cadbury is my brand of choice. It's nice that he's old school as a man as well as a journalist, knowing flowers and/or candy are the old standby when you've pissed off a woman, since he's done it a lot. Not that it's helped through his four marriages, since unfortunately he hasn't mastered the art of *knowing* when he's pissed off a woman.

"I wasn't mad at you," I said, grabbing the bar and unwrapping it. "But I'll take it. Thanks, Dad."

"Jenna gave me a little lecture on the care and feeding of women who change their appearance."

"That why you've been divorced four times?"

He shrugged. "I've never been good at lying. My last wife asked me if her jeans made her ass look fat, and I said, 'No, your fat ass makes your ass look fat.'"

"Ouch." I broke off the corner of the bar and popped the chocolate, savoring the smooth cocoa that ran down my throat.

"Wife number three threw a lamp at me when she changed her hair and got this God-awful perm. She looked like a friggin' poodle."

"What did you say that time?"

"You *paid* for that?"

I leaned back in my chair and smiled at him. "Glad to know I'm not the only one in the room with no social skills."

"I didn't mean it that way, Cupcake. I meant as a reporter you have to be—"

"Actually, you were spot-on, Harry. I really never learned to be a girl."

"Well, you sure as hell look like one now." He reached over, stole some of the chocolate and looked at my laptop screen. "This what Jagger gave you?" He bit off a piece of chocolate.

I nodded. "Might as well be hieroglyphics. I'm gonna need help deciphering all this."

"If that's the case, you know who to call."

The color drained out of my face as I broke out in a cold sweat. A bale of cotton instantly filled my mouth as I sat up straight. It was the only person in the world I truly feared. I shook my head. "No, Harry. Please don't make me."

"You know if there's something fishy in those books she'll find it."

I grabbed my old-fashioned Rolodex and started frantically spinning it. "I'll find someone else. I know plenty of people—"

"Not as thorough as her."

I spotted a business card that might help, pulled it out and held it up in front of him. "How about my friend at the SEC?"

Harry shook his head and stood up. "Suck it up, Cupcake, and walk down the hall."

My heart rate kicked up and I knew it wouldn't slow down until I got it over with.

I was off to see the Inhuman Resources troll.

***

The Inhuman Resources troll is ironically named Glenda. I say ironically because she's anything but the good witch.

I'm not sure who first called her a troll, but she looked the part. The woman wouldn't even need a Halloween mask with that hooked nose. About five feet high and wide, Glenda wore a permanent scowl on her forty-year-old round face, which was accented with a hairy mole on her chin. Her beady dark eyes glared at you from under the bushy unibrow. She was currently dressed in the summer dowdy collection, featuring a bulky black sweater buttoned up to her many chins. Her office was a ten-by-ten windowless room with bare white walls and no pictures on her desk. And it was always freezing in there.

The photographers in the newsroom despised her. Frank said she lived under a bridge near a toll booth on the Garden State Parkway and reached up to snatch small children while their parents were looking for change. Steve contended she had little red circles all over her body from where men had touched her with ten-foot poles.

I gently tapped on the open door to her office, standing rigid like a kid summoned to the principal's office. She looked up from her paper-covered desk, and I wondered if she heard my heart slamming against my chest.

"I thought you'd be here sooner," she said, in a heavy German accent that sounds like a female version of Arnold Schwarzenegger.

"Excuse me?"

"It's only inevitable after you changed your... *look*." She leaned over her desk and pulled a form from a bin marked "sexual harass-ment". "Come and fill these out—"

"I'm not here to file a complaint."

She frowned, looked disappointed. "If you don't it will keep happening."

"No one's harassing me." I slowly tiptoed into her office, nearly knocked over by the scent of her cheap perfume in which she had obviously bathed. "I was wondering if I could borrow your *attention to detail* skills to help me on a story."

She furrowed her unibrow. "You want *my* help on a *story*?"

God, it was hard to breathe. It was like a damn potpourri factory exploded in there. "I'm working on a piece about a government agency possibly cooking the books. And I know your expertise on finding accounting errors is unsurpassed."

"I'm pretty busy."

Oooh! I've got an out! "That's okay. I can take it to someone else." I spun around and headed for the door.

"I'm busy, but I can find time to take a look."

I turned back to face her. "Really, I don't want to burden you—"

She put out her hand, palm up. "Give me what you've got."

I handed her a copy of the zip drive and filled her in on the story. "I appreciate your help on this."

She nodded. "Is this story for today?"

"No, I'm just beginning to research it. Might be weeks or even months."

"Okay. I'll look at it and get back to you by the middle of next week."

"Thanks, that will be fine," I said. I turned and headed out the door, breathing in the fresh air of the hallway and thinking I needed a big glass of wine even though it was ten in the morning.

***

After a Monday dealing with trolls and Celine Dion songs, I wanted a treat, so I hit the Italian deli down the street from my apartment. I walked down the block with a big brown bag of goodies which included my dinner for the evening, a foot-long meatball sub. The smell was driving me crazy so I picked up my pace. I wanted to tear into the thing the minute I got through the door, but I had to remember to drop the blinds lest anyone see me devour it like a yeti. I stuck my nose into the bag and took a big whiff of it and the giant hunk of imported provolone that sat next to it and atop all sorts of delicacies, which included a slice of tiramisu for dessert.

And when I looked up, the smell disappeared and turned to sewage.

He was heading right toward me.

"Oh, you gotta be friggin' kidding me," I said to myself. "Not again."

Vincent was walking in my direction, holding a bag of groceries while eating an apple. He looked up, saw me, slowed to a stop a few feet in front of me, and stopped chewing.

"Are you stalking me?" I asked.

He swallowed. "Yeah. I always prey on innocent women with a sack full of produce. Mangoes lure 'em in like you wouldn't believe. Want one?"

I stood up straight and glared at him, my arms wrapped around my bag. "Then please explain why you're here."

"Uhhh... let me think. Oh, yeah. I live here."

"You live on *my* block?"

"No, I live on Staten Island but I shop here. It's a nice walk. And I wasn't aware this was *your* block."

I stood there with my mouth hanging open. This couldn't be happening. "So we're *neighbors*?"

"I'm two blocks over. I get my produce at Vinnie's and then I hit the deli on the way back." He stuck his nose in the air in the direction of my grocery bag. "Smells like you've already been there."

"Yeah."

He glanced into my bag. I leaned back. "Hmmm. Foot-long sub. You gonna eat all that yourself?"

"You implying I'm fat?"

"No way. You look great."

"Maybe I'm saving half for tomorrow."

"Uh-huh. Right. Those things don't re-heat well. So, where do you live?"

"Why should I tell you?"

"So I can avoid your building, which I would assume you'd appreciate."

I cocked my head toward my apartment building a few feet away. "Right there. And there's a doorman to prevent any ne'er-do-wells from getting in."

"*Ne'er-do-wells*?"

"Look it up."

"I know what it means." He started walking past me. "Have a good night, Cupcake."

I whipped my head around. "You haven't earned the right to

call me that!"

He put up one hand in a half-hearted wave and moved on. Then, just when I thought I was done with him, just when I turned and headed to my building, he struck again. "You know, you're beautiful when you're angry!"

I was so pissed off I turned around and glared at him, and of course he was wearing that shit-eating grin again. I put the bag down, yanked the meatball sub out of it, ripped open the paper covering the top, and took as big a bite as possible.

CHAPTER ELEVEN

"Here he comes!" I sat up straight and smiled as Scott spotted me from the door.

"Down, girl," said Serena.

"Mmmmm. Very cute," said Ariel.

Roxanne looked at him skeptically with narrowed eyes. "We'll see."

Scott was wearing dark slacks, brown tasseled loafers, and a royal-blue polo shirt. He had a tan windbreaker slung over his shoulder as he made his way through the bar, looking like an ad for casual menswear. He smiled as he arrived at our table. "Hi guys."

"You're right on time," I said, shooting a look at Roxanne, who seemed determined to use one of her peremptory strikes for any flag that's even in the palest shade of red. I took care of the introductions as he sat down. A waitress spotted the new arrival and quickly visited our table. Scott ordered a beer and asked if the rest of us needed anything. We were already sufficiently lubricated, though I was so nervous I could have used an alcohol IV.

"So," Roxanne said, "how long you been a Mets fan?"

"Since I was a kid."

"Really," said Roxanne, and I could tell she was ready with more gotcha questions than a biased political reporter. "Be nice if they got back in the World Series again."

"Yeah, it's been awhile," said Scott. "Haven't been there since two thousand."

"Yeah, but that was a great subway series."

He furrowed his brow. "You kidding? They lost, four games to one. Bad enough to lose the series, but to the Yankees? That was hard to take."

I tilted my head back and stuck my nose in the air, then shot Roxanne a quick *so-there* smile.

The small talk flowed smoothly for the next forty-five minutes, and I was getting more relaxed as I hadn't seen any red flags run up the pole, though Roxanne had certainly greased the damn thing.

Scott took a quick look at his watch. "Well, we'd better get going."

"Yeah, the subway will be packed," said Roxanne, even though it wouldn't be since the Mets don't draw many fans. She was fishing again.

"I arranged for a car," said Scott, who pointed toward the window. I spotted a black Town Car with a driver in a suit and tie standing by the fender.

"That's so thoughtful," I said, then gave Roxanne another *so-there* look.

"Not wild about the subway for a night game," said Scott. "There are a few dicey stops on the number seven line."

"Well, have a good time," said Ariel.

"Hope the Mets win," said Serena.

"Not a sure thing these days," said Scott, who got up from his chair. "So, you guys got anything interesting planned for the rest of the evening?"

"Yeah," said Roxanne, who looked at the other two. "And we need to get going if we're gonna meet Will and Vincent."

Great. Hung jury.

***

We headed out of Citi Field after a rare Mets win and the temperature had suddenly taken a dive. I'd forgotten to bring a jacket and wrapped my arms around my waist as the chilly air filled my lungs. Scott noticed, took off his windbreaker and draped it over my shoulders.

"Thank you," I said, as we headed for the car.

"Little brisk for June."

"Well, I'm cold-natured. I can get goose bumps in July."

Scott tossed the foul ball he caught into the air and caught it as we walked. He didn't really catch it during the game, but our seats behind the visiting dugout were so sparsely populated he managed to grab a ball that landed three rows down.

We reached the Town Car and the driver opened the door for us. It was running and I was hoping the heat was on.

"Nice way to travel to a game," I said, as I got in and discovered it was warm and toasty inside.

"I use this company a lot. Not as expensive as you might think," he said, sliding in next to me. The driver closed the door and Scott handed me the ball. "Here, souvenir of the evening."

"No, that's yours. You caught it."

"I didn't *catch* it. It wasn't even moving when I picked it up. Besides, I got a foul ball about five years ago and one's enough. That one I actually caught."

"Well, thanks. I've never gotten one." I turned the ball over in my hand, a perfect sphere except for a small dent where it was hit. The leather was smooth, the red laces rough and the feel took me back. I adjusted it so that it was between my thumb and first two fingers, which were across the laces.

"You got a decent curve ball?"

"Nah, just brings back memories of playing with my brothers. But I don't throw like a girl."

"It would be okay if you did."

We cruised out of the parking lot easily, the thin crowd not making for much of a bottleneck. The ride back to Manhattan was quicker than normal, with little traffic on a Saturday night. The conversation continued to be relaxed and easy, as it had been all night. He was sitting close to me, near enough for me to get a whiff of his light cologne. The driver pulled up to our building. Scott reached into his pocket, pulled out a twenty-dollar bill and handed it to him. "Thanks, Bill. I can get the door."

"Thank you, Mr Shepard. See you soon."

So now, after what had been a terrific evening, I felt my heart hit a speed bump as I considered what was going to happen next. The questions flew through my mind much too fast as I got out of the car.

He's sending the driver away. How's he getting home? Does that mean he thinks I'm going to invite him in and he's sleeping here?

My friends have told me to limit him to one goodnight kiss with no invitation inside to my apartment. Do I blow off the advice since my gut is telling me he's okay? (And I really want to jump his bones.)

If I don't invite him in, will he get turned off and not ask me out again? (And I really want him to ask me out again.)

And what was the deal with Roxanne's comment about meeting Will AND Vincent? Serena and Ariel didn't say anything, so did that mean they agreed he could go either way?

Scott lightly took my arm as we walked about fifty feet past the fountain with the colored lights to the front of my building.

I had no friggin' idea what to do and said nothing.

Thankfully, he broke the silence as we reached the door. "I had a great time, Belinda."

I turned to face him. "Me too. I... uh..."

Before I could say anything he moved closer, gently took my chin, tilted it up while slipping his other hand around my waist, pulled me close and gave me the best, longest kiss I've ever had. I dropped the baseball, heard it bounce.

I hate to be cliché but I grew weak in the knees as he leaned back a bit, his hand sliding from my back to my side. "Whoa," I said softly.

He smiled. "My feelings exactly. I take it we can go out again?"

"Oh yeah," I said, without any hesitation.

Big smile from him. He picked up the ball and handed it to me. "Okay, slugger. See you in the morning."

"Huh?" Was this his way of inviting himself inside?

"At the shelter," he said.

"Oh, I forgot. Tomorrow's Sunday."

"Well, see you then. Good night." He leaned over, kissed me lightly on the cheek and walked back toward the street where he stuck out his arm and hailed a cab.

I turned and slowly entered the building, still in somewhat of a trance from the kiss. Trying to figure out if he sent the car away because he thought I would invite him in. That made the most sense, but then again, if he had the driver stand by it would tell me he didn't want to come in... aw, hell, it was too much to think about as I headed across the black and white marble floor to the elevator.

"So, details," came a familiar Brooklyn accent from behind me.

I looked over and saw Roxanne, Serena and Ariel sitting on the couch at the far end of the spacious lobby. "You guys are *waiting up for me?*"

"Well... yeah," said Ariel.

"What're you, my parents? Have you been here all night?"

"No," said Serena. "We kept an eye on the game and then figured it would take you at least a half hour to get here. We got here about ten minutes ago."

"So," said Roxanne, "enjoy the tonsillectomy?"

"You *saw* that?"

"There's a great view of the front door from this couch," said Ariel. "We were just taking in the pretty fountain and you happened to walk into our line of sight."

I rolled my eyes as I began to squeeze the life out of the baseball. "What a steaming pile of horseshit! You guys are spying on me!"

"We prefer to call it *preventive surveillance*," Serena said.

"You guys don't trust me!"

"Not after seeing those puppy dog eyes when Scott walked into the bar, we don't," said Ariel.

"So what would you guys have done had I broken your rule and invited him in? Tackled him in the lobby?"

"Honestly," said Roxanne, "the way you were looking at him you wouldn't have even noticed us."

"Meanwhile," said Serena, as she whipped a legal pad out of her purse. "Details."

I folded my arms, still holding the baseball. "The Mets won, five to two. Helluva game."

"Be serious," said Ariel.

"Fine," I said, taking a seat on the end of the tan leather couch. "He was a perfect gentleman. Never laid a hand on me until we pulled up here."

"So," said Serena, "during your three hours at said baseball game, did the defendant—"

"The *defendant*?" I asked.

"Sorry, but that will have to suffice for lack of a better term. He *is* basically on trial," said Serena. "Continuing with my previous line of questioning. Is it therefore your contention that he is sincerely a gentleman or simply playing the part?"

"Well, during the seventh inning stretch we sneaked into the upper deck since it was empty and had sex behind the foul pole. Other than that he didn't touch me."

"You think this is funny," said Roxanne.

"No, I think you're all being ridiculous," I said. "Look, we enjoyed the game, we talked baseball, he asked me a lot about my job and the stories I'm working on. He seemed genuinely interested and even offered to help me with one that involves financial stuff. He drank one beer all night and took me to one of the clubs to get something to eat." I held up the baseball. "He got a foul ball and gave it to me. Anything else?"

"Yeah," said Ariel. "Did he ask you out again?"

I nodded. "He did but didn't specify any particular date or activity. Besides, we can talk about it more tomorrow morning at the shelter."

Roxanne exhaled and her face dropped into a frown. "You really like this guy, don't you?" She sounded resigned to the inevitable.

"I do. It was the best first date I've ever had. We seem to be on the same page."

"Very well," said Serena, clicking her pen and putting it back in her purse. She looked at Ariel and Roxanne. "After considering the events as related to us and combining that with our cocktail hour impressions, I believe she can move forward with this potential relationship."

"I agree," said Ariel.

Roxanne looked right at me. "As long as you're careful."

"I'm a big girl," I said.

"Yeah, we've heard that before," said Roxanne.

"Meanwhile," said Ariel, "we'll re-visit the catch and release program this coming weekend."

I furrowed my brow. "But I've already found someone nice to date."

"You need to play the field until you've mastered your new skills," said Serena. "Just because you had one good first date doesn't mean you're... fixed."

"You don't want to put all your eggs in one basket," said Roxanne, suddenly perked up. "Besides, Scott may be playing the field right now as well."

And that comment sucked the energy out of me. It was something I hadn't considered, didn't want to consider, but her point was valid. His "stupid" question at lunch about me being attached would have been just as valid coming from me. I mean, the guy's beyond cute, obviously well off and polite. He wouldn't have trouble finding a date. "Okay, I'll buy that. By the way, what was the deal with the codes tonight? Meeting Will *and* Vincent?"

"Ariel and I thought he had potential," said Serena. "But you know Rox has that built-in bullshit detector."

I turned to Roxanne. "So you sensed something bad?"

She shrugged, her look turned serious. "I dunno. He seemed a little too perfect."

"I think you're biased," I said. "Can you at least give him the benefit of the doubt for a while?"

"He's on a short leash," she said. "But if he hurts you, I'll kick his ass."

CHAPTER TWELVE

Seeing the zip drive on my desk Wednesday morning got me off to a great start. And when I read the note under it, I knew nothing could ruin my day.

Belinda,

I took a look at the documents and honestly don't have the expertise to decipher all this. You need someone who is a financial advisor, or someone who knows the inner workings of managing funds.

Sorry I couldn't be of any help.

-Glenda

You're probably wondering why I was thrilled about Inhuman Resources hitting a dead end on the Councilman Jagger story. Two reasons. First, I wouldn't have to deal with the troll again, and second, I kinda sorta know a guy in the financial world who will be taking me out this Friday. Actually, three reasons. I actually had something in writing with Glenda saying she's sorry about something, which will go into my scrapbook of *amazing shit I've run into in the news business*. Frankly I was surprised she couldn't find anything, but hey, I've got plenty of other stories in the hopper, and the thought of working together on a story with Scott sounds intriguing.

Meanwhile, Harry asked me to drop by after the morning

meeting. I could tell he still isn't used to the new me, but I made it a point to turn some kick-ass stories in the last week, so I was still *one of the guys* even if I was wearing the dreaded skirt.

I tapped on his open office door and he looked up from the pile of papers on his desk. "You summoned me, noble one?"

"C'mon in, Cupcake." He was smiling, so I knew this wasn't anything bad. "You're certainly on a roll the last few days. Really great work."

Now Harry already said that in the morning meeting, so I knew something else was coming. He always says something good when something bad is about to follow. It's his one-man version of good cop, bad cop. "Thanks, Harry. So... what's up?" I slid onto the chair opposite his desk.

He shook his head as he picked up a stack of large yellow cards, which I knew to be requests from the promotions department. "I hope these won't take time away from your primary duties."

"They never do, Harry." Though honestly, promotions rarely requested me for any kind of personal appearance.

"Well, keep that in mind." He flipped a yellow card at me like a Vegas blackjack dealer and I caught it. "Cancer Fund wants you for a fashion show."

"They need an emcee?" I looked at the card.

"Nope. They want you as one of their models." He flipped another card at me. "Apparently someone from the Mets front office spotted you at a game recently and wants you to throw out the first pitch in the future."

I looked at the card. "Cool! And I get a jersey with either my name or Brass Cupcake above the number."

Another card flew in my direction. "Beauty pageant wants you for a co-host." Flip. "Makeover show wants you as a guest." Flip. "Tree lighting at Rockefeller Center in November." Flip. "Guest ring announcer for a fight in Atlantic City." Flip. "Judge at the Coney Island hot dog eating contest." He finally stopped flipping cards at me as I straightened them all into a stack. He folded his hands, dipped his head and looked at me over his glasses with what I call the *serious dad* look. "Young lady, I'm sorry if this reporting gig is going to play havoc with your promotional escapades."

I couldn't help but be flattered by all the requests, but tried my best not to smile. And I knew I'd better not, because when Harry starts a sentence with "young lady" you know he's not kidding. "Escapades" he usually reserves for newsroom romances, most recently in the case in which two people were caught semi-nude in an editing booth after the late newscast. "C'mon, Harry, you know me better than that. And I'll keep them to a minimum. Just the charity stuff. And the Mets game because I go there anyway. But that's it."

He nodded slightly. "Very well. But see what you started?"

"Again with the see what you started? Have my stories been of the kick-ass variety since my makeover?"

"They have."

"Then why are you worrying so much about my makeover?"

"Because I've seen the fame thing go to people's heads before, and I don't want it to happen to you."

"I've been well known in this town for a long time, Harry. I'm already famous."

"Not for your looks. This is different."

"What, you want me to change back into frumpy girl?"

"That barn door has sailed." That's Harry's metaphor combination of "locking the barn door after the horse has been stolen" and "that ship has sailed." He shook his head again and flipped me a large sheet of paper which I recognized as the overnight ratings. "Every time your stories run the numbers go up. Besides, if you suddenly reverted back to, as you call her, *frumpy girl*, I'd have to add two extra people to handle the complaints."

I looked at the overnights and saw a definite spike in the shows I was on, particularly in the fifteen-minute segments in which I had appeared. "As you said, I've had some great stories lately. That's all this is."

"That's not it, and you know it. You could have found Jimmy Hoffa or an alien from Area 51 with your old look and not gotten numbers like these." He stood up and started pacing behind his desk, then looked at the floor. "Dammit, Cupcake, why'd you have to turn out so pretty?"

I had to admit, I got a kick out of Harry's indirect compliments. "You don't like the higher ratings?"

He shrugged and looked away. "I like 'em fine, and corporate is over the moon about you. It's just... well, you've always been special to me. I never had a daughter, you know. And I feel like I've lost you."

I actually got misty at that one. It was the first time I'd ever seen Harry get sentimental about anything. I stood up and tossed the index cards back on his desk. "You'll never lose me, Harry. In fact, now I've got even more to prove."

He turned to face me. "How's that?"

"I have to keep showing people that I'm *not* just eye candy."

"I know that won't be a problem."

I moved around the desk so I was closer to him. "Harry, why is this bothering you so much?"

"Because you remind me of a reporter from a long time ago."

"Really? Who?

"Me."

And they say there's no crying in news.

***

Scott handed the menu back to the waitress and then his eyes grew wide.

"Oh, hell! I can't believe I forgot to call him back."

"Someone important?"

"Big client." He looked at his watch. "Yeah, but thankfully he's in California so it's still business hours out there."

He began to fidget in his seat and I could tell he wanted to make the call but was too polite to interrupt our date. I sensed he was waiting for permission so I gave it. "Well, what're you waiting for? Give him a holler."

"You don't mind?"

I waved my hand as if shooing a fly. "Nah, go ahead." I picked up my wine glass. "But I'm getting a head start."

"Okay," he said, pulling out his cell. "It'll just take five minutes." He started to get up. "I hate people who talk in restaurants, so I'll go outside."

"No problem, I'm not going anywhere."

"I'd better not find another guy in my seat when I get back."

"You have nothing to worry about."

He looked at his phone and his face dropped. "Oh, you gotta be kidding. My cell's dead."

"Relax, you can borrow mine," I said, as I fished it out of my purse and handed it to him.

"You're a life saver. Five minutes, no more, and I'll be back."

I sipped the wine as he headed for the door. Amazingly, my three friends approved my bringing Scott back to my apartment after dinner and a movie with the stipulation I ask for his input on Councilman Jagger's tip. (Who knew the Inhuman Resources troll would actually provide me with a way to move the relationship along?) They actually liked my idea of asking him to help out with my story, so that will be my "excuse" to invite him in.

Though as Roxanne dutifully noted, vampires have to be invited in before they bite their victims.

I personally thought it was a great idea and wouldn't put too much pressure on the guy, though after that kiss last week he probably wouldn't mind a more private and lengthier session. I had also gotten pinky swears from each of the girls promising they wouldn't be camped out in my lobby or use the Hubble telescope to do their "preventive surveillance." (However, knowing Roxanne's "connections" in the Sicilian world, I'm considering having my apartment swept for bugs.) But they insisted that breakfast with the guy is off the table. I must say that the sensible girl in me agreed that sex after two dates is rushing things a bit. Though my body has been arguing with sensible girl, reminding her she's been the equivalent of a sexual camel for several years and has basic human needs.

An hour and a half later the conversation had gone well; easy and not at all forced. He chose a place somewhere between casual and fancy, comfortable with good food. I was fat and happy as I daintily dabbed my red lips with a napkin and placed it on the table. Our movie would start at nine and it was eight-thirty, so I decided to drop my little hint and ask for his assistance.

"I meant to ask you," I said. "About your financial expertise. I need a little help."

"You need me to look at your 401k or something?"

"No, that's doing well. I've been working on this story that's hit a dead end. Someone is possibly cooking the books with the city's pension fund, and the person at the station who's great at finding stuff like that came up empty. She said I needed someone like a financial advisor to take a look. So, I was wondering..."

He smiled. "You want my help on one of your stories?"

"If you wouldn't mind taking a look. I don't want to impose."

"I'd be happy to." Suddenly his eyes filled with worry. "I don't have to be on camera or anything, do I?"

"No, not at all. I just need someone who knows the recipe for cooking books and can find the ingredients."

His face relaxed. "That's cute. Recipe for cooking the books. Dash of corruption, pinch of greed."

"I love that! I'll use it in the story if it pans out. Anyway, I brought my work home with me, so... would you mind taking a look after the movie?"

"Sure, not a problem." He checked his watch. "Speaking of which, we need to get going."

He asked the waitress for the check and I couldn't wait for the movie to end even before it had begun.

***

I placed two glasses of chilled white wine on the coffee table as Scott whipped through page after page of economic information on my laptop.

"Anything jump out at you?" I asked, as I sat close to him on the couch, presumably to get a look over his shoulder at the laptop. But when I inhaled his Polo cologne I wasn't thinking of balance sheets but satin ones. (And yes, I hired a maid so the bedroom does not look as though looters have rummaged through it.)

"Everything looks very professional, and I don't see anything out of the ordinary. For the amount of money you're talking about I would expect to see something blatantly obvious. But honestly, at first glance it looks like everything is legit."

"Hmmm. Is there anything else I might look for?"

He shook his head. "I know this would be a great scandal, and I would love to be part of one of your stories, but I don't think there's anything here. Sorry."

"Don't be. If there's no story then there's no story. The Councilman wasn't sure of anything either." I snapped the laptop shut, placed it on the coffee table, grabbed the wine glasses, and handed one to him. "Meanwhile..." I held up my glass for a toast. "To... new beginnings."

"To new beginnings." He clinked my glass and we each took a sip. "Mmmm. Great wine."

"Thought you'd like it."

"Any other financial statements you need me to look at?"

"Nope."

He turned his body a bit so that he was facing me. "Want me to balance your checkbook? Roll your loose change?"

I shook my head and smiled as my heart rate kicked up a notch.

"You're off the clock, Mister. You are free to do with your leisure time as you wish."

"Good." He took my glass from me, placed both on the coffee table, then turned back and pulled me onto his lap.

***

Roxanne leaned forward and studied my face closely as I slung my purse over the barstool.

"Whaaaat?" I asked as I sat down. "Did I screw up my makeup?"

She turned to Ariel and Serena. "She's okay."

"I'm glad you approve, but okay with what?"

"You didn't have sex," she said.

"What, you got a camera in my apartment now?"

"No, you don't have that *glow*."

"Glow?"

"Hard to explain," said Roxanne. "But I know it when I see it, so don't try to sneak it past me."

"So, how'd it go?" asked Ariel. "Scale of one to ten."

"Eleven," I said, with a huge smile.

"Eleven with no sex," said Serena. "I can only image what a five must be like. His-and-her oil changes followed by an evening watching C-Span."

I wrinkled my nose at her. "You'll all be happy to know he wants to take things slowly."

"So, you brought him home..." said Roxanne, leaving her words hanging in the air like a question mark.

"He checked out the documents from my story, we had some wine, and made out like teenagers for about two hours."

"Fully clothed?" asked Roxanne.

"No, I dressed up as a nun and he wore a suit of armor. Left me with a damn rash, so I bought him a Zorro costume for our next date."

102

"So how did the night end?" asked Ariel.

"Well, he had to go out of town this morning and had an early flight, so we just called it quits around one."

Serena nodded. "And he'll see you again... when?"

"Two weeks. He travels a lot."

"Terrific," said Roxanne, suddenly more upbeat. "That'll free you up for some catch 'n' release."

"Seriously guys, do we really need to do this? I've found a nice man and it's going well—"

"And you have nothing to compare him to," said Serena. "Let me explain this to you from a chocoholic point of view, since you may actually understand that. If you'd never had chocolate and I gave you a Hershey bar, you'd say it was terrific, and there's no reason to try anything else. But if you ate Hershey bars for a while and I gave you a Cadbury, all of a sudden you'd realize there were lots of choices out there. And you needed to find the best one by trying them all."

"Are you saying Scott is a Hershey bar?" I asked.

Ariel reached across the table and patted my hand. "She's saying he may or may not be your Cadbury. But you'll never know unless you visit the candy store. He could be a Cadbury, or he could be stale Halloween candy."

"So," I said, "if I can keep all this straight, I need to make sure Scott is a Cadbury bar Will and not a trick-or-treat Vincent."

"We got too many friggin' metaphors in this project," said Roxanne.

"I'm just glad you didn't use M&Ms and their *melts in your mouth, not in your hand* slogan."

They all cracked up at that one.

And just when I was about to present my closing arguments against the catch and release program, we got interrupted by what may have been *the* total package.

The total package's name was Todd, and he turned out to be nice enough to get the "all clear" from the three amigos via the Will code. Honestly, I think they were all drooling so much they could barely concentrate.

Of course I'd been thinking of Scott the whole time I was talking to... what's his name? Oh yeah, Todd.

The guy looked like he was computer generated. Six-four, built like Superman, short dark hair, deep-blue eyes. A lean, rugged face with a slight five o'clock shadow. Maybe thirty-five.

We went dancing after we left the bar, and he cut the rug pretty well, though our height difference was a bit of a problem. I like guys under six feet, as I don't care to get a stiff neck when I kiss someone. With this guy I was looking into his chest and needed to crane my neck to make eye contact.

The dance club was just a few blocks from my building and it was a nice night so Todd decided to walk me home.

He got a lot of looks on the dance floor and is probably every woman's dream, but I didn't *feel* anything. He was polite, funny, smart... yet there was no "it" factor as we say in television. With Scott, I felt it. This guy? Nothing. If he were working in my newsroom, he'd be known as a Ken-doll.

As we approached my building I knew I wasn't going to invite him in. And I was trying to figure out a polite way of not giving out my phone number. (I actually considered giving him the direct line to the Inhuman Resources troll because a conversation with her would be like a cold shower to the tenth power.)

We crossed the street and arrived at my front door. I turned to face him. "Well, this is it. I'd invite you in but I've got an early story tomorrow."

"Sure, no problem."

Wow, that was easy.

Suddenly he bent down, wrapped one arm around my waist,

and effortlessly lifted me into the air so we were eye to eye. His lips moved toward mine but I leaned back. "Hey!"

"What?"

"What are you doing?"

"Giving you a good night kiss. Or trying to."

I looked down and saw my feet dangling a foot off the ground. "Put me down."

"C'mon, Belinda."

I tried to wriggle free by pushing his shoulders but it was like shoving a stone wall. "Put me down or I'll scream. And my doorman will kick your ass."

He dropped me instantly. "Geez, what a frigid bitch." He turned on a dime and walked away.

Just like that.

I straightened my dress and headed quickly to the door.

I wished Scott would get back quickly.

Because I had decided that tomorrow I was going to tell my friends the catch and release season was over.

CHAPTER THIRTEEN

Every year Roxanne invites me to her family's Fourth of July picnic. And every year I seemed to be tied up with something, hanging with my brothers, or out of town.

But this year I promised her I'd accompany her to Brooklyn for what she calls "a real Sicilian Fourth." Not sure what that means, but I know the food will be good. Besides, she's done so much for me lately (despite the spying) I figured I owed her one.

Her family compound (her description, not mine) was a large brick Georgian home on the shore with a big back yard that had a terrific view of Manhattan. A cluster of huge maple trees surrounded the house like a natural canopy. Her extended family is what I expected: big, loud and full of hugs. As the lone redhead in a sea of raven-haired *paisans*, I certainly stuck out, but they were making me feel like an honored guest. Though I needed an interpreter for all the Italian slang and hand signals.

I took a bite of grilled Italian sausage, which certainly had a kick to it in the spice department and may have been the best I'd ever tasted. Throw in homemade red wine, a giant antipasto, three kinds of pasta and tomato basil salad, and it beat the hell out of hot dogs and burgers.

I leaned back in my chair under one of the maples, taking a break before getting seconds. The weather was perfect for the fourth, a sunny, cloudless day in the mid eighties. A light offshore breeze sent the smell of salt water my way. I'd worn a pale-blue cotton dress that was perfect for an afternoon at the shore.

Roxanne plopped down in the chair next to me and noticed my plate was empty. "Get enough to eat?"

"Yeah, and I'm taking a break before I go in for round two. This is wonderful. I'm sorry I've missed it all these years."

"Well, clear your calendar in the future because you're always welcome here."

"Your family is terrific, Rox."

And the moment those words left my mouth, I saw *him*.

I leaned toward Roxanne and lowered my voice. "You didn't tell me *he* was going to be here."

"I told you my family was all going to be here, and he's a big part of it. This is his mother's house, after all."

"Wonderful." I rolled my eyes as I saw Vincent prop open the back door, then disappear back into the house. "I wish you would stop trying to fix us up."

"I'm not trying to do anything."

"You're full of it."

What I saw next was something I didn't expect.

A wheelchair occupied by a frail, gray-haired elderly woman slowly came into view, with Vincent pushing it.

"Who's that?"

Roxanne sipped her wine. "That's his mother."

"So what's the deal?"

"She's an invalid. Can't walk any more or do much of anything. But her mind's still sharp."

"So her husband takes care of her?"

Roxanne shook her head. "He died about ten years ago. Vincent's an only child, so it's been tough on him. He lives here two days a week, the rest of us cousins all take turns, and thank God there's plenty of us. He couldn't bear to put her in a nursing home and he knows she wouldn't want to go to one. Those places are basically waiting rooms to die."

"Really," I said, as my emotions downshifted. I watched as family members got up and walked over to greet Vincent's mom. Her face lit up, but she struggled to lift her hand when they all bent down to hug or kiss her. When the receiving line dispersed, Vincent wheeled her past the grill so she could see what was cooking, then over to the table for a look at all the dishes that were laid out. Her face beamed. He leaned down and listened to her, nodded, grabbed a plate, then filled it as she pointed to various foods with a shaky hand. He wheeled her up to the long picnic table, put the plate in front of her, and started cutting a piece of sausage. Then he picked up a piece with a fork and began to feed her. She looked at him as she chewed, with a look right into his soul, with a look only a mother and son can share. For once, I wished I could see his eyes.

"She can't feed herself?"

Roxanne shook her head. "Not any more. They've got a live-in retired nurse for the bathroom stuff and medical care. She's just hanging on. Terminal. Doctor says she could go any time. This is definitely her last Fourth of July."

I couldn't stop staring at the scene. Vincent patiently waited as his mother took forever to chew a small bite, then fed her more or gave her a sip of wine through a straw. Her eyes were locked on him the entire time.

"You wanna meet her now?"

"Absolutely," I said. I put my plate on the table as I got up.

I followed Roxanne as we headed in her direction. Vincent looked up and saw me, gave a slight smile, then turned back to his mother.

His mother's face brightened when she saw Roxanne. "Roxy!" she said in a gravel voice. "I was wondering if you were here."

"You know I wouldn't miss it, Grace," she said, then leaned down to kiss her on the cheek. "Grace, I want you to meet a very good friend of mine. This is Belinda."

Roxanne stepped aside and I crouched down and took her hand. "Nice to meet you, Mrs. Martino," I said in a loud voice.

"I'm not deaf, honey, my body's just shot to hell."

I couldn't help but laugh. "Sorry."

She struggled to point at me, her index finger shook. "You're the one from TV."

I nodded. "That's me."

She managed to reach out and touch my hair. "Oooh, such a beautiful red."

"Thank you."

She looked up at Roxanne. "You do her hair, Roxy?"

Roxanne smiled. "You know my work, Grace."

She looked back at me. "Oh, it's just gorgeous." She reached out to Vincent and touched his forearm, then turned to face him. "Vincent, is this the girl you told me about?"

His face turned red as the pasta sauce and his eyes grew wide. "Uh, yeah Ma."

"Such a beautiful girl. She's even prettier than you said."

Face got even redder. "Yeah, I know."

***

The hours between dinner and the fireworks were filled with card games and loud conversation. The kids were off in one section of the yard, which had been turned into an old-fashioned bocce court. Meanwhile, Vincent had been avoiding me since his mother outed him. Every time I got anywhere remotely close to him he quickly headed in the opposite direction.

Probably because he knew I had a little bit of the upper hand here. And it was about damn time.

"Time for charades!" yelled Roxanne.

A dozen or so adults gathered on the lawn as Roxanne shook an old fedora. I wasn't sure what was going on but decided to play along.

"Okay," said Roxanne, "usual rules apply. I'll pick the teams out of the hat." She drew out one slip of paper after another, pairing people off. Finally she reached in and called my name. I was looking around to see who was left as a possible partner, when she reached into the hat, unfolded a slip of paper, and shot a big smile at me. "Your partner is Vincent."

Something tells me the fix is in. Nah, she's not trying to fix anyone up.

Roxanne was the timekeeper with a clipboard and a stopwatch. I hadn't played this pantomime game since I was a kid, but I remembered you have to silently act out whatever you're given and get your partner to identify it. I watched the other teams and quickly picked up the signals for movies, songs, famous people, etcetera.

"Belinda and Vincent are next," said Roxanne.

"I'll let him go first," I said. "Haven't played this in awhile."

Vincent got up, reached into the hat, pulled out a slip of paper, looked at it, then handed it back to Roxanne.

She looked at him and he nodded, then turned to me. "Annnnnnd... go!" She clicked the stopwatch.

Vincent took his right hand and rolled an imaginary camera while he looked at me through the circle he'd made with his left hand to represent a lens.

"Movie!" I yelled.

He nodded. He pointed to himself, then to Roxanne. He did it again and I got it immediately.

"My Cousin Vinny!"

A chorus of "aw, c'mon" filled the air as Roxanne clicked the stopwatch. "Ten seconds. Impressive. That should be hard to beat."

"That was way too easy," said one of the other relatives.

"Hey, he picked it out of the hat," said Roxanne, who then shot me a wink. "You're up, Belinda."

I stood up as Vincent passed me and sat down. I reached into the hat, grabbed a slip of paper, looked at it and handed it back to Roxanne. I nodded at her, then turned to Vincent.

"And... go!"

I held one fist near my mouth, placed the other hand on my stomach, and opened my mouth wide.

"Music!" Vincent said.

I pointed at him and nodded. Then I pointed strongly at myself.

"Devil in a blue dress?"

Everyone laughed as I gave him a nasty look. I pointed at myself again.

"Not a song?"

I nodded.

"A singer?"

Bigger nod. I pointed to myself again, then made an hourglass motion with my hands.

"Female singer?"

Nod.

Vincent bit his lower lip as he looked off to the side, thinking. "A reporter who sings?"

I gave him an incredulous look and put my palms up as if to say *are you kidding me*? I pointed at myself again.

"You... Belinda! Singer named Belinda!"

I nodded with a big smile.

"Belinda Carlisle!"

I clapped my hands as Roxanne hit the watch. "Thirty-four seconds, you guys are in the lead."

"Fix!" yelled someone on another team.

"Shaddup, she pulled it out of the hat," said Roxanne.

***

It was dark by nine, with no moon, the only light provided by the tiki torches scattered around the lawn. Dozens of lawn chairs had been scattered facing the water to offer everyone the best view of the fireworks.

I was about to sit next to Roxanne when Mrs. Martino locked eyes with me for a moment and gently waved me over. I walked to her wheelchair, situated in the middle of the lawn chairs and crouched down beside her. Vincent was nowhere in sight. "Can I get you something, Mrs. Martino?"

"Just yourself, honey. Sit down next to me during the fireworks."

I could see matchmaking ran in the family and I was going to let Roxanne have it on the way home. But the woman had such a sweet smile I couldn't refuse. "Sure." I grabbed a seat in the lawn chair next to her, noting the one on the other side was empty.

Belinda Carson, you've chosen the Daily Double!

I'll take Italian mother fix-ups for a thousand, Alex.

The answer is... he's sitting next to his mom for the fireworks show.

I heard patriotic music wash across the water and knew the fireworks were about to start. So did everyone else, as people took their places.

Of course Vincent walked by me, smiled sheepishly, and sat down next to his mother.

He took her hand. Then she took mine. It was tiny and cold, the hard creases of her skin rough against my hand. She looked at me and smiled with those knowing eyes.

The fireworks began, exploded high in the sky and reflected off the water. It was like having a giant mirror for the Fourth of July and was a spectacular effect.

I took a look at Vincent's mom, whose face was filled with the wonder of a small child as Vincent wrapped one arm around her shoulder, his face next to hers. The lights reflected off her face, giving her an almost ethereal, angelic effect. Suddenly she didn't look old and terminal.

All I could think of was Frank the photographer's favorite line about shooting video, about the subtle difference between sight and vision.

It had to do with seeing things in a different light.

It was approaching midnight as we rode back to Manhattan in Roxanne's four-door burgundy Chrysler land yacht. She was one of the few people I knew who had a car in the city, as the price of parking is prohibitive and often a lot more than a car payment. But she "has a deal" with someone who owns a garage, and I knew that meant it was one of those look-the-other-way under the table arrangements with someone who has a last name ending in a vowel.

"So," she said, waiting in line to pay the toll, "have a good time?"

"It was a blast. Really unique."

"Anything in particular?"

"Oh, you know, the food was great. The old-fashioned games. Your family is wonderful. What a bunch of characters. And the view of the fireworks was spectacular. I loved the reflection off the water. Really unique perspective."

"Glad you liked it. Anything else?"

Now I knew she was fishing and the fix really *was* in. "Nah, that pretty much covers everything."

"Uh-*huh*." I didn't say anything, as I knew she was doing a slow burn by the little twitch in her lips. Ten seconds passed. "So, Vincent's not a monster, huh?"

"I *knew* it! You set me up again!"

"I didn't set anybody up. I told you my whole family would be there, and he's part of the family."

"What a steaming pile of horseshit. You're still trying to get us together. You fixed charades. You even enlisted the guy's mother!"

"You know, for such a smart girl, sometimes you're a real *stunad*."

"A what?"

"Stoo-nad!" She looked at me and tapped a knuckle on my head. "Italian for stupid idiot! I try to fix you up with a great guy and you treat him like shit!"

"Hey, he's the one with the snotty remarks—"

"Only because of your attitude."

"He told me I was unapproachable."

"You wanted the truth!"

"Not *that* kind of truth!"

"Who do I look like, Jack Nicholson telling you that *you can't handle the truth*? Oh, like he's supposed to know there are different degrees of truth for the Brass Cupcake that don't apply to everyone else? You asked him what he thought and you said you were a big girl so he told you. You get in his cab and he calls you a fabulous babe and you won't take a compliment or a free ride. The guy goes to adopt a cat and you give him a hard time. A friggin' cat! How many guys do you know who like cats!"

"I don't know—"

"Stunad!" She slapped the back of my head.

"Ow!"

"He's a great lookin' guy who makes good money and he takes care of his invalid mother for goodness sake!"

"I'm sure he can find a nice girl—"

"Yeah, lots of girls out there would understand the situation with his mom. I figured if anyone would, you would. He has no life between work and her. I thought the least you could do... eh, fuhgeddaboudit."

The traffic moved and Roxanne finally got through the EZ-PASS lane which had been anything but easy. She stared straight ahead and I could tell she was really steamed by the death grip she had on the steering wheel.

"That's really nice how he takes care of his mother," I said.

"The man's a friggin' saint."

Another long pause as we picked up speed.

"He really told his mother about me?" She nodded but didn't say anything. She gave me a sideways glare. I got a major dose of Catholic guilt.

"He actually *likes* me?"

She looked at me for a second and said, "Stunad," softly.

I went to bed more confused than ever. Was Wing Girl simply a *stunad*? Had the Brass Cupcake lost her identity? And who the hell was Belinda?

Meanwhile, was sensible girl really being sensible? Or was she just a horrible judge of character?

Inquiring minds wanna know.

I turned out the lights thinking that when I was frumpy girl without any men interested in me life was a hell of a lot simpler.

But not more exciting.

CHAPTER FOURTEEN

Some people pay hundreds of dollars an hour to talk to a psychiatrist.

Reporters get personal advice free, from photographers. Often whether they want it or not. When you spend most of your day in a news car, you can only talk about your story for so long, so you end up having these incredible conversations about life that can often last for hours.

While Harry has been my "TV dad" since my real one passed away, Frank the Chief Photographer has been my sounding board.

Frank Hansen has been in the business for twenty years, and he has a surprisingly normal life away from the station. The television news business has an alarmingly high divorce rate (as evidenced by Harry's four-monthly alimony checks), but Frank has lived a comfortable life with his high school sweetheart since he got out of college. Forty-two, about five-eleven and solidly built from carrying gear all his life, he's got that rugged blue-collar look which is appropriate since he favors those pale-blue chambray shirts. His weathered face courtesy of working outdoors is complimented by salt-and-pepper hair that creeps over his collar and deep-set hazel eyes. Those eyes see stuff no reporter can, as he consistently turns out spectacular video for my stories, with incredible shots that make your jaw drop. Frank can shoot a blade of grass and make you feel guilty about cutting the lawn. And, like all photographers, he was born with the sarcasm chromosome.

I've worked with Frank more than any other shooter (that's slang for photographer) and he's been like an extra big brother, very protective of me when we've been in dicey situations. He knows my reporting style, what kind of shots I like, and, most important, when something's bothering me.

So when I slid into the passenger seat of his news car and shut the door, he was already facing me.

"You okay?" he asked, with that big brother look.

"Yeah."

He cranked the car. "Bull. There's a whole bunch of new shit going on with you, and you've got that faraway look lately." He pulled the car out of the lot and headed for New Jersey, the location of our story for today.

"Lately?"

"Lately. Since you turned into a *news babe*."

"I just care a little more about how I look of late. But thank you for the compliment."

"Pffft. There's more to it than that. You're different. If I didn't know you better I'd guess you were in love."

"Why do you assume I can't be in love?"

"Aha!"

I hate it when people use reporter's tricks on me.

"So who's the guy?"

I started to blush. "We've only been out a few times, but, I mean, he's really nice and old-fashioned. Not pushy or anything. I like him a lot, but it's not love... yet."

"Name, age, occupation, details." (Like I said, he's protective of me.)

"His name is Scott Shepard. He's a financial consultant, a little older than me, never married."

"You meet him since you became a news babe?"

I slapped him on the arm. "Stop calling me that!"

"Eh, I'm just bustin' your chops, Cupcake. I know that buried underneath the hair and the makeup and the skirt, my take-no-prisoners superheroine is still there."

"Thank you."

"By the way, speaking of skirts, all the shooters now say you've got the best legs in the station. Who knew?"

"Thank you again."

"So, you like this guy, huh?"

"Yeah."

We stopped at a red light and he turned, studied my face. "But…"

I frowned. "But… what?"

"There's something else in the equation."

"Dammit, shooter, how the hell do you know this stuff?"

"Marriage will do that to you. You like this guy but the second guy has you confused."

"No, he doesn't."

"Aha! There *is* a second guy!"

Dammit! Tricked again.

"I've only been out with Scott. Well, that's not exactly true. I went out with another jerk I met at a bar once but he's long gone."

"So you like this guy Scott but someone else is on your mind."

"Not really on my mind. Just under my skin."

"Like the Sinatra song?"

"Definitely not."

"So who is he?"

"You know my friend Roxanne?"

"The hairstylist? Yeah. What about her?"

"She's been trying to fix me up with her cousin."

"And…?"

"We met and it was like oil and water. But I kept running into him and he pushes my buttons every time I see him. And then I went to Roxanne's family Fourth of July picnic and I saw him in a different light. He's actually incredibly decent. I guess in the back of my mind I've been wondering if I'm a really bad judge of character."

"So you're thinking you might be wrong about both of them."

"No. Maybe. I dunno. This is all uncharted territory for me. I've rarely even had one boyfriend, let alone a bunch of guys interested in me."

"So you're thinking about this other guy... what's his name?"

"Vincent."

"You're dating Scott and you're thinking about Vincent."

"Yeah. No. You're confusing me."

The light turned green and we moved forward. "Love is confusing sometimes."

"No shit. I think I was better off before I became a news babe."

"No you weren't. Some guy out there deserves a terrific girl like you. I was beginning to wonder if you were going to end up in a convent."

"You're not the only one."

"So what are you gonna do?"

"About what?"

"The Scott and Vincent situation."

"There *is* no Scott and Vincent situation."

"Yeah, there is. The sooner you realize it, the better."

***

I had just gotten off the set after another terrific story when the tip line started ringing. I'd grown to hate the thing, as ninety percent of the calls had something to do with my appearance. The voice mails had been piling up, as I hadn't answered it for two days, so I figured I'd better pick up the phone.

"Tip line, this is Belinda."

"Belinda, it's Councilman Jagger."

"How are you, Sir?"

"I'm wondering if you've been able to turn up anything on

that issue we discussed."

"Not really. I've had a couple of financial types look at it and nothing out of the ordinary turned up."

"Interesting."

"Sorry, Sir, I know that's not what you wanted to hear."

"Belinda, I don't want to tell you how to do your job, but I know something's not right."

"Anything in particular making you think that way?"

"When I got in this morning, someone had slid a note under my door. Belinda, it was a threat."

Now my radar went up. "And that note said?"

"Stop looking into the pension fund if you want your family to be safe. And if you give this to the police, you face the consequences."

"Geez." This was getting serious. "Have you called the police, FBI?"

"No, quite frankly I'm afraid to. Obviously I'm being watched and my phone is probably tapped. I'm calling you from a disposable cell phone."

"How would anyone know you were looking at the fund?"

"Obviously they saw you when you came into my office and if the phone's tapped or my office is bugged they know why. And let's face it, when anyone sees you visiting a politician they know it's not a social call."

"Tell you what, sir, I'll keep digging because obviously there's something going on. Meanwhile, give me the number you're calling from and I'll give you my personal cell."

We exchanged numbers and I told him I'd get back to him.

And now the story I thought was a dead end had jumped to the front burner.

I had to talk to Harry.

CHAPTER FIFTEEN

I had lunch with Ariel today, who said I looked "excited as a schoolgirl."

Which was probably accurate, since Scott was flying back today. And, barring the usual Friday night rush hour gridlock at LaGuardia, I would be seeing him for dinner.

So when my cell rang and I saw "unknown" on the screen, my face dropped. Scott was the only person who called me with a blocked number. I was thinking the worst: flight delay, cancellation, hijacked to Cuba, ran off with a stewardess, you name it. "Hello?"

"Hey, my flight's about to board and I wanted to touch base."

My smile returned. "Glad you're on time. So we're still on for tonight?"

"Yeah. Listen, I had an idea. I've got a car picking me up at the airport and I was thinking, how about I have the driver pick you up first, then get me at the airport. Then we can go right to dinner after I get off the plane?"

I liked the way this man thinks, and in my business any man who can manage time and logistics was impressive. "That sounds terrific. I should be done at the station by five-thirty."

"Great. The car will be waiting for you. So how's your week going?"

"Pretty good. Broke a couple of big stories. Hey, I got another tip on that one I had you check out. Would you mind looking at it again?”

“I didn’t see anything wrong the first time, but sure.”

“Great. See you in a few hours.”

“Looking forward to it.” I heard the boarding call in the background. “Hey, gotta go.”

“Okay, bye.”

I hung up and headed to the makeup room since I had to record a few teases on set.

One look in the mirror told me I did indeed look as excited as a schoolgirl.

***

I was bouncing on my feet as the parade of passengers from Scott’s flight moved past the security checkpoint. I was trying my best not to look too excited, honestly I was, but I’m afraid my poker face wasn’t very convincing.

I couldn’t help it. I missed the guy.

Finally I spotted him, wearing a dark suit, tie loosened, pulling a red carry-on bag.

And when he spotted me, his smile told me he was just as excited.

He picked up the pace and moved toward me, let go of the bag and gave me a hug, then pulled back and said, “Much nicer to look at than a limo driver with a sign.”

“Thank you. You look good too.”

“Yeah, right. I’m wiped out. But glad to finally be home.”

“Did you check a bag?”

“Nope, they only lose ‘em anyway. And I don’t want to waste forty-five minutes staring at a carousel.”

“Great. Let’s get out of here.”

Sensible girl was apparently dating sensible guy. Which, I must admit, was a tad disappointing to that other slutty girl sitting on my shoulder who kept reminding me I should spend the night with the guy after three dates. Though he'd mentioned twice he liked the slow pace that our relationship was taking.

What the hell. I'd been a camel this long, I could go without water a little longer.

Dinner went well, but Scott kept yawning during dessert and I could tell the guy was fried. Then he fell asleep halfway through a killer science fiction movie. And let's face it, if it was gonna be the first time with him it would be nice if he wasn't comatose.

So we decided to meet up tomorrow night for a Broadway show. Hopefully he would be well rested.

For what, I had no idea.

CHAPTER SIXTEEN

Two weeks later, I was back where we started, camped out at Ariel's place with that dreaded whiteboard looming like a grim reaper. My friends told me that while I've made significant progress, it was time for a "review" and we needed to go over some "to-do" list, whatever that meant. At that point the only thing I wanted to do was Scott.

It was rainy and miserable outside so we settled on pizza and decided to stay in for the rest of the evening. I was loving the double supremes Roxanne ordered, which naturally cost nothing since she had another "deal" with the pizzeria owner. The steaming pies were loaded down with Italian sausage, pepperoni, onions, black olives and dripping with cheese. Of course if we did this at my place it would have been paper plates and bottles of beer all the way, but at Ariel's we were eating our slices off bone china and sipping white wine in goblets that cost more than most people's utility bills.

Ariel, as you probably expected, ate her pizza with a knife and fork. Sterling, naturally. Luckily Roxanne and Serena ate it the normal way, with their hands, so I couldn't be accused of a culinary faux pas that would send Mrs. Baymont into the etiquette version of vapor lock.

After two slices Ariel daintily dabbed her lips with a red linen napkin (the color chosen so it wouldn't show any red sauce stains) while the rest of us continued to tear into the pizza. "Okay, let's get started." She stood up, grabbed a dry erase marker from the ledge of the whiteboard, uncapped it, then wrote "Progress Report" on top of the board. She turned to face me and smiled. "Wing Girl, you've made tremendous strides since we started this project."

"Oh, now I'm a project," I said, sipping the sweet wine.

"You're the dating equivalent of Boston's Big Dig," said Roxanne, who flashed a sinister smile.

"Funny," I said.

"But not too far off," said Serena, as she grabbed another slice from the box. "Though that took more than twenty years."

"Let's begin with the positive," said Ariel, "by listing the improvements."

"Her new wardrobe is spectacular," said Serena.

"No argument here," I said, as Ariel wrote "wardrobe" on the board. "And I can't tell you how many compliments I've gotten on my hair."

Roxanne smiled and said, "I meant to tell you, I've had a few clients come in and ask for the Belinda Carson."

My eyes grew wide. "So now I'm a *style*? Wow."

"Just like Jennifer Aniston had *The Rachel*, you have *The Belinda*."

Ariel wrote "hair" on the board, then added "makeup". "I'd like to add you've gotten much better with your makeup lately."

"Thank you. I've been practicing a lot."

Ariel then wrote "table manners" on the board. "And I'm so proud of you, Wing Girl. You're able to dine in public and can identify all of your forks."

I took a huge bite of pizza and said, "Thanks," with my mouth full.

"Cute," said Serena. "Brings back such warm memories of your days eating like a cave girl."

Ariel then wrote "men" on the board and sat down. "Now,

sweetie, where do we stand with Scott?"

"We?"

"It's the editorial *we*," said Serena. "But remember, we all have supreme veto power if he steps out of line. Or we can go with the nuclear option if we have to."

My face tightened. "I'm almost afraid to ask. *Nuclear option?*"

"Roxanne kicks his ass if you fail to obey our veto," said Ariel.

"I'd like to know what you think of him first," I said, launching a pre-emptive strike in keeping with the nuclear theme.

"He made a good first impression," said Ariel, "but I haven't really gotten to know him. I did like the Town Car for the Mets game. That was a nice touch. Didn't put you in harm's way on the subway."

"I agree," said Serena. "He seemed like a good guy, but we've got a long way to go."

"Again with the *we* thing," I said, as I turned to Roxanne. "I can't wait for your assessment of the guy. Not that I'm going to be surprised."

She shrugged. "Jury's still out," she said, then took another bite of pizza.

"Why is the jury out with you?" I asked. "He treats me well, he's a gentleman, he volunteers at the shelter. He has a good job—"

"You ever seen his office?" asked Roxanne.

"He works out of his home," I said.

"Uh-*huh*," said Roxanne. "Probably lives in his mother's basement."

"Lots of people work out of their homes," I said. "What is it about him that you don't like? You've been wanting me to cut him loose from day one."

"Don't know yet, but my bullshit detector went off the night I met him. I'm just telling you to be careful."

"I really haven't had to," I said.

"Speaking of which," said Serena, "how many dates have you guys been on?"

"Six."

"Six and still no sex," said Serena. "Odd."

"He's just old fashioned," I said.

"Opening a door for a woman is old fashioned," said Ariel. "Not even asking for sex after six dates is a priest."

Roxanne nodded. "Like I said, there's somethin' about this guy. A man who doesn't even try to nail a girl after half a dozen dates, well..."

"It is rather curious," said Serena. "But after reviewing all the feedback and in light of the tonsillectomy after the first date, I surmise we should allow Wing Girl to move forward. For the time being."

Ariel nodded. "Agreed."

Roxanne rolled his eyes. "You know where I stand. Dude's still on a short leash with me."

"Meanwhile," said Ariel, turning toward me, "are you sure you won't reconsider the catch and release program?"

I shook my head. "No way. That aerial first kiss attempt from Todd was enough."

"Damn, he was hot though. I would have at least taken him for a ride before throwing him back," said Roxanne.

"You would," I said.

"So I guess that takes care of the men category," said Ariel.

"Not really," said Roxanne.

"Oh shit," I said. "Here it comes."

"Someone else reaalllllly likes her," said Roxanne.

I dropped my slice of pizza on my plate. "I'm *not* going out with Vincent."

"Interesting," said Serena. "Rox, please continue presenting your evidence."

"He talks about her a lot," said Roxanne. "But he might be giving up. The other day he told me he thought she was out of his league."

I was about to take another bite of pizza but that comment

stopped the slice in mid-air. Hmmm. I must admit I was sorta flattered. "He really said that?"

She nodded. "He said you were probably too pretty and could get any guy you wanted. But his mother went on and on about you after I brought you to the picnic."

"She met his mother?" asked Ariel.

"Yep," said Roxanne, "and Wing Girl over here made quite the impression. Ever since it's Belinda this, and Belinda that, and oh that beautiful red hair, and she's so gorgeous, and she's just perfect for my Vincent." Then she raised her hands like she was being held up. "But hey, you're out of his league, so why I even brought it up, I don't know."

More Catholic guilt. "I'm not out of his league, I'm just interested in someone else."

Roxanne turned to Serena and whispered, loud enough for all to hear, "She likes him, she just doesn't know it yet."

***

Doing nothing but investigative reporting all year can sometimes leave you feeling like your brain is hooked up to jumper cables. So every once in a while Harry takes me off the beat for a day and lets me knock out a fun feature.

And since everyone in the station knows I'm a sci-fi geek, I've been assigned to cover the massive convention in Manhattan that always attracts, to use a sixties term, a few "far out" characters. Harry sends me to do this every year, since he says I am "the only one in the newsroom who knows the difference between a Cylon and a Klingon." (Though from him saying that, I've always wondered if he's got a set of Spock ears at home.)

Frank loves shooting these conventions because, in his words, "It brings out the serious whack jobs who actually *want* to be abducted by aliens." And sure enough, as we made our way through the convention hall, there were plenty of fans in costume who made you wonder if Bellevue had endured a mass escape of its mental ward. Though for many, these costumes were their everyday outfits. In my opinion, there are two types of sci-fi fan. The first, and most common (that would be me), are those who simply enjoy the escapism and the wondrous possibilities without going so far as to wear antennae on days other than Halloween. The second, a smaller but very noticeable fringe group, are those who truly believe that the fiction part of sci-fi is actually real, and that if they talk into their communicators long enough, someone, somewhere, will actually beam them up. To where, God only knows.

So far we'd managed to interview a woman with green hair, electric-blue hot pants and matching halter top who claimed she was a cheerleader for a football team on Venus; a teenage boy wrapped entirely in tin foil with a face painted silver who said this was the only way to prevent aliens from invading his body with nanoprobes; and a four hundred pound guy dressed as Batman who didn't notice a sticker someone had slapped on his back reading "you have exceeded the weight limit of your costume".

With enough loons on tape, Frank set about gathering video for the story. I was at his side, spotting interesting things to shoot, when I heard a familiar voice from behind call my name.

Vincent. Again.

I turned around and saw him smiling at me. Thankfully he wasn't dressed as an alien, but in sharply creased khakis and a pale-green oxford shirt. I didn't want Roxanne to call me *stunad* again so I made an effort to be polite. "Hi, Vincent. What are you doing here?"

"Just took the morning off for the convention."

"*You* like science fiction?"

His eyes lit up. "I love science fiction. Have since I was a kid."

Somehow I didn't believe him. I figured Roxanne tipped him off that I'd be here and this was another of her fixes. "Roxanne tell you I was gonna be here?"

He shook his head. "Haven't talked to her in a few days."

"Hmmm. You really a sci-fi fan?"

"Why else would I be here?"

Okay. One way to find out if this was a Roxanne set-up. "So, did you see that model of Captain Kirk's ship over there? The Millennium Falcon?"

"Kirk's ship was the Enterprise. The Falcon was Han Solo's from Star Wars. I thought everyone knew that."

That was an easy one. Let's try something harder. "Duh, I mixed them up. So, what's your favorite Trek movie?"

"A tie between Wrath of Khan and The Voyage Home. Can't beat those even-numbered movies. Though I really liked the re-boot from a few years ago."

"What's the name of Ripley's cat in the first Alien movie?"

Vincent looked at me quizzically. "The cat's name is Jones. Why?"

"Who played Starbuck in the original Battlestar Galactica?"

"Dirk Benedict. What, are you a judge in the trivia contest or something?"

I shook my head. "Just wanted to see if you were really a sci-fi fan."

"Well, I am. And obviously you are as well." He looked up at the ceiling a moment, then back at me. "What was the name of the actor in Voyage to the Bottom of the Sea who was also the lead in the original movie version of The Fly?""

"David Hedison. What did the robot always say to warn the kid in Lost in Space?"

"Danger, Will Robinson." He flashed a knowing smile. "Seriously? That the best you got?" He made a *come closer* motion with his hands. "C'mon, girl, let's rock."

Frank returned from shooting video. "You wanna interview this guy?"

I put up my hand, still looking at Vincent. I raised one eyebrow. "In the movie Stargate, James Spader eats a candy bar. What kind—"

"Clark Bar. In the original Day the Earth Stood Still, what does Michael Rennie use for money?"

"Diamonds. What kind of pet does Sarah Connor have in the original Terminator?"

"Iguana."

Frank shouldered his camera. "Damn, I need to be shooting this for the Christmas party."

We went back and forth like this for five minutes, eventually attracting a crowd. I became oblivious to the fact that Frank was rolling tape on the whole thing. Through it all Vincent not only answered every obscure question I could throw at him, but he hit me with some serious sci-fi tidbits only a fanatic would know.

Finally Frank interrupted. "Guys, I'm out of tape. How 'bout you two call this a draw?"

We both relaxed as the crowd applauded, then began to disperse.

"You two know each other?" asked Frank.

"Yeah. Sort of," said Vincent, who then stuck out his hand. "Vincent Martino."

Frank raised both eyebrows and smiled as he shook his hand. "Ah, you must be the Vincent I've heard so much about."

Vincent looked at me and gave me a huge smile. Now I was the one turning beet red.

***

Thankfully our news car was parked in the garage underneath the convention hall so no viewer would be able to see my impending explosion. I'd been holding it in through gritted teeth, forced a smile as we made our way through the crowd while wishing I had an alien mask.

In television news, no one can hear you scream.

The only noise you heard in the musty garage were the echoes of my fast heel clicks on the pavement. I got to the news car way ahead of Frank, turned, folded my arms, stuck out one leg in front of the other like a pissed off parent, and glared at him.

He noticed. "What?"

I waited for him to unlock the trunk and place the camera inside before I moved toward him and shoved a finger in his chest. "You embarrassed the hell out of me! Geez, I cannot *believe* you did that!"

He started to back up, as he obviously noted the fire in my eyes. "Did what?"

I wrinkled my nose and lowered my voice in an attempt to imitate him. "Ah, you must be the Vincent I've heard so much about."

"That embarrassed you? Seriously?" He kept backing up toward the front of the car. I kept following him.

"You told him I was *talking* about him."

"Yeah, so what. You *were* talking about him."

"Not like *that*!" Frank continued walking backwards around the front of the car and I kept following him.

"Like *what*?"

"Like... like... like I'm talking about him as if I like him! He doesn't need to think I like him!"

"Why, because you do?"

"Augh!" I put up two hands and shoved him backwards. Now he was back at the trunk, beginning his second lap around the car with me in steamed pursuit. "Get this straight! I! Don't! Like! Him!"

"Coulda fooled me."

"What makes you say that?"

"You two had this... I don't know, this *thing* going. Like couples do. You were competing but you were having fun. It was great to watch. You obviously have a lot in common if you both know the name of the cat in Alien. Geez, who the hell remembers that stuff?"

I started waving my arms like a lunatic. "It's a FAMOUS CAT because RIPLEY risked her life TO SAVE IT! It was IMPORTANT to the PLOT!"

Finally Frank stopped walking backwards at the front of the car and put out one hand to stop me, then took me by the shoulders. "Hey, you need to settle down." He looked right into my eyes. "This isn't about trivia or famous cats, is it?"

I shook my head and bit my lower lip as my eyes grew moist. I tried to exhale my tension. "No. I'm sorry," I said, as my voice cracked with emotion. "I don't need to yell at you, Frank. But like I said he pushes my buttons like no one ever has."

"Because he answered every question you threw at him and you got stumped by a couple of his?"

I threw out my lower lip in a pout. "Yeah. Sonofabitch beat me. It pisses me off."

"Geez, I'd hate to see you get in an argument over something serious." I looked down at the ground. "C'mere, Cupcake." Frank moved closer and gave me a strong hug, being the big brother he had always been for me at the station. I leaned my head on his shoulder as he patted me on the back. He held the hug a moment, then pulled back, still holding me by the shoulders. I was still looking down. "Hey, look at me." I wiped my eyes as I looked up. "It's okay to like more than one guy, kiddo. Not after you get married of course, but now it's fine. And he sure likes you, I can tell that."

"How?"

"Because he looks at you the same way I look at my wife."

***

We had finished editing what turned out to be a hilarious feature story and I was about to leave the dimly lit editing booth when Frank said, "Hold on a minute."

I stopped and turned around. "What? I forget something?"

"I want you to watch this." He put another tape in the playback

133

deck, then rolled it.

It was the scene of Vincent and me having the trivia showdown. "Do I have to?"

"You don't even need the audio." He hit the mute button. "Pay attention to the way you're looking at each other."

What I assumed would look like a trivia war was completely different. Frank had been the fly on the wall, capturing, as he always did, what I could not see.

Vincent and I both smiling, almost laughing, as we fired question after question at each other. He getting really excited when he stumped me; my eyes growing wide and filling with delight as he struggled to find an answer.

His eyes intently focused on mine, and mine on his. So focused the crowd around us did not exist.

The tape ran out. Frank hit the eject button, got up, handed me the tape and patted me on the shoulder as he left the edit booth. "Yeah, Cupcake. You really hate the guy."

CHAPTER SEVENTEEN

So now it was August and I was on date number eleven with Scott. It would have been a lot more but he travels so much I've had to take what I could get. I missed him when he was gone and really enjoyed spending time with him. Our makeout sessions were terrific.

Yet something was missing.

Yep, you guessed it. He still hadn't ventured into my bedroom. And the sexual camel in me wanted her hump.

Ariel was beginning to think this was odd.

Serena already *knew* this was odd.

And I don't really need to tell you what Roxanne thought, do I? To quote her, "Ten dates and you don't even have to go to confession? Fuhgeddaboudim!" (That's forget about *him* instead of forget about *it* for those of you who are New York accent-challenged.)

After our latest dinner together it was decided that I would have to be pro-active and draw the guy a road map. And if he still didn't take the hint, I've been encouraged to grab him by the hand, drag him into my bed and take him.

Now, while I've always considered myself a strong woman, especially considering my line of work, I'd never reversed roles when it comes to men. No date for the Sadie Hawkins dance, never asked a man for a phone number or even to lunch. So initiating sex has me, well, to be honest, a little apprehensive. I didn't exactly have a pair of thigh-high dominatrix boots in my closet. (When I mentioned that to the girls, Roxanne said that if I did possess such a pair, they'd be flats.)

Being subtle was not my forte, as you already know. So Serena said when the time was right I should say nothing and lead him to my bedroom.

If he still didn't take the hint, well, I'm baffled.

So we were at my place after a wonderful dinner in Little Italy and a hansom cab ride through Central Park. That's an old-fashioned horse and buggy. Talk about romantic, and under a full moon, no less, on a beautiful summer night. So I figured the mood was perfect.

My old-fashioned regulator clock on the wall had just struck midnight and I was in my usual position, straddling his lap while the only light in my apartment was provided by a ton of candles. I'd been doing everything I'd seen a stripper do in the movies and still there'd been no indication he wanted more. Oh, I knew he was enjoying himself, breathing heavily with his hands all over me. I tried unbuttoning his shirt, loosening his belt, whispering dirty in his ear, expecting him to simply lift me up and carry me away, but we were still stuck in neutral.

Finally, rather than take Serena's advice, I stopped mid-grind, sat up straight and looked at him.

"Something wrong?" he asked.

"Uh... yeah. Actually, I'm seriously beginning to wonder if there's something wrong with *me*."

"Are you kidding? You're the best girl I've ever dated. You're smart, beautiful, a great kisser, we have a lot in common—"

I put up one hand. "Let's back up a bit to that great kisser part. Since you seem to be really enjoying our makeout sessions and my arguably amateur attempt at a lap dance, I will connect the dots and assume you would really enjoy making love to me."

His face went blank, the color drained. He looked away and

said nothing.

I grabbed his face and turned it back so he was looking at me. "Don't you want me, Scott?"

He nodded with a sheepish look on his face. "More than you can possibly know."

"Because I sure as hell want you." I got off his lap, stood up, took his hand and pulled. He didn't budge. "Well, c'mon. Do I have to send you an engraved invitation?"

He patted the couch cushion next to him with his other hand as his eyes suddenly filled with sadness. "Let's talk a minute."

Now I was totally confused as I sat down and he took both my hands. The man I've known with all the confidence in the world looked like a frightened teenager. "Scott, what's wrong?"

"Belinda, there's uh... something you need to know about me."

Oh, shit. Every possible crazy explanation was flying through my head. He's impotent. He used to be a woman. He's got herpes or some weird STD. His Johnson is microscopic.

And then he hit me with something I never considered.

"I'm, uh, very religious and, well, there's really no other way to say this. I believe in waiting for marriage."

Annnnndddd... cue the cold shower.

To say my jaw dropped would be an understatement. And after he left, all I could think of was my original want list on that whiteboard. I should have clarified what I meant by "a decent guy."

Sonofabitch, I really am dating the Pope.

***

I could've predicted the words that would come out of Roxanne's mouth after I delivered the news. "You're friggin' kidding me! He's a friggin' virgin?"

Serena's mouth hung open from shock. Ariel, who had been standing up, plopped down on the couch like she was gonna pass out. "Oh dear," she said, pressing her forehead with the back of her hand like a movie star on a fainting couch.

"*Oh dear*? More like *oh shit*," said Roxanne. "How old is this guy?"

"Thirty-three."

"Looks like your bullshit detector needs to be recalibrated for virgins," said Serena, who then turned to me. "So what happened after he told you this?" She playfully slapped her cheek. "Sorry, your honor, I withdraw the question. Obviously *nothing* happened."

"Well, we talked about it a while, he said he hoped I wouldn't break up with him because things were going so well."

Ariel rubbed her temples as she stretched out flat on the couch. "And you said..."

"What could I say?" I said. "The guy poured his heart out to me. I told him it was okay—"

"Oh, shit," said Roxanne.

"What?" I asked.

Roxanne rolled her eyes. "Seriously, are you telling me you're willing to wait for this guy? What's your current definition of foreplay, thirty minutes of begging? You should run so fast you leave skid marks."

Serena got up, sat next to me and took my hands. "Wing Girl, you need to cut your losses. I know you like him, but in this day and age, and at his age, that's ridiculous."

I bit my lower lip. "But we're so compatible. He's such a gentleman, we have so much in common, we have fun together—"

"You aint havin' the right kind of fun," said Roxanne.

"And you have no idea what he's like in bed," said Ariel. "That's one big chance to take if you're serious about this guy."

"He's a helluva kisser. I'm sure he'll be fine in the bedroom."

"You can't know that," said Serena. "That's like saying a car that idles well will be great on the highway before you even test drive the thing. He might not even be able to shift out of park."

"So what do I do?"

"I'd roofie the guy," said Roxanne.

I glared at her. "C'mon, Rox. Be serious."

"Hey," she said, "I *am* being serious. He won't remember a thing and you'll find out if he's any good. He'll still think he's a virgin. Victimless crime. Problem solved."

"I can see the headline in *The Post*," I said. "*Brass Cupcake Date Rapes Men*. I need some real help here. But I will not break up with him, so forget your veto power. Not yet, at least."

"Well, then," said Ariel, "If you're dead set against cutting him loose, I have an idea that will force him to sleep with you."

***

If you'd asked me which of my friends was the most devious, I would have answered Roxanne in a heartbeat.

Little did I know that a manipulative Scarlett O'Hara wannabe resided in the head of Ariel Baymont.

She pulled every trick out of the single woman playbook and set what she thought will be a foolproof sex trap.

There was no Plan B. I honestly didn't know what I'd do if this over-the-top seduction doesn't work. Because it absolutely had to work.

Ariel was also taking a hands-on approach to this, as she would play a vital part to blow up Scott's morality play. Serena said it should work. Roxanne said if it didn't, the guy's a eunuch.

I had rented a convertible for a seemingly innocent trip to a beach club in Connecticut. I'd told Scott to bring a few changes of clothes, since we might go hiking, out to dinner, whatever. In reality the changes of clothes were for the next day. He offered to use his car service, but I told him I liked driving, I missed it, and wanted to drive along the shore with the top down.

So we'd been cruising along, wind in our hair, enjoying the sunshine and salt air as we arrived at Ariel's beach club in Eastern

Connecticut around ten in the morning. I pulled up under the massive white canopy and a young, hunky valet immediately opened my door for me, said, "Welcome to the Baymont Club," and took my keys. (Yeah, Ariel's mom owns this too. I think she might actually own the entire State of Connecticut, but I'm not sure.)

Ariel was waiting at the top steps to the main pavilion and bounded down the stairs as we arrived. "Hey, you made it! Glad you could come." She gave me a hug, then moved around to greet my date. "And Scott, so nice to see you again."

"Nice of you to invite us."

"Well, grab your bags and I'll show you where you can change. The sun and surf are waiting for you."

Scott grabbed both our carry-ons from the back seat, hauled them up the steps, extended the handle on mine and placed it in front of me.

Ariel pointed to the right. "Scott, the men's locker room is right there. We'll meet you on the beach in the red cabana."

Scott headed to the changing room while Ariel led me into the women's locker room. "Does he have any clue?" she asked.

"He thinks we're just spending the day and heading back tonight."

"Great. You didn't forget the bikini and shoes?"

"Of course not."

"Good. Take your time changing. We want him to already be there when you make your entrance."

I know this sounds hard to believe, but it was my first time wearing a bikini even though I've always been slender, so I was a little self-conscious. But Roxanne helped me pick it out and said that no man would be able to ignore me in a bathing suit that leaves little to the imagination. The four-inch cork wedges added a beauty-pageant-swimsuit-competition-bimbo effect to the outfit. And Roxanne said no red-blooded man can resist a bimbo, virginity be damned.

I emerged from the dressing cubicle and Ariel was already waiting for me, striking in her own modest two-piece. "Wow."

I looked at myself in the mirror, a five-nine calendar girl in a black string halter bikini. "Damn, I feel naked."

"That's the whole point, grasshopper. If he won't take your clothes off in the bedroom, we'll show him what he's missing. Wow, your hair looks great with the black." She looked at her watch. "Okay, he should be there by now."

"I'd better not end up on *Page Six* in this."

"Don't worry, this club is far away from the prying eyes of the best telephoto lens. That's why so many celebrities are members."

We headed out to the cabana. The beach wasn't terribly crowded, the advantages of belonging to a club with a ridiculously expensive membership fee. (Rumor has it that children pitch Kruggerands for amusement.) It was a little odd walking through sand in the wedges, but I managed. We made our way to the red cabana, and I saw Scott was already reclining in an Adirondack chair, reading a newspaper.

He looked up as we arrived and I could tell from his bug-eyed look he was impressed. He whistled and simply said, "Damn, Belinda."

I played dumb. "What?"

"You're... I mean, geez, you could be a bikini model." He couldn't stop staring at me.

"Why thank you, kind sir." I handed him a bottle of sun block, sat down on the edge of his chair, and turned my back to him. "Do my back. Redheads are very fair-skinned and we burn easily, so you might have to do this more than once."

I looked up at Ariel. She winked and checked her watch. "Okay, you're all set here. I've got to go meet some other guests so I'll see you at twelve on the patio for lunch."

"Okay," I said, as Scott started applying lotion to my back. Well, applying wasn't the word. He seemed to be massaging the lotion into my skin. "You've got great hands. If you ever get tired of the investment thing, you could be a masseur."

"Not a bad idea if all the customers looked like you."

He finished my back and handed me the bottle. I sat in the chair next to him and made a slow, sensual production number of rubbing lotion on my legs, stomach, and boobs, which were about to explode from a bikini top that I thought was too small but Roxanne assured me was necessary. I put on sunglasses and an oversized straw hat, then leaned back and let the sun warm my body, which was glistening from the lotion.

He wasn't paying attention to the newspaper.

****

Lunch was served on a patio with a spectacular view of Long Island Sound. A few sailboats skimmed the calm waters in the distance and an occasional seagull flew by. The round, glass-topped tables sat under large white umbrellas, while one waiter flitted endlessly about refilling everyone's glass of champagne.

Mrs. Baymont joined us for lunch, and Scott got on her good side by standing up and pulling out her wicker chair when she arrived. She was watching me like a hawk, smiling each time I used the proper fork. The cold lobster salad was amazing, and the other courses to die for. Personally, I wanted to gorge myself on the dessert bar, but being in a bikini I didn't want to look like one of those idiots from Hollywood who walk around in a skimpy two piece while eight months pregnant. (I mean, seriously, have some class.) I was ready for a nap but I knew that wasn't in Ariel's plan. I was supposed to take Scott for a long walk on the beach.

At one point Scott excused himself to go to the rest room, and Mrs. Baymont leaned forward. "Dearie, he seems like such a fine young man."

"I think so too."

"But Ariel says you're feeling a little... anxious."

"Not exactly the word I'd choose, but accurate."

"You know, back in the day, this was not considered unusual."

Ariel smiled. "Mother, *back in the day* doesn't exist anymore."

Again with "back in the day." Was Mrs. Baymont one of Harry's ex-wives, and did that make Ariel... nah. The champagne had made me silly.

Mrs. Baymont raised one finger. "Alas, times have changed. But the art of seduction has not. I would surmise, Belinda, that looking the way you today do he would find you hard to resist."

"We can only hope, Mrs. Baymont," I said.

"If I may offer one small bit of advice. That is, if you wouldn't mind accepting it from someone who was courted..." She looked at Ariel with eyes slightly narrowed. "Back in the day."

"Sure, Mrs. Baymont," I said.

"Well, over the years morals have changed, but one thing has remained a constant when it comes to courtship."

I leaned forward, as I waited for this secret handshake. "And that would be?"

She dropped her voice into one I'd never heard, one dripping with lust. "Men always want what they can't have. Be a bit aloof, and he'll be begging for it."

Ariel's eyes grew wide in shock. "Mother!"

Mrs. Baymont shrugged and returned to her normal persona. "I'm just suggesting that if this little plan of yours today doesn't work, that perhaps Belinda might not be as... available... in the future."

"I believe this is called *playing hard to get*," I said.

Mrs. Baymont smiled. "Yes, dearie. Worked back in the day with Ariel's father, should work just as well today."

"You pulled this on Dad?" asked Ariel.

"I did. Always remember that absence makes the heart grow fonder. Might even make it more..." She raised one eyebrow. "... anxious."

***

The rest of the day went according to plan. A long walk on the private beach, a little rolling around in the sand when we were totally alone, dinner and dancing on the veranda complimented by a spectacular sunset and cool offshore breezes. But my heart rate was beginning to rise as we grew closer to the key point of Ariel's plan.

The band signed off at ten o'clock. Ariel moved toward us on the dance floor as we headed back to our table, then handed me a key. "Here's your room key at the bed and breakfast across the street."

Scott furrowed his brow. "I thought we were driving home tonight."

"Oh, you have to stay," said Ariel, her eyes begging. "Tomorrow's the regatta!"

"That's right, I forgot," I said, turning to Scott. "It really *is* spectacular." I dipped my head and looked up at him through my long eyelashes, then playfully thrust out my lower lip. "Can't we stay? Pleeeease?"

He smiled and nodded. "Sure, it's a little late for a drive home anyway."

"Terrific," said Ariel. "See you at breakfast then."

"Thanks for everything," I said as my eyes met hers while I tried my best not to smile like the Cheshire cat.

Of course, always the worrier, I thought, that went way too easily. He didn't ask for a separate room, or one with twin beds.

Maybe this was it.

We picked up our bags and strolled across the street to the old three-story Victorian bed and breakfast. (Conveniently owned by Mrs. Baymont.) A cheery young clerk greeted us, looked at our key and directed us to the third floor. Scott dutifully carried both bags up the stairs.

I opened the door to our room and it was clear this was the most expensive suite in the place. Moonlight spilled in through the windows that wrapped around the room, illuminating the antique four-poster canopy bed.

Thankfully, it was the only one.

Scott still acted like this was nothing out of the ordinary. He placed our bags on a bench and flicked on a light. "Wow, gorgeous room. Tired?" he asked.

"A little," I said, as I moved toward my suitcase and unzipped it. "I'm going to get ready for bed."

"Yeah, me too." He kicked off his docksiders, then began to unbutton his shirt as he moved to the window and took in the view.

I grabbed the seduction uniform provided by Roxanne, headed to the bathroom and locked the door.

I hoped that when I emerged he wouldn't be able to hear my heart trying to escape my chest. I took a quick shower, tried my best not to get my hair wet. The warm water shot through the shower massage setting felt wonderful and relaxed me a bit. I was nervous as a virgin at an Aztec sacrifice (ironic, huh?) as I slipped into the red lingerie and matching stilettos Roxanne had picked out, then teased out my hair as big as possible. A little makeup, some fresh lipstick, and I was ready to go.

I'd been in there ten minutes, but paused to take a look at the total package in the mirror.

I had to admit, I looked like a complete slut.

But, as Roxanne said, that was the whole idea.

Sensible girl was outta here for the night. I took one deep breath and opened the door.

The only light was provided by the moonlight. Scott was already in bed.

His loud snoring filled the room.

***

The sunrise was gorgeous. It had been years since I'd seen one without working, without setting up for a crack of dawn live shot. TV people know a sunrise takes two minutes and eight seconds from the time the sun first hits the horizon until it clears it. But there was no clock this time, as I took in the golden fingers of light that shot oranges and reds across the sky while the waves gently lapped the shore. The water has always had a calming effect on me.

But this time it did not.

I was the only person on the veranda at that hour, as I sipped fresh squeezed orange juice and occasionally speared a piece of chilled fruit from a bowl provided by a cheerful waiter who was way too perky for the hour.

I, on the other hand, am not a morning person, and was certainly not perky. I was confused. How did a day that had gone so perfectly end up the way it did? How a guy I seem to be so in tune with couldn't answer the one question I wanted him to answer. A life outside the bedroom with Scott would seem to be wonderful. Inside? Who knew? Would sex be of the thong-on-the-ceiling-fan and claw-marks-on-the-bedpost variety, or the version where I counted the ceiling tiles and replayed my previous night's story while the man on top robotically performed? Imagine being patient and then having a huge letdown on your wedding night, then having to live with that till death do you part.

The possibilities made my head hurt. And since I couldn't sleep, I figured communing with nature might help.

It wasn't working.

I'd been there two hours when I heard gentle footsteps on the marble floor and the familiar voice.

"Uh-oh," said Ariel, who grabbed a chair opposite mine and looked into my face. "Don't tell me..."

I frowned as I shook my head.

"No lift off?"

"Hell, no countdown at all," I said. "Mission was scrubbed."

"What happened? I specifically got you a room with one bed and no couch. Did he sleep on the floor?"

"Oh, he slept in the bed with me. But he was out cold and snoring when I came out of the bathroom in Roxanne's *every man's fantasy* outfit."

She reached across the table and took my hands. "Oh, sweetie, I'm so sorry."

A single tear rolled down my cheek. "What's wrong with me, Ariel?"

She wiped the tear away with her thumb. "Nothing, sweetie. Nothing's wrong with you. In fact, you're better than ever. He's just something we didn't expect. There's nothing in the playbook for this scenario."

"But we're so perfect when we're together."

"I know, I can see the way you two look at each other and how well you get along. Hey, look at it this way, at least he's not a guy who sleeps around and is cheating on you."

"At least then we'd know if he liked sex."

"I'm sure he will like it. At some point." She looked out at the Sound. "You still staying for the Regatta?"

"I guess so. How would it look if I demanded to go home? I mean, he already told me where he stood. I really thought when he didn't raise an eyebrow over the sleeping arrangements that he might bend."

"You know something? Maybe my mother is right."

"About what?"

"About absence making the heart grow fonder. Is he in town next weekend?"

"Yeah."

She sat up straight and stuck her nose in the air. "Then you have plans."

"I do?"

"And nothing specific. You just have plans. We're gonna make him miss you so much he can't stand it."

"I would think a thirty-three-year-old virgin would be ready to explode like Mount Saint Helens anyway."

"Maybe so. But let's talk about it when we all get home."

CHAPTER EIGHTEEN

Serena's eyes grew wide and I could tell she'd had a revelation. "Oh my God!" She dropped her fork into her salad plate. "I figured it out!"

My spoonful of soup hovered in mid-air. "Well, don't keep me in suspense, 'cause I sure as hell haven't."

"You're the *guy* in this relationship!" she said.

My face tightened as I put the spoon back into the bowl. "Excuse me?"

"Don't you get it?" she said. "You're the guy! You're the man! The roles are reversed!"

"Wow, you're right!" said Ariel. "We've been approaching this as women, when all along we really needed to think like a guy!"

My palms went up in surrender. "I'm sorry, I still have no idea what you're talking about."

Roxanne took one of my hands. "Serena's right. You're the one who's the pursuer."

"That doesn't make any sense," I said.

"It makes perfect sense," said Serena. "This is the classic 'guy trying to be the first one who nails the virgin' scenario. It's more than a courtship, it's a quest."

"So let me get this straight," I said. "First, you guys pull out all the stops giving me a makeover because I look like a librarian and act like Cro-Magnon girl. New hair, new makeup, contacts, entire wardrobe. Then you take me to charm school, during which I have to identify every frigging type of fork in a place setting while spooning my chowder from the back of the bowl. And after all that, after you've taken the Brass out of the Cupcake, after you've *froo-frooed* me up so much that I don't even recognize myself in the mirror and turned me into a slutty seductress with everything but a riding crop, *now* you're telling me I need to act like a man?"

"Yeah," Serena nodded. "That about sums it up."

"You three have completely lost your minds."

"No, we haven't," said Ariel.

"So," I said, "I'm supposed to go find my old clothes at Goodwill—"

"You're missin' the point," said Roxanne. "The makeover stuff stays. You don't have to look like a man, just act like one. It's always the girl trying to preserve the virginity, not the guy. And it's always the guy trying to get the girl to give it up. The roles are simply reversed. You're the girl trying to get the guy to give it up so you can pop his cherry."

"That's such a genteel way to put it," I said.

"Somewhat crass, but accurate," said Serena.

"So what do I do?" I asked. "Demand that a man have sex with me or I'll break up with him?"

"That would be a first in the annals of dating," said Ariel. "But no."

"What then?" I asked.

"I know exactly who you need to meet," said Serena. "They'll know what to do."

***

I decided to throw myself into my work. Don't get me wrong, I've always been dedicated, but I needed to take my mind off my frustration. Or, in my case, kick some serious political ass to compensate for Scott not grabbing mine.

Today's story, I had decided, was going to be a slam dunk. It was a simple case of a government housing official dodging complaints from residents of an apartment building who'd had no water or utilities for weeks, while living in horrible conditions. Obviously the guy was covering for (and receiving kickbacks from) a slumlord who lives out of state. By law he can force the guy to make repairs and turn on the juice, but he's been elusive.

However, the intrepid Brass Cupcake discovered that he would be eating lunch at his desk today and his secretary, a linebacker version of the Inhuman Resources troll, heads out to gorge herself at a lunch trough every day promptly at eleven-thirty.

Frank and I were staked out outside his office in our news car, as we waited for her to go to lunch before we struck with tape rolling.

"You got that look today," he said, as he sipped his coffee.

I turned to him. "What look?"

"That *don't screw with me* look. Haven't seen it for a while."

"This story just pisses me off."

"Yeah, me too. It's not right what they're doing to those people." He sat up straight as the linebacker troll emerged from the office. "Hey, here she comes."

We waited a minute until she walked to her car and drove off, then leaped into action. Frank opened the trunk, grabbed his camera, tossed me a wireless stick microphone and off we went.

We made our way through the glass doors into a lobby that was empty except for a black sign filled with names and office numbers. I quickly scanned the thing and found our target. We moved through the lifeless government office, down the musty hallways which were exposed cinder block, but as was the case in most city buildings, were painted vomit green. Finally we reached the office. "Hiram Silver, Housing Authority" was stenciled on the glass door. The outer office was empty, as expected. We quietly entered, moved to his office door and I gently knocked.

"Come in."

Frank hit the record button on his camera, kicked on the light attached to the top, and I opened the door.

Silver, a fifty-year-old chubby munchkin with a white beard who might have had a future as the Travelocity Roaming Gnome on retirement, stood up immediately when he saw us. "Whoa. How did you get in here?"

"I knocked; you said come in," I said.

He moved toward me. "Get out."

The man was maybe five feet tall, and with my heels I towered over him. I grabbed him by the shoulders and gave him a shove. He landed in his swivel chair, which rolled backward until it came to a rest with a thud against a book case. I moved quickly toward him and put my hands on the arms of the chair so he couldn't escape. "Listen to me, you little shit, you're either going to do one of two things. You're going to either give me an interview and explain why you don't get a court order to help the people in Remington Towers, or you're going to march your puny little ass across the street and *get* that court order."

The man was wide-eyed, as he obviously never expected an assault like this. "Who do you think you are? I don't have to do anything—"

"And if you don't, your wife is going to receive some very incriminating photos of you and *your friend* in the mail."

The bravado drained from his face as fear flashed into his eyes. "How... how do you—"

My eyes narrowed into gunslinger mode with a touch of the death stare. "It doesn't matter. So what's it gonna be, court order, or special delivery? FedEx can have the photos in your wife's hands by four-thirty. Tick-tock."

His face broke out in a sweat. "Okay, okay. I'll get the court order."

"Courthouse. Right now. And we're gonna follow you."

He nodded. "Okay, let's go." I released the chair as he stood up. "I don't know what the hell you call journalism these days—"

I jabbed one finger into his chest. "This isn't journalism, it's justice. Look, I'm in a pissy mood and if you so much as mention this to anyone at my station or anyone else, the photos will be in the mail. In fact, I might just deliver them personally to Miriam."

The mention of his wife's name (it pays to do your homework) sent him into full-fledged-flop sweat mode as he put his hands up in surrender. "Okay, okay, you've made your point. As long as I don't ever see you again."

"Just do your job and you won't. But remember, I'll always have those pictures."

***

As we emerged from the courthouse my soul felt healed from righting a wrong. The Brass Cupcake threw back her cape and strutted to the news car, head held high.

"Holy shit, Cupcake, where the hell did all that come from?" asked Frank.

I shrugged. "Hey, you said I had the look today."

"You had the look, but I didn't know you had the look of a mob enforcer. Geez, shoving him into a chair and blackmailing the guy? I was half expecting you to break his kneecaps."

"Eh, I thought about it, but I forgot to bring my baseball bat."

"What the hell's gotten into you?"

"Hey, we got the story, the people get their utilities and their building fixed."

"You do know you crossed a line back there."

"Why Frank, whatever are you talking about? I'm just being an aggressive reporter. I tripped and accidentally knocked him back."

"Yeah, right. Tripped, my ass. Don't worry, I'll erase that part of the tape."

"I knew you would."

"I'm worried you'll break *my* kneecaps if I don't." We reached the car and Frank popped the trunk and began loading the gear into it. "So how in the world did you get incriminating photos of the guy?"

"I didn't."

He stood up straight. "Excuse me?"

"Reporter's trick. Look, just about every politician has some honey on the side, and I had it on very good authority that he's a sleazeball and is having an affair, so I took a shot."

"You gotta be kidding me! You don't have anything on the guy?"

I shook my head and smiled ear to ear. "Nada. Bupkes."

"Damn, Cupcake," he said, as he moved to the front of the car. "Remind me never to play poker with you." We both got in the car and he cranked it up. "May I ask what has gotten you into this, as you said, pissy mood?"

My hands tightened into fists as my heart rate kicked up a notch. "Just stuff."

"Anything I can help with?"

"Like I said, just stuff that's going on in my life."

"You know you can talk to me—"

"The guy I'm dating won't have sex with me, all right? I want sex, dammit! And I want it now! I'm just... frustrated!"

Frank leaned back into his bucket seat and closed his eyes. "I need to wake up. Damn, this is one weird dream."

***

Feature reporter Stan Harvey was on the phone when I got off the set. "Yes, ma'am, I'll tell her. You hang in there. Bye." He looked up at me as I reached my desk. "Phone call from a woman in that building, thanking you for saving them."

"Yeah, nice when the good guys win," I said.

"It's why we do what we do. Speaking of which..." he pointed to the monitor that was broadcasting our newscast. "Happy endings all around. I had a warm fuzzy today." (A "warm fuzzy" is a nice heartwarming story that in theory makes you feel, according to news consultants, *warm and fuzzy. Warm* I get; *fuzzy*, I have no clue.) "Here it comes."

I liked Stan's stories so I sat down as the commercial ended and Jenna's flawless face filled the screen.

"Finally tonight, a heartwarming story about transportation, of all things. Stan Harvey shows us how getting from one place to another means an awful lot to some people."

The story began with a standard shot of Manhattan streets and lots of traffic zipping by as Stan voiced-over the video.

"Getting around town is simple as taking the bus, the subway... or hailing a cab. But for some, simply flagging down a taxi is impossible."

The video cut to a shot of a young woman in a wheelchair, heading out of her front door and down a ramp as Stan's voiceover continued.

"Gretchen Haver is paralyzed from the waist down, and needs to visit a special clinic in Queens once a month for treatment. Until now, getting there has been a major ordeal."

The shot cut to one of those handicapped vans, which was painted in the familiar canary yellow used by New York taxicabs.

And then Vincent's face filled the screen as he greeted the woman.

"Vincent Martino drives a cab, but this isn't just any taxi. It's a specially equipped one designed for the handicapped. Patients call it the "angel cab", and it transports people like Gretchen free of charge across the city when they need medical attention."

I couldn't believe it. I was riveted as I watched Vincent help the woman navigate her wheelchair onto a lift which placed her in the van. The shot dissolved into one showing him wheeling her into a doctor's office. She smiled as he told her he'd be back in two hours to pick her up.

"I don't know what'd I'd do without the angel cab," said the woman. "It used to take me hours to get here. It's such a wonderful thing that company is doing."

"What's easy for me is very difficult for people like her," said Vincent. "I'm happy to help in a small way. It's just a few minutes out of my day. It's really no big deal."

Stan's voiceover continued. "It may be no big deal for Vincent Martino, but for Gretchen Haver, the angel cab is a life-saver. And the tips he receives are priceless."

I watched in amazement as the story continued, as it showed Vincent giving Stan a tour of the specially equipped van, then picking up the woman from the doctor's office and taking her home. She gave him a strong hug after he wheeled her back into her house.

The story ended, dissolved to Jenna's face. Her soft smile told me she was obviously touched by the story.

She wasn't the only one.

***

The "people" I needed to meet were supposed to already be in Serena's apartment after dinner. Apparently they lived in her building, just down the hall, and could offer some "unique insight" into my situation, whatever the hell that means. I was guessing that they're shrinks, but knowing Serena and how she and Roxanne love to plot weird stuff, they could be gypsies conjuring up a love potion. (If so, I'd gladly use it.)

I already heard conversation in the apartment when I knocked on the door. Actually, it's not an apartment, but what I call a "lair" as Serena's bedroom was equipped with enough seduction material to stock an adult toy store.

She opened the door wide enough for me to see the couple seated on her red leather couch. "Hey, right on time."

"I work in TV, I'm always on time."

She closed the door behind me and ushered me into the living room, which was not decorated for seduction but rather looked like a lawyer's office. Bold green wallpaper with red stripes, gleaming cherry hardwood floors, a large window framed by exposed brick. The furniture was classic, with everything from an old-fashioned secretary to an armoire that served as a home to a television set. "Belinda, these are my neighbors, Daniel and Virginia."

The man stood up to shake my hand. "Hi, Belinda, nice to meet you." He was about thirty and six feet tall: a real beach-boy type with sandy hair, pale-blue eyes. Solidly built with an angular face and a warm smile.

I shook his hand and that of his wife, a tall knockout with big green eyes and a mound of soft brunette curls that hit her shoulders. She had classic high cheekbones and a wide smile, while dressed in a very conservative outfit: a knee-length skirt that showed off long, killer legs and a long-sleeved blouse that was no doubt hiding a supermodel's rack. "Nice to meet you both," I said.

Serena poured me a glass of wine and gestured toward the matching love seat opposite the couch. She picked up her own wine glass and took a seat next to me. "I asked Daniel and Virginia over tonight because they went through a situation very similar to what you're going through now."

I felt my face flush a bit, embarrassed as you can imagine that Serena had explained my "situation" to complete strangers. "Okay," I said, not thinking of anything else.

Daniel picked up the ball. "Virginia and I have been married three years. We met when we were both twenty-five and dated two years before we got married."

"You look very happy together," I said, as I noticed he was holding her hand.

"We have an amazing relationship," said Virginia. "But it almost didn't happen."

"You mean you almost didn't meet?"

"No," said Virginia. "I was a virgin when we started dating."

"Wow," I said. "Twenty-five's a long time to hold out." Thirty-three was even longer.

"Well, I'm Catholic," she said, "and when your mother names you Virginia Mary, you get the idea how strict my parents were."

I laughed a bit. "I'm Catholic as well, so I know about guilt. Anyway, go on."

"Well," said Daniel, "we start going out and I just know she's the one. I mean, everything clicks. We have everything in common, love spending time together—"

"I know the feeling," I said.

"But," said Daniel, "I was having a problem with her wanting to wait for marriage."

"Having a problem?" said Virginia, as she patted his knee. "Poor man was ready to explode."

"I understood her religious beliefs," said Daniel, "but I was a little worried. You know, that we'd get married and the sex would be awful. I mean, I loved her and all that, but..."

"So what happened?" I asked.

"I could tell he was losing interest," said Virginia.

"I was not," said Daniel.

"That's how it looked to me."

"It was just, well, beyond frustrating to be around her sometimes, knowing the date would end with the equivalent of a cold shower. And in the back of my mind I was wondering if maybe I might be making a mistake taking such a big chance. I mean, you're talking about spending the rest of your life with someone."

"So he started avoiding me," said Virginia.

"Not so much avoiding," said Daniel. "But I guess I was subconsciously putting a little distance between us."

"Obviously they worked it out," said Serena.

Virginia nodded. "I could tell I was losing him, and I knew I'd never find a better man. So..." she smiled and looked at the ceiling.

"So...?" I said.

"I caved," she said. "I told Daniel I was ready and it was terrific."

"What about your strong religious beliefs?" I asked.

She shrugged. "I went to confession." We all laughed as Daniel put his arm around her shoulder. "Anyway, the point is that I thought I was going to lose Daniel. And that outweighed the other stuff."

"So," said Serena, "while Daniel wasn't really playing hard to get, it had the same effect."

"But the roles are reversed for me," I said.

"Boggles the mind," said Virginia. "You're gorgeous."

"Thanks, so are you."

"And how old is this guy?" asked Daniel.

"Thirty-three," said Serena.

"Good God," said Daniel. "I'm surprised he can function. I mean, it's different for men."

"How so?" I asked.

"He needs a little more *scheduled maintenance* than I do," said Virginia.

"Hey, it's tough living with a babe," said Daniel. His wife smiled and gave him a little hug. "But, anyway, I would suggest that if you two feel the same way as we did, you need to put a little distance between you and him."

"Worked for me," said Virginia.

"To be quite honest and with all due respect to my wife," said Daniel, "if a guy doesn't want to have sex with a woman who looks like you, he's either an idiot or he's gay."

***

I was beginning to think that between Harry and Mrs. Baymont, I should have been born back in the day.

Mrs. Baymont told me that back in the day women patiently waited by their phones, hoping for a man to call. No caller ID, no answering machines, no cell phones. You either waited by the phone or took the chance of missing the call... and maybe the man of your dreams. (It sounded more dramatic when she said it.)

I was doing the same thing tonight, but for the opposite reason.

Scott was scheduled to fly back into town. And as he had during the time we'd been dating, would no doubt call as soon as he stepped off the plane.

And when he did, I would be ready.

I had my legal pad next to my phone, filled with notes and strategies that I would no doubt use to make my absence make his heart grow fonder. Or at least more frustrated.

I was to follow these guidelines:

-Do not sound excited when he calls. Sound indifferent.
-Use "dead air" whenever possible, letting the conversation die at various points.
-Do not, under any circumstances, agree to meet him tonight. Tell him you need "alone time."
-When he wants to discuss activities for the weekend, say "I have plans." Do not be specific.
-Tell him you'll touch base with him next week, then don't. When he does call, tell him, "I forgot."

This might sound like a recipe to kill a relationship, but at this point my desperation outweighed the possibility that Scott would take a hike. Personally, I thought he was as in lo— Oh, my God, I almost said it. That he *liked me* as much as I liked him. How about that? A *woman* being unable to commit for a change?

Now at this point you might think I'd be nervous, but after kicking some serious ass with that housing authority gnome this week, I was feeling pretty cocky. I was also in the process of eating some hellacious kung pao chicken, which was not only clearing out my sinuses but kicking up my adrenaline like a six pack of Red Bull.

C'mon, Scott. Call. Let's rock.

From now on if you want this girl, you're playing by my rules.

I was halfway through the chicken and into my second beer when "unknown" showed up on my cell. I assumed it was him.

I answered, trying to sound as bored as possible. "This is Belinda."

"Hey, it's me." He sounded upbeat.

Long pause. "I'm sorry, *who's* calling?" (That was Roxanne's suggestion.)

"It's Scott."

"Oh, guess it's a bad connection." I said nothing else. No *"How was your trip?"* No *"Would you like to come over and make out?"* No *"May I stop by your place and dress in two hundred dollars-worth of lingerie that will knock you out like an Ambien?"* Nothing. Dead air for five seconds.

"Yeah. Uh, anyway, I just landed and wanted to see if you're up for a late dinner, or maybe dessert or a drink?"

"Eh, not tonight. I kinda need some alone time right now."

"Everything okay?"

"Everything's great. Just need a quiet evening."

"Oh. Okay." I could tell from his tone he was a bit disappointed. "Anyway, for this weekend I was thinking—"

"Oh, I'm sorry but I already have plans both nights."

"Going out of town?"

"Nope, just have plans." Thank God this wasn't a Skype call, or he would have seen me with a huge grin.

"Okay. Well, I, uh, guess I'll see you at the shelter Sunday."

"Won't be there this week. I'm sure you can handle it. Tell you what, I'll call you next week."

"All right. Well... have a good night."

"You too." I hung up, then let out a shriek, got up and did a happy dance. Then, since I'd taped the whole thing, I replayed it and marveled at how well the whole thing worked out.

Finally, I got a third beer.

Because after all that, I still missed the guy. But, as Mrs. Baymont said, you have to look long term when it comes to relationships. I just hoped long term wasn't more than another month.

CHAPTER NINETEEN

By three o'clock on Thursday afternoon, Harry had endured enough of my sneezing and coughs that sounded like I was a two-pack-a-day smoker and sent me home. I felt like shit, I sounded like shit, I no doubt looked like shit and I probably would have infected the whole newsroom with whatever crap I was carrying. And the last thing Harry needed was a skeleton crew. "Go to the doctor and don't come back until you're well," he said. I wanted to tough it out and Harry appreciated my devotion, but he was right.

Fortunately my doctor understands my career and lifestyle, and managed to sneak me in for an appointment. Oh, joy, I had the flu along with some other sinus stuff going on. He wrote me a couple of prescriptions and told me to stay in bed for a few days, at least until Monday.

The last thing on my mind was a date with Scott. Who, in case you're wondering, still hadn't called me.

The light of the day was fading behind growing storm clouds, and all I wanted to do was take my medicine, crawl into bed and sleep forever. I had the taxi drop me off at the drug store two blocks from my place, got my scripts filled, and decided to hoof it home despite the cold, raw weather. I buttoned up my light jacket, which had been a poor choice considering the quickly changing temperature and headed home, wind slapping me in the face. I thought about hailing a cab for the two blocks, but didn't see one. What the hell, it was just a five-minute walk and I could be home before a taxi wandered by.

And then my heel got stuck in a grate right outside the pharmacy and broke off. My ankle bent at a ridiculous angle, pain shot up my leg and I crumpled to the ground.

Meanwhile, cue the rain.

"Can this day get any worse?" I said, as I looked at the broken heel stuck in the grate. I had two choices. I could either walk home with one leg four inches shorter than the other, or ditch the other shoe and go barefoot on the cold pavement, which was probably littered with glass and God knows what else. Just what I needed to help me get well, running around without shoes like Bruce Willis in *Die Hard*. I tried to push myself off the ground and stand up, but the pain in my quickly swelling ankle shot that idea to hell.

It was starting to rain harder when I heard, "Miss, are you all right?"

I turned around and Vincent was trotting toward me.

At this point my you-gotta-be-kidding-me thoughts were pointless. I needed help, and I didn't care who it was.

He recognized me as he arrived. "Oh, it's you. I saw you fall from down across the street and when you couldn't get up—"

I pointed at the two pieces of my shoe as that damned red sole taunted me. "My heel broke off, I think I sprained my ankle real bad and I've already got some sort of plague," I said, holding up my prescriptions.

"Well, we need to get you out of this weather. You think you can stand up?"

"I tried that already. Maybe if you give me a hand." I shoved the prescriptions in my purse and slung it over one shoulder.

"Sure," he said, as he slipped one arm behind my back and under my arm. "Try to stand. Lean on me."

The rain was starting to fall harder as Vincent helped me to my feet. I leaned on him and then slowly put some weight on my sprained ankle. The pain was excruciating. "Owwww!"

"Okay, this isn't going to work," he said. Then in a quick motion he reached under my legs with one arm while the other was still supporting my back and lifted me easily.

"What are you doing?" I asked.

"Getting you out of this weather," he said.

I started to argue, but realized he was right, that this was the only way to get me home. He was carrying me effortlessly and I knew he'd have no problem lugging my hundred and fifteen pounds two blocks. I wrapped my arms around his neck to hold on, felt the taut muscles of his broad shoulders.

He made a right turn off the sidewalk and headed into an apartment building.

"Where are you going?"

"I'm taking you home," he said.

"I don't live here."

"I know. *I* live here."

"Can't you just take me to my place?"

He kept walking toward the front door. "Look, it's starting to pour, you're sick, you can't walk, it's getting cold, my cab's four blocks away at the garage and I'm not gonna carry you two more blocks through this rain and get you soaked to the bone. You want an upgrade to pneumonia?"

I shook my head. "No."

"Then let me help you."

"Fine, but don't treat me like some damsel in distress."

"You are a damsel. You are in distress. Hence, by deductive reasoning, you are the proverbial damsel in distress. And right now I'm the only white knight you've got. So shut up, I'm rescuing you."

A burly, middle-aged doorman opened the door to his building as he carried me inside. "Need any help, Mr. Martino?" he asked. "I've got a wheelchair in the back."

"I'm good. She just took a fall."

The warm air of the lobby hit me and felt wonderful. My clothes were pretty damp, but not soaking wet. Vincent carried me to the elevator. "Hit the up button, will you?"

I reached out and tapped the button, which turned red. A few seconds later the doors opened and we got inside. "Floor, please," I said.

"Four."

"Fourth floor, linens and house wares." I hit the button, the doors closed and we headed up.

"What did the doctor say you had?"

"The flu with a sinus infection thrown in. I have bad allergies."

"Yeah, me too."

The elevator moved fast. Two minutes later we were at his door. "Oh, geez," he said.

"What?"

"Fish the keys out of my right pants pocket, will you?"

Oh, great. "Can't you just put me down for a minute?"

"Remember how it hurt the last time?"

"Point taken." I twisted my body around so I could reach into his pocket and get the keys. I expected some sexual double entendre, but he didn't say anything as I unlocked the door and pushed it open, then reached out and flicked on the light switch that was just inside the door. The apartment was not what I would have expected from a cab driver. It was beautifully decorated in art deco furniture and matching prints, with gleaming light hardwood floors underneath the black sofa and loveseat. A large aquarium was bubbling on a coffee table against the far wall as tropical fish provided color. And the place was spotless. No underwear on the lamps, no empty pizza boxes on the floor, no stuff you'd expect from a bachelor. There was even a faint smell of pine, as if the apartment had just been cleaned. Hell, the apartment was nicer than mine. "Beautiful place," I said.

"Thanks. Rox picked out most of the stuff. She has great taste." He carried me past the kitchen, through the living room and down a short hallway into a bedroom. The huge windows provided enough light to see. He'd been carrying me for a good five minutes, yet wasn't even breathing hard. He gently lowered me onto an ornate brass bed, flicked on a lamp that sat on a night stand, then walked to a closet. He returned carrying some clothes and handed them to me. "Rox left these sweatpants here a while back when we were decorating so they should fit you. All I've got for your top half is one of my sweatshirts. It'll be big but it's warm."

"What do you expect me to do with this stuff?"

"Get out of those wet clothes, get into these and get under the covers."

"You expect me to stay *here*?"

He pointed to the window, which was being pelted by rain. "You wanna go back out in that?"

Common sense hit me. I shook my head.

"Didn't think so. Look, Belinda, I know I'm not your favorite person, but you're one of Roxanne's best friends and she'd smack the living shit out of me if I didn't take care of you. Besides, I couldn't look myself in the mirror. The sooner you get well, the sooner you can go home. So get out of those wet clothes and into bed right now." He was looking at me like Harry does when he calls me *young lady*.

"Yes, sir," I said softly, suddenly a little girl who was obeying a parent.

He reached for the end table and hit a switch on a control box. "I'm turning on the electric blanket. It warms up pretty quick."

I looked up at him and was at a loss for words. For me, that was becoming a fairly common occurrence with men. Why was this man being so nice to me when I'd treated him like dirt?

His tone softened. "Have you eaten dinner?"

"No, I've been kinda queasy all day. But I am pretty hungry."

"And you sound awful. Think you can handle some soup?"

"Yeah, that'd be great."

"I'll go heat some up. And get an ice bag for that ankle. Meanwhile, out of those clothes and under the covers." He headed out of the bedroom and closed the door.

The situation boggled the mind. I wanted Scott in *my* bed and somehow I've ended up in Vincent's with him waiting on me like some weird combination of Sir Lancelot, Florence Nightingale and my dad. If I didn't know better I'd think Roxanne had sabotaged my heels and seeded the clouds to make it rain. (And while I'm on that train of thought, it occurs to me she probably tipped off Stan about the angel cab story.)

I peeled off my wet clothes, managed to get my now-ballooned ankle through the leg of the sweatpants, and threw on Vincent's sweatshirt, which I swam in. I slid between the covers into the soothing warmth provided by the electric blanket, then pulled them up to my neck. I was in a cocoon of heat, which was beginning to warm me to the bone. The room had a soothing effect on me. The deco theme didn't carry through to the bedroom. The walls were painted pale green, the ceiling a light beige, not as glaring as the bright white you see on most ceilings. There was an old rolltop desk in one corner, an oak dresser in another. A distressed leather chair sat next to the bed. A few prints of seashore scenes adorned the walls, giving the room a beachy feel.

Ten minutes later he tapped on the door. "You decent?"

"No, I'm a cheap slut." My voice was now filled with gravel.

"Funny." He cracked open the door and moved through it carrying a bed tray with a bowl of soup. "At least the flu hasn't killed that famous attitude. Sit up a bit."

I propped two pillows behind me and sat up. Vincent placed the tray over my lap as steam rose from the bowl. "Thank you." I looked at the soup, which I didn't recognize. "What is this?"

"Italian meatball soup. Some people call it wedding soup. It's little meatballs and a tiny pasta called *pastine*, which is what they feed Italian babies. It's good when you're sick because there's all kinds of spices in the meatballs and the broth. Garlic, fresh parsley, basil, pepper."

I picked up my spoon, dipped it into the bowl and took a sip. My mouth filled with a combination of rich chicken broth and garlic from the little meatballs. "Oh, that's wonderful. Who makes this?"

"It's... homemade."

"So who made it?"

"Me."

"You just whipped this up in ten minutes?"

"No, I made a big batch a while ago and always keep a bowl in the freezer for when I'm sick. I zapped it in the microwave."

I took another bite, which warmed my insides. "You really made this?"

"There is a vowel at the end of my name, Belinda. You forget Italians are obsessed with food."

"Well, this is a wonderful obsession."

"I forgot the ice bag. Be right back."

I continued my attack on the meal and thought this was the best soup I'd ever eaten. I was wondering if the little meatballs were this good, how great would the big ones be with sauce and a big plate of pasta?

He returned a few minutes later, just as I finished the soup. "Somebody was hungry. You think you can keep it down?"

"Yeah. That was perfect. Thank you. It really warmed me up."

"Let's take a look at that ankle." He removed the tray and put it behind him on the floor, then sat on the foot of the bed and pulled back the covers. "Whoa."

"Yeah, I know."

"It's pretty swollen." He grabbed a pillow from a nearby chair, placed one hand under my calf and gently lifted my leg, then propped my ankle on the pillow. I knew I wasn't going to run a marathon in the next few days. "Think you can handle some ice?"

"Give it a shot."

He slowly placed the ice bag on my ankle, watching my face the whole time. I cringed a bit from the cold, but then my face relaxed. "That okay?"

"Yeah."

"Let's leave that on for ten minutes, then back under the covers you go."

"Yes, Doctor."

He reached down to the floor and grabbed the tray. "You wanna watch TV, need something to read?"

"I'm pretty tired. Think I just need to sleep."

"That's probably best. I'll be back to get the ice bag."

Ten minutes later Vincent returned, removed the bag and inspected the ankle. "Looks a touch better, but it'll take a while. The best thing to do is to stay off it. Not that you're going anywhere anyway." He looked at my face. "You're pale as a ghost. Are you hot?"

"So I've been told. If I wear a skirt that's short enough."

"Well, obviously your one hundred fifty IQ backside is feeling fine."

"That your way of calling me a smartass?"

"You're very perceptive. But I meant temperature with my original question. Is your body very warm?

"Yeah."

He covered my ankle with the blanket and tucked it in, moved toward the front of the bed, sat on the edge and placed his hand on my forehead. "Geez, you're burning up." He opened a drawer on the end table, pulled out a thermometer and began shaking it. I opened my mouth and he put it in. He sat there and smiled at me as he waited. I would have smiled back if I didn't have the thermometer in my mouth.

Finally he pulled it out and held it up to the light. "A hundred and one point seven."

"Yikes. So is it feed a fever, starve a cold, or the other way around?"

"No idea. In this household we just feed everything." My eyes were already at half mast and he noticed. "You wanna sleep now?"

I nodded.

"I hate to ask this, but do you need me to carry you to the bathroom before I turn out the light?"

I started to laugh. "No, I'm good in that department."

"Okay, just yell if you do." He pulled the covers up under my chin and tucked me in. A memory of my dad doing the same thing flashed through my mind, generating more warmth than the blanket. "G'night."

He turned out the light and started to head out when a twinge of guilt hit me. "Vincent, I'm sorry I'm putting you out."

He was backlit by the hallway light, but I could see him shaking his head. "You're not putting me out."

"Where are *you* sleeping?"

"The sofa is a hide-a-bed. Very comfortable. I'll be fine. G'night."

"Good night. And... thank you."

He shut the door behind him. The sun, what little there was one of it, had gone down and taken the last remaining light in the room with it. The only noise was the sound of rain steadily hitting the window.

I closed my eyes and instantly fell asleep, feeling safe, protected... And confused.

***

I cracked open one eye and saw the clock on the nightstand with the red digital numbers. Nine-thirty.

I had slept fourteen hours straight.

I stretched my eyes open and yawned. A look out the window told me it was still overcast and raining pretty hard.

I started to wake up, and became aware of my horrible trench mouth and achy joints. My back was absolutely killing me.

And I needed the little girl's room. I threw back the covers, hoping the swelling on the ankle had gone down so I could hop to the bathroom. But it was just as swollen as the night before.

Dammit, I needed help. And there was only one port in this storm.

I heard the talk radio station playing in the other room and knew he was up. "Hey, Vincent!" I yelled, still hoarse.

I heard footsteps and then a tap on the door. "You decent?"

"No, I'm a wanton harlot."

He was laughing as he opened the door. "Belinda, you have a visitor." He looked back into the other room. "C'mon, she's right in here."

Oh, shit. The last thing I needed looking like this was company. I quickly grabbed the covers and pulled them up to my neck as a very familiar cat bounded into the room and jumped on the bed.

"Gypsy!" I relaxed immediately as the cat moved toward me and started to purr. "I'd forgotten you adopted her. She looks great." I started to pet her, as she nuzzled my arm and looked at me with those beautiful pale-green eyes.

"Well, she's a little ticked off at me. She usually sleeps in here at the foot of the bed, but the door was closed." He ducked back out of the bedroom and returned carrying crutches. "Sleep okay?"

"Like a rock. Where'd you get those?"

"I remembered my neighbor had a broken leg last year, and turns out she still had these. She's about your height, so these should work. I assumed you wouldn't want me carrying you back and forth to the bathroom."

"Yes, even the damsel in distress has her limitations when it comes to accepting help. Thank you."

He sat down on the edge of the bed. "How you feeling?"

"Everything hurts. Not just the ankle. My back is one big knot."

"Well, you've got the flu, so you're gonna be achy." He looked at the ankle. "Looks like you need some more ice. You hungry?"

"Starving."

"Protein is good when you're sick. Bacon and eggs?"

"Bring it on." He got up to head to the kitchen. "Oh, can you bring me my purse?"

"Sure thing." He left the room, then quickly returned with my stuff, which he placed on the bed. "Hey, your phone was buzzing last night but I didn't want to wake you up."

"I appreciate that."

"Okay, let me get breakfast started. You're okay on crutches?"

"I've had 'em before. Thank you, Vincent."

He left the room and closed the door behind him. I pulled my cell phone from my purse and saw I had missed one call.

From "unknown number."

Sonofabitch.

Scott had called.

***

After a terrific breakfast in bed Vincent returned wearing a jacket and holding an umbrella. "Off to work?" I asked.

He shook his head. "I took the day off."

"What for?"

"I wasn't going to leave you here all alone. Somebody has to take care of you."

"You didn't have to burn a vacation day on my account."

"Hey, I'm tight with the boss. Anyway, I gotta run to the store. You need anything?"

"I think I'm good. I'm gonna call Roxanne and have her bring me some clothes. My laptop. She's got a spare key to my apartment."

"Okay." He reached in his pocket, pulled out a slip of paper and placed it on the end table. "That's my cell number just in case."

"Just in case what?"

"In case you suddenly get real sick, fall down, whatever. I don't think you will, but best to be safe."

"So this is the younger, high-tech version of *I've fallen and I can't get up?*"

"Basically."

"You're a regular boy scout, aren't you?"

He shrugged. "Back in a few minutes."

172

"Okay." He left the room, and I waited until I heard him shut the door to the apartment. I pulled out my cell and quickly called Roxanne.

She picked up after a couple of rings. "Hey there, Wing Girl," she said. I heard music in the background as well as scissors snipping away and knew she was at the salon.

"Got a minute to talk?"

"Sure. God, you sound horrible."

"I've got the flu."

"Ewwww. You need anything?"

"Yeah, I was wondering if you could go by my apartment later and pick up some clothes, my toothbrush, a few other things."

"Sure." Short pause as it obviously dawned on her what I was asking. "Wait a minute. Where the hell are you?"

"Well, you're not going to believe this, but I'm at your cousin Vincent's apartment."

I heard her excuse herself from the client, the music faded and a door closed. I knew she was in her office. "Did I just hear you say you were at *Vincent's* place?"

"It's a long story, but yeah. I broke a heel last night, sprained my ankle outside his apartment, it was raining, I was sick, he carried me inside—"

"Holy shit!" Long pause. "Wait a minute, last night? You spent the night with Vincent?"

"I spent the night *in his apartment*. I'm real sick and he put me in his bed and made me meatball soup and has been taking care of me and keeping me warm."

"Yeah, I'll bet."

"That's not what I meant! He's keeping me warm with an electric blanket."

"So where's he sleeping?" I didn't need Skype to see the devilish look on her face.

"On his sofa bed."

"Oh, poor guy. That thing's a torture rack."

"Really? He said it was comfortable."

"Pffft. I spent a night on it once. You may as well sleep on the sidewalk. So anyway, does this mean—"

"It doesn't mean anything, Roxanne, he was just being nice because I couldn't walk and I'm sick and it was raining."

"Just being nice. Sure, hun, whatever you say."

"Roxanne!"

"Hey, your words, not mine."

I needed to change the subject. "Meanwhile, Scott finally called last night and I've gotta call him back."

"Let me get this straight. Vincent rescued you, took you in, is taking care of you, and you're gonna call another guy for a date?"

"Uh... yeah, that about sums it up."

"Wow, calling one man back from another man's bed. Aren't you the wild child? You got some serious *cojones*."

"It's not like that!"

"Oh, so you're not calling one man from another man's bed?"

"Yeah. No. Dammit, Roxanne, I'm in a situation here!"

"Yeah, that's a good word for it. You sound like one of my clients who says *it's complicated* when I ask about their love life. Look, I gotta go but I'll bring your stuff by this afternoon. Meanwhile, stay in Vincent's bed and let him keep you warm." I heard her sinister laugh as she hung up.

I could hardly wait for her visit.

That painful conversation out of the way, I now had to call Scott back before Vincent returned and I didn't know how long he'd be gone. Dammit, I should have called him first. I quickly dialed his number and he picked up on the first ring.

"Hey there."

"Hi, Scott. Sorry I didn't get back to you last night. I went to bed real early."

"Are you sick? You sound awful."

"I've got the flu."

"Ugh. Geez, I'm sorry you're feeling bad. I was going to see if you wanted to catch an opera tonight, but I guess that's out of the question."

"I'm afraid I'm not going anywhere for a few days. Doctor wants me to stay in bed until at least Monday."

"Well, okay. You get well and we'll do something when you're better. I really miss you."

"I miss you too."

"Okay, talk to you later. Bye."

"Bye."

I felt better, having gotten that taken care of. And apparently just in time, as I heard the key in the door and knew Vincent had returned.

And then I realized Scott had not asked if I needed anything or offered to take care of me. It shouldn't have bothered me, but it somehow did.

***

I slept most of the day and woke up around four in the afternoon, hobbled to the bathroom on crutches still feeling lousy and sore, and then decided to wander out of the bedroom. Thankfully Vincent had left the door cracked, so I pushed it open with the end of one crutch. I heard the faint sound of a baseball game and recognized the Mets announcers. I made my way into the other room and found Vincent at the kitchen table, keeping an eye on the game while rolling little meatballs and dropping them onto a metal cookie sheet.

He noticed my arrival and looked up. "Hey, what are you doing out of bed?"

"Needed to get up and move around for a while. I'm going right back. What are you doing?"

"Making a batch of meatball soup. You ate the last bowl and you're gonna need more."

175

The table was covered with bowls, a garlic press, bread crumbs, and about six jars of spices along with the cookie sheet. "You didn't have to do that. It looks like a lot of trouble."

"It's no trouble. I love to cook and you need to get well." He finished rolling the last of the beef mixture, got up, picked up the cookie sheet, walked to the kitchen and slid the meatballs into a large steaming pot. "It'll be ready in a half hour."

"Great, I'm hungry again."

"Feeling any better?"

I shook my head. "Not much. Still pretty sore."

"A hot bath would probably loosen you up."

"So, you like your women loose?"

He shook his head and smiled. "Oh, man. It never ends with you, does it?"

I wiped my runny nose with the back of my hand. "Nah, it's part of my charm. The smartass chromosome is dominant in my family."

"Well, it suits you. So, you want me to run you a hot bath after you eat?"

"Yeah, that sounds good."

He cocked his head toward the bedroom as he washed his hands in the sink. "Go get back in bed. I'll bring you some soup when it's ready."

"Yes, sir."

"Oh, Roxanne stopped by. She peeked in on you but you were dead to the world. She dropped off a bunch of your stuff. Clothes, your laptop. I'll bring it in for you."

"Thank you, Vincent."

***

Two bowls of soup, a thirty-minute hot bath and some fresh clothes later, I was back under the covers. Apparently Disney bluebirds had changed the sheets while I was in the tub, while my outfit from yesterday had seemingly been washed and ironed by magical elves and was hanging on the back of a closet door.

Vincent tapped on the bedroom door. "You decent?"

"No, I'm a cheap bimbo."

He laughed as he entered the room. "I guess this will be our running joke for the weekend. Did the bath help?" He sat down on the edge of the bed. His hand landed close to mine.

"Yeah. My back's still pretty tight, though."

"Some Bengay would probably make you feel better."

"Yeah."

He reached into the night-stand drawer and pulled out a tube of the muscle rub, then handed it to me. "Here you go."

He started to get up. Much as I hated to do it, I desperately needed to ask for another favor, one that would involve his hands on my body. "Uh, Vincent, I can't exactly rub it on my own back."

He playfully slapped his forehead with his palm. "Duh. Right." He took the tube back from me. "Okay, sit up."

I sat up and scooted forward while he sat on the bed behind me. My heart raced a bit as he squeezed some Bengay on his hand. I was expecting him to tell me to take my sweatshirt off, but he simply ran his hand under it and gently rubbed the stuff all over my back with a very light touch. I peeked at him over my shoulder and saw that he was focused on my back. No sleazy comment, no creepy smile, no hands going where they weren't supposed to be. My back began to warm up as the stuff took effect and he pulled my sweatshirt down.

"Thank you."

"No problem. Need anything else?"

"Well, I slept all day. Could I watch a little TV?"

"Sure." He grabbed the remote from the end table, fired it at the flat screen on the wall and handed it to me. He watched as I scrolled through the guide. "Not much on Friday nights these days. Then again unless you like reality shows there's not much on any night of the week."

"No kidding, I hate that garbage. You got any movies?"

"I got a ton of movies. What are you in the mood for?"

"Sci-fi, what else? But no zombies or vampires, I'm not into that. And no fantasy either. I hate those quests that last three hours. Just fire the damn phasers and be done with it."

"I agree. That's why I like Kirk better than Picard on *Star Trek*. Shoot first and ask questions later instead of talking your enemy to death."

"Plus, Picard had less sex than Spock on that show."

"True enough. Kirk nailed an alien babe in almost every episode. Anyway, I've got a whole Netflix franchise on hand in the other room. Be right back."

Just as he left, my cell phone rang. I saw Ariel's number and answered it. "Hi there."

"Hey, Wing Girl, we miss you!" said Ariel. I could tell she was on speaker as I heard a party atmosphere in the back and knew they were at a bar or restaurant.

"How ya feeling?" asked Serena.

"Not great, but a little better. My fever's dropped a little bit."

"Sorry I missed you when I came by," said Roxanne. "But you were sawing through a cord of wood and out cold."

"Yeah, I've been sleeping a lot. Thanks for bringing my stuff."

"Do you need anything else?" asked Ariel.

"No, I'm good. And I don't want any of you to catch this bug. It's really awful. By the way, I'm not buying any more red-heeled shoes."

"They don't design those things to walk across grates," said Roxanne.

"Then they should come with a warning," I said.

"Heard from Scott?" asked Serena, who I knew damn well already had the answer to that question since I had told Roxanne he'd called. But I played along.

"Yeah, he called last night but I was asleep. I called him back today. He wanted to go to the opera tonight, but obviously when I told him I was really sick we couldn't. He said we'll do something next week when I feel better."

"Did he offer anything?" asked Ariel.

"How do you mean?"

"You know, to come over and take care of you, if you needed orange juice, stuff from the drug store, things like that."

"Nope. Just said he'd see me when I got well."

"Ariel, that's a silly question," said Roxanne. "I mean, why in the world would she need Scott to bring her stuff when she's already got someone who *adores her* waiting on her hand and foot? Who *isn't a virgin*."

Just what I needed while bedridden, more Catholic guilt. I heard them giggling. "You guys think this is funny."

"We're just getting a kick out of your current situation," said Serena.

"That I'm sick as a dog and have the flu?"

"No," said Ariel. "What bed you're in and who's taking care of you. It's funny as hell. You've raised irony to an art form."

"I'm glad you all find this so amusing."

"Lighten up, Wing Girl," said Serena. "Enjoy the butler service. We love you."

"Get well, kid," said Roxanne. "Stay warm."

She had to throw that in. "See you guys next week," I said, and ended the call just as Vincent returned with a huge box of DVDs.

"You weren't kidding," I said, looking at the box which must have contained over a hundred movies.

"How else would I know all that sci-fi trivia?"

"So, you got a Starfleet uniform in that closet?"

"I have to draw the line somewhere. I made a model of the Enterprise when I was a kid, but that's about as far as it went. I stick with movies and books. And the annual convention. I get a kick out of those whackjobs in costume."

He set the box on the edge of the bed and I chose a bunch of movies I hadn't seen in a while, along with some all-time favorites. I handed him one from the fifties.

"Forbidden Planet, a classic," he said, as he moved toward the Blu-Ray player under the flat screen. "I love this movie. First appearance of Robby the Robot."

"Yeah, that's right," I said, as he loaded the disc. The movie, being an old one, started immediately, so there weren't a ton of previews to sit through.

"And Anne Francis is pretty damn hot. I mean, for an actress in 1956 to wear that sort of a dress—"

"You *would* notice that."

"Why else would women wear short skirts if they didn't want men to notice them? I believe you brought up the hemline issue when I asked if you were hot."

"Fine, point taken."

"Okay, enjoy," he said, as he started to head out of the room.

Something wasn't right. I had to start being nicer. "Aren't you gonna watch it with me?"

He stopped and turned to face me. "I figured you'd want to be by yourself."

I reached out and patted the chair next to the bed. "C'mon, big boy. Anne Francis in a short skirt."

"Well, if you're gonna twist my arm."

***

After a Friday night triple feature (including our friend Jones the cat) I slept late, and so did Vincent. Poor guy was probably exhausted from being my slave and he was already doing this stuff for his mother. My fever was beginning to break, down to one hundred even, and the swelling in my ankle had gone down significantly. I still needed the crutches, though, as it was tender.

Meanwhile, I was ravenous. I absolutely devoured an entire

foot-long meatball sub Vincent picked up from the deli, along with all the other incredible food he put in my path. Mrs. Baymont's rules went out the window for the time being, as pure animal hunger trumped etiquette. I was, however, pleased that feeding a fever seemed to work best for me. And if you're going to get stuck in someone else's apartment when you're ill, pick an Italian.

I was also getting a little bored. Loafing and watching movies is nice, but I was married to my job and beginning to miss the rush of the big story. I decided to spend the afternoon trying to catch up on work and doing as much investigating as possible from a bed. So I fired up my laptop and started looking at some of the stories I was working on when Vincent knocked on the door.

"You decent?"

I had a good one ready for him. "No, I'm a trashy jezebel."

He opened the door. "Jezebel, haven't heard that term in a while. Then again, wanton harlot isn't exactly a popular catch phrase these days." He noticed the laptop. "Catching up on e-mail?"

"Working on some stories."

"Oh, anything interesting?"

"All of my stories are interesting."

"I didn't mean it that way."

"I know." I looked at the screen, filled with the ever-frustrating documents provided by Councilman Jagger. "This one story in particular has me stumped."

"Can I take a look? I'd love to know how you people put stories together."

I nodded at the chair next to the bed. "Sure, c'mon." He moved to the chair and sat down as I slanted the laptop so we could both see it.

His face tightened as he looked at the long list of names and pension payments they were receiving. "What exactly is this?"

"You know who Councilman Jagger is?"

"Yeah, sure."

"Well, he called me a while back and told me he thinks

someone's skimming from the city's pension fund. He gave me all these documents. I was hoping to find out where the money's going, but I'm not a CPA. So far all the financial people I've had take a look at it have come up empty, and it's just a bunch of names and numbers to me."

"Why does he think someone's skimming?"

"Well, the city moved newer employees to a 401k a few years ago, the theory being that the older people collecting pensions would eventually die off and save the city money. But after three years, Jagger says he's not seeing the savings he expected. So he thinks someone's cooked the books."

"Maybe people aren't dying off as quick as they expected. People are living longer, you know. Maybe those people... what are they called? You know, those insurance people who figure out the odds of people dying?"

"Actuaries."

"Yeah, maybe they miscalculated."

"That's possible, but here's the key that keeps me going on this story. Jagger's been threatened, told to stop nosing around in the pension fund. So something's definitely there. We just haven't been able to find it."

"Are the police involved in this?"

"Jagger's afraid to contact anyone. He's pretty sure his office is bugged. He's been calling me from a burner phone he's so worried."

Vincent's face took on a look of recognition as he pointed at the screen. "Hey, that's my cousin Stefano."

I looked and saw the name Stefano Salvatore DiBlasio on the screen. "He must have worked for the city."

He nodded. "Yeah, maintenance guy for the school system. He was kind of simple-minded, went to a special school, but the guy could fix anything. They loved him down there. He was sort of a mechanical savant, for lack of a better term." Suddenly he furrowed his brow. "This must be an old list, right?"

"No, Jagger said it's up to date. Why?"

"This is the list of people receiving pension payments?"

"Uh-huh."

"Right now?"

"Yeah, why?"

"My cousin Stefano died two years ago."

My eyes grew wide as I looked closer at the screen. "You sure that's him?"

"Of course it's him. How many people named Stefano Salvatore DiBlasio do you think there are working for the city?"

"Maybe his wife's receiving the payments."

"Uh-uh. Stefano never married." He pointed at the screen. "Scroll over to the address. I wanna see if they're mailing checks to his old house, since his sister who took care of him still lives there."

I slid the spreadsheet over to the right. "Post office box in Queens."

Vincent shook his head. "That doesn't make any sense. He lived in Brooklyn his entire life. And we had direct deposits set up for him so he wouldn't lose his checks." He looked closer. "The rest of the information is right. That's his birthday, Christmas Day, I always remembered that. Stefano used to say he got shortchanged because his birthday fell on Christmas. And that's the day he retired. We threw him a big party."

Suddenly I had an idea. "Hold that thought." I did a search of the documents for the post office box, number 504 in Queens.

More than six hundred names popped up.

"That's where the missing money is going..." I grabbed his arm. "Holy shit, that's it!"

"What?"

"All these people are getting their pension checks delivered to the same address. And I'm willing to bet they're all dead and the computer doesn't know it, so it's still cutting checks. Oh my God!"

"Well, that would make sense," said Vincent. "But how would someone cash that many pension checks made out to dead people?"

"Obviously whoever's doing this works in a bank or has some

way to do that. Maybe has an accomplice. But whoever it is, his ass is mine." My eyes gleamed as the adrenaline known as a "big story" shot through my veins.

He noticed. "You look like you're suddenly feeling a lot better."

"Yep." I turned to face him. "A big story has healing powers, especially when you catch the bad guy. And *you* broke the story, Vincent."

"I didn't do anything—"

"Yeah, you did. I never would have found this without you. Oh, this is gonna be too easy."

"How so?"

"Not only do we know what the scam is, now we know the thief's address. We just have to wait to see who picks up the mail."

***

By Sunday morning I felt I had really turned the corner. My ankle was back to normal and I could walk without the crutches, though I was still favoring them. The aches were almost gone, but my back was still a bit stiff. I considered asking Vincent to take me home, but one look out the window at the steady drizzle and steam coming out of tailpipes told me it was a bad idea for the butterfly to leave her cocoon. The last thing I needed was a health setback before I could break this story. And I was determined to get well because I wasn't giving this story to anyone.

I had no idea if Scott called, since my cell died. I'd forgotten to have Roxanne bring the charger and I wasn't going to ask her to run another errand on a Sunday.

So last night I borrowed Vincent's phone and after talking with Councilman Jagger and my contact at the FBI, I discovered we had to break it Tuesday, the first of the month.

Because that was the day the pension checks arrived in the mail. Surely whoever was behind this scheme would be showing up at that post office in Queens. You don't let that amount of money sit untouched in the hands of the morons who work for the postal service.

So it was Tuesday or bust, as far as my health was concerned.

I was under the covers drying my hair with a thick, fluffy black towel. The now-famous red tangles had been matted and soaked with sweat since my fever broke overnight. I didn't have a hair dryer, and apparently neither did Vincent, so I got it as dry as I could and would have to wait for the principles of evaporation to work their magic. While I was waiting I heard the familiar tap on the door.

Ooooh, I got a good one for ya.

"You decent?"

"No, I'm an easily seduced trollop."

Vincent entered, laughing a bit. "Did you stay up all night thinking of that one?"

"Nah, just till one in the morning."

"An easily seduced trollop, huh?"

"Are there any other kind?"

"Of course *I* wouldn't know. But I have heard stories."

"Uh-huh. Right."

He sat down on the edge of the bed. "So how you feeling today?"

"A lot better. Still a little sore, but I think I can go back to work tomorrow."

He grabbed the thermometer, shook it, and stuck it in my mouth. "Well, let's see. It was an even hundred last time, right?"

I nodded.

"You wanna watch the Giants later?"

Big smile, big nod. "I tawt you had tikets," I said, trying to get the words past the thermometer.

"Don't talk yet." He waited a minute, then took the thermometer out and held it up to the light. "Ninety-nine and a half. Much better, but not all the way back. You're probably right, one more day of rest and a few more feeding frenzies and you should be good to go."

"Hey, you're the one bringing all the great food in here."

"I was kidding. I like a girl who can clean her plate and still be skinny."

"I'm not skinny."

"I carried you in here, remember? Trust me, you don't weigh anything. Hey, what were you trying to ask me before?"

"Oh, about the Giants. I thought you had tickets. Those things are expensive. I don't want you to miss the game."

"I do have tickets, but it's a road game today. Four o'clock, San Francisco."

"Oh, right, I forgot. Tough game. They need this one to make the playoffs. And the Cowboys have to lose."

"Yeah. You want me to do your back before I start breakfast?"

"Do my back?"

"With Bengay."

"Oh yeah, sure. That would be great."

"Scoot up a bit."

I sat up and slid forward as Vincent grabbed the tube and started applying relief to my back. I didn't peek over my shoulder because I trusted him. And I decided I was definitely getting a massage when I got better.

"So, all the dominoes in place for your story? You were working the phone quite a while last night."

"Yeah, and thanks for letting me use yours. I had to call my boss and my FBI contact to get it all set up. The Feds will have a surveillance van across the street and they'll let me and a photographer stay inside until the guy shows up. Since it's Sunday and the post office is closed today they're busy setting up a hidden camera inside right now. They're also sweeping Jagger's office for bugs." I turned my head to look at him. "By the way, you cannot tell a soul about this."

He made the classic zipper motion across his lips. "No problem. I'm a vault."

I turned back as he continued applying the lotion. "Anyway, tomorrow I meet with the Feds and we go over logistics, the ground rules. And then Tuesday... well, make sure you watch at five o'clock. It's a huge exclusive, if we get it."

"I've already got your newscast set on the DVR. It tapes every day."

"Oh, really?" I peeked over my shoulder, but couldn't see his face.

He finished putting the stuff on my back and pulled down my blue sleep shirt. "Uh, yeah, I uh, have watched your station for years." I turned to face him and saw his face redden a bit. "I'll go make you something to eat. Right back."

***

I used my credit card and ordered pizza for the game, a pre-emptive strike as I knew Vincent would want to cook for me and he had to be sick of providing room service by now. Besides, I'd eaten him out of house and home and figured I should re-stock his fridge and do something nice for him when I got well.

Did I really say that?

Meanwhile, despite my dead cell phone I had Scott's number committed to memory and thought I'd let him know I'd be back in action tomorrow. I was hoping he'd called, and it was driving me crazy.

He picked up after about five rings. "Hello?"

"Scott, it's Belinda."

"Oh. I didn't recognize the number."

"My cell died yesterday and I'm using another phone. I didn't know if you'd called."

"No, I was going to touch base with you today. How are you feeling? You sound like yourself."

"Much better. I should be back at work tomorrow."

"Glad to hear it. Think you'll have enough energy for dinner

187

tomorrow night then? I really miss you."

"Dinner sounds great. Not sure if I should kiss you, though. You might catch something."

"You're worth the risk. Listen, I've got a few things to take care of in the morning and I'll call you tomorrow with the dinner plans. By the way, I also have something important to tell you. I think you'll be happy."

"Oh, really? Do I get a hint?"

"Nope, has to be face to face."

"Sounds great. See you then, Scott."

"Can't wait. Bye."

The call ended just as Vincent entered the room and saw me hang up the phone. "Still working on your story?"

Luckily he wasn't familiar with my *hand in the cookie jar* face. "I'm, uh, setting up things for tomorrow." (Hey, don't roll your eyes. It's the truth. Kinda sorta. Fine, I'll go to confession.)

"I gotta tell you, you're really dedicated. Sick in bed and you're still working the story. There should be more reporters like you."

Now I really needed to go to confession. "Thank you."

"So what are you in the mood for regarding dinner?"

"I already ordered a pizza for the game. It should be here any minute."

He frowned. "You didn't have to do that—"

"And you didn't have to play nursemaid and cook for four days. Believe me, I owe you a lot more than a pizza. I want you to sit back and enjoy the game this afternoon. Take a break, Vincent. Put your feet up. You're not my butler. You've still gotta do this stuff for your mother after I'm outta here."

"Well, okay."

"By the way, how is she?"

He shrugged and a bit of sadness crept into his eyes. "Ah, you know, good days and bad. At least her mind is still sharp. I'll see her tomorrow night. Thank God I've got a big family to help out."

The doorbell rang. "Dinner is served!" I said.

"Thanks, Belinda. That was really thoughtful of you." He headed out to answer the door.

Yeah. Thanks, Belinda. A really good looking guy who obviously has a major crush on you has treated you like a queen for four days and you make a date with another man. Calling from his bed. On his phone, no less.

Even going to confession won't make the guilt go away.

***

"Geez, tackle somebody!" My own words seemed to echo off the walls of Vincent's bedroom.

He started to laugh. "Geez, maybe I'd better take your blood pressure instead of your temperature. And I thought I got worked up during these games."

"They're just so damn frustrating! They should have put this game away in the third quarter, but nooooo! It's never friggin' easy with the Giants! They've gotta make you sweat right down to the end."

"They do win their share of Super Bowls."

"And even those go right down to the wire! It's never simple with these guys! A fourteen-point lead and it's almost gone! If the Niners kick a field goal we've got overtime. Just what I need."

"I think you need a beer."

"I can't! I'm taking frigging medication! Damn flu!"

And then one of the Giant cornerbacks intercepted a pass and headed for the end zone.

"All right, go! Go!" yelled Vincent.

"C'mon, c'mon, c'mon! Somebody block for him, dammit!"

The cornerback wove his way through the tacklers and made a flying leap into the corner of the end zone. The ref signaled touchdown and I slumped back against my pillow.

"Okay, you can relax now," said Vincent. "They're up by ten

with thirty seconds to go."

"I'm not relaxing till it's all zeroes. I don't trust the bastards. There could be a kickoff return, an onside kick. The fat lady hasn't sung yet."

As it turned out, that was enough for the win. We decided to stay up and also watch the Sunday night game since I was too wired to fall asleep anyway. We rooted against the evil Cowboys who did their part for the Giants' playoff hopes as they lost. (Somehow I take perverse joy in rooting for a team to lose.)

I looked at the clock and saw it was almost eleven. "Guess I'd better turn in. Back on the clock tomorrow."

"Yeah, sounds like you've got two very busy days ahead of you. What time do you have to be in?"

"Nine."

"What time you want me to take you back to your place?"

"Is seven too early?"

"Not at all. I gotta be in at seven-thirty. I'll have the cab outside at seven." He started to leave the bedroom. "Well, g'night."

"Vincent, wait a minute."

"Yeah?"

"I can't thank you enough for everything you've done these past few days. I really owe you one."

"I may hold you to that." He started to shut the door, then it opened again. "Well, go ahead, you little traitor."

Gypsy the cat ran in, bounded on the bed and curled up at the foot. I reached down to pet her as he closed the door, scratched her head a bit, then got back under the covers and turned out the light.

I didn't get to sleep for an hour.

CHAPTER TWENTY

Ninety-eight-point-six.

"I think we can officially discharge you," said Vincent. He put the thermometer back in the drawer. "You're good to go." He smiled at me, but his eyes had a tinge of sadness.

I pushed back the covers. "I feel like I've been sick for weeks."

"Just a few days. I know you can't wait to get to work on that story."

"I think it helped me get well a little faster. But not as fast as your incredible soup."

"There's a lot left over. You're taking some home. You don't want a relapse." He got up and headed to the door. "I'll bring the cab around in about ten minutes."

"You know, you really don't have to do that, Vincent. I can walk two blocks."

"You don't need to push it with that ankle. I gotta go to work anyway, and it's on the way."

"If you insist. But I'm leaving you a big tip."

"Sorry, you know the rules about that."

He headed out the door and I threw on some clothes. I planned to shower and get dressed in my own apartment. I grabbed my clothes, laptop and purse and hauled everything to the bedroom door. I turned and looked back at what had been my home for the past few days. It looked like a disaster and there was no way I could leave it in this condition.

And then I started cleaning. Quickly.

I made the bed, folded the towels, picked up the tissues that seemed to be everywhere, put the half dozen used glasses in the dishwasher, and tried to leave it looking decent. He'd still be washing everything to kill the flu germs, but at least I didn't want him to think I was a total slob. I didn't want him to think I'd taken advantage of him. I didn't want him to think—

It hit me while I was tidying up and stopped me dead in my tracks.

I was worried about what Vincent thought of me.

I shook my head, chalking it up to the flu, and walked to the front door. I stopped to pet Gypsy for a minute, then headed out.

***

Vincent pulled up to my apartment building after a one-minute ride, got out of the cab, ran around and opened the door for me before I had a chance to do it myself.

"Thank you," I said, as I gathered up my stuff and got out of the cab. The weather had cleared, it was warming up and sunny, and the fresh air felt great as it filled my lungs.

"Well, good luck on that story. I'll be watching."

"Can't wait to nail whoever's behind this. I did the math, it looks like several million over the past few years." I looked at my building, then turned back to him. "Vincent, again, I can't thank you enough for taking such great care of me this weekend. I... uh... I have to admit I really misjudged you. And I'm truly sorry for the way I treated you before. It was wrong and I apologize. You've always tried to be nice to me and—"

"Hey, I kinda had you pegged wrong too. Bygones."

"Despite the fact I had to get the flu to do it, I'm glad I got to know you better."

"Me too."

An awkward silence followed. Did I give him a hug, shake his hand, what?

He deserved better. I leaned up on my tiptoes and kissed him on the cheek. "You're a good man, Vincent Martino. See you around the neighborhood."

"Yeah, you too."

I headed toward the front door with a spring in my step, having gotten my life back, on the way to a kick-ass story. Then, just as I reached it, I turned back. "And remember, I owe you one..."

But he was already gone.

***

I was walking on air as I entered Harry's office and noted he already had company.

"Hey, welcome back," he said. "How you feeling?"

"Pretty good, though I'm kinda on low power. I'll feel a lot better once we put this story to bed." I turned to the man who had gotten up and extended his hand. "Nice to see you again, Special Agent Willis." I shook his hand.

"You too, Belinda. And thank you for getting us in the loop on this."

"Hey, couldn't do it without you."

Special Agent Sean Willis had worked with me over the years on a handful of stories, and I liked him because he understood my job and that one hand washes the other. I gave him tips, he gave me exclusives. He was a Fed who knew the value of sometimes looking the other way and occasionally bending the rules. Willis was about forty and resembled an accountant, slender with thinning brown hair, a weak chin, and deep set hazel eyes. Of course he worked in the white-collar division, so he didn't resemble the usual linebacker types that often seemed to be favored by the Bureau. But he wore the traditional dark suits, white shirts and muted ties that didn't attract attention.

Frank tapped on the open door, walked in and closed it behind him. "Agent Willis, nice to work with you again."

"You too, Frank."

"So what's the deal on the deal?" asked Harry, using one of his favorite phrases as everyone took a seat.

Willis pulled a small notepad from his inside jacket pocket and flipped it open. "Well, we set up surveillance in the post office yesterday, with cameras in the lobby and one pointed right at the post office box in question. But the lobby is a long way from the box, so the main camera is on the box. The postmaster has been briefed and we're going to have an agent behind the box and one near the boxes posing as a customer sorting through his mail on a table. The checks will be wrapped with a rubber band, though one of the envelopes is bogus and contains a GPS in the event he should get away. But he won't. There's only one way out of the building and we've got that locked down."

"I'm just hoping he shows up tomorrow," I said.

"Oh, he will," said Willis. "Would you leave that kind of money hanging around in a post office box?"

"No way," I said. "What time does the mail get sorted?"

"It's all out by nine thirty at the latest," said Willis. "When it's sorted the clerk turns on a red light above the boxes to let people know the mail has all been delivered. Our cameras will transmit a signal to our surveillance truck across the street. Frank, it's the usual set-up where you can plug directly into the live feed. You'll need two record decks. And we'll be recording anyway, so you have a backup just in case."

"Terrific," said Frank. "That worked great the last time."

"Now," said Willis, "as soon as the mail is picked up, we've got six agents in place to arrest him. Belinda, we'll take a little time reading him his rights before we walk him to a car to take him in. That should give you guys enough time to get your gear, get out of the van and get some video, ask a few questions."

"Sounds good," I said.

"So what's the penalty for something like this?" asked Harry.

"A very long time in federal prison," said the agent. "At least twenty-five years, maybe more."

"So any idea where the money is?" I asked.

"We traced last month's cancelled checks and found out this morning they were all cleared at the bank across the street at the same time. The funds were then deposited to an account with an electronic link to one offshore. Both accounts are still active."

"So they're making a deposit and sending the money out of the country," said Frank. "Makes sense."

Willis nodded. "The minute the checks clear, the cash gets transferred. The account here is registered to a bogus name and address, and we're waiting on a call back from the offshore bank."

"Any chance you can get the money back?" asked Frank.

"There will be a lot of red tape, and it might take a while, but probably. Of course, there's no telling how much the thieves have already spent. We don't even know how much has been stolen, for that matter. Our forensic accountants will be working on that, and they might have to go back a few years. Meanwhile, we found bugs in Councilman Jagger's office and on his cell phone, which we're leaving in place. We don't want the thieves to think we're on to them. We assume there are at least two people, maybe more, with someone in the bank and someone working in the Councilman's office. It has to be an inside job since there's no possible access to the computers that control the pension fund from outside the office building."

"How many people have access to those computers?" asked Frank.

"Supposedly half a dozen, but it wouldn't be too hard for someone to hack into them from inside the building if they knew what they were doing."

"How's Councilman Jagger?" I asked.

"A little shaky, but he'll be okay. We have an agent in the office today and tomorrow posing as a consultant who will be spending a lot of time with him."

"Why not keep Jagger at home if someone's threatening him?" asked Harry. "Let him call in sick."

"We don't want anything out of the ordinary," said Willis. "It has to look like a normal day since we think someone's on the inside. We don't want to spook them. If they get out of the country, they could clean out the offshore account and be gone forever. So, any other questions?"

"I do get an exclusive with the guy after you book him, right?"

"Absolutely. That's assuming he hasn't lawyered up and will talk to you. We'll wait on the press conference until six-thirty, after your newscast is over."

"Thank you," said Harry. "I appreciate that."

"Least I can do for such a great tip. Listen, if we take these people down, we're talking tens of millions of dollars you're saving the city." Willis got up and we all followed. "Belinda, you and Frank meet us at my office at seven-thirty, and you can ride with us."

"Thank you, Agent Willis," said Harry. Willis nodded and left the office. "So, assuming your thief is of the incredibly greedy type and is eager to pick up his mail, we should have this story in the can for tomorrow night."

"We can only hope," I said. "Harry, you can't tell anyone about this until they catch the guy."

"Not even the producers," he said. "Don't worry, Cupcake, everything stays in this room."

***

I was anything but relaxed as I got ready for my date. Yeah, I know what you're thinking. One more night and then cut Scott loose if he doesn't get with the program. Wing Girl has been patient enough with him. Why in the world would she stay with a guy who may or may not be good in the sack but she won't know that unless she walks down the aisle? That's a pretty big risk.

The answer is an old one: the heart wants what the heart wants.

But sadly, when it came to love, my heart suffered from an irregular heartbeat and I'd been wondering if someone needed to hit me with the romance defibrillator and yell, "Clear!"

I waited for Scott to pick me up, excited to see him for the first time in two weeks. I'd missed the great rapport we had, how we seemed so perfect together and have everything in common.

And yet one concern kept sneaking past the rose-colored guards in my brain, asking the question that'dw been driving me crazy. The question, and this may surprise you, is one that has nothing at all to do with sex.

Why didn't Scott offer to take care of me when I was sick?

I know, I know, I was probably worrying about nothing. Maybe he was working, maybe he had to travel, maybe he had to see an important client and didn't want to get the flu. But Ariel was right to ask about it. He didn't even offer. And the more I thought about it, the more it bothered me.

That little red pennant kept trying to sneak up the flagpole, but those rose-colored guards kept getting in the way when sensible girl tried to raise it.

Meanwhile, there was the other question. What did Scott want to talk about tonight? It sounded important, he sounded as though I'd like it. Was it an engagement ring? An offer to elope? How would I answer if he's going to propose? (No frigging clue.) Would he finally throw his religious beliefs to the wind and take me? Inquiring minds want to know.

My locomotive of thought was interrupted by the doorman's buzzer telling me Scott had arrived. The rose-colored guards declared martial law, and every concern went sailing out the window while I went flying out the door.

His face lit up as I emerged from the elevator. He moved quickly across the lobby toward me and gave me a strong hug, nearly lifting me off the floor.

"Wow, I missed you too," I said. Apparently absence had made his heart grow fonder. Hopefully something else, too.

He broke the embrace and took my hand, then led me to the door, seemingly out of breath and in a hurry. "Two weeks is too long."

"Agreed."

"You look like you're feeling fine now. You over the flu?"

"Pretty much. But I was miserable for a few days." I wanted to add, "And you didn't even offer to come by and give me a back rub or make me some chicken soup," but I caught the words by the tail.

"Well, glad you're better tonight since I have to fly out tomorrow night."

"Again?" I asked, as the driver opened the door for me and I started to get in.

"Just for two days, then we can spend the whole weekend together."

"I'll clear my calendar," I said, as he slid in next to me and the driver shut the door.

***

Scott ordered dessert for both of us and handed the menu back to the waiter. "So I've been meaning to say you're looking especially beautiful tonight. As opposed to your everyday stunning version."

I couldn't help but feel special. The restaurant was as romantic a place as you could imagine. Candles provided the only illumination in the room. The light seemed to dance in the crystal chandeliers that hung from the ceiling every ten feet. A piano player offered soft instrumentals, which added to the relaxing mood. The waiters were all outfitted in white tuxedoes, some busy preparing flaming desserts tableside. The patrons were dressed to the nines. I thought back to my pre-makeover days and could only imagine how I would have stuck out had I worn what Ariel called "the Hillary Clinton fall collection" to a place like this.

Scott seemed to glow, as the flicker of the candlelight reflected off his tanned face. "You're looking very handsome yourself. As opposed to your everyday good-looking version. And this is such a nice place."

"Glad you like it. I must say, Belinda, you look really... upbeat. I mean, for someone who just got out of a sick bed."

"Well, I had cabin fever today after being cooped up since Thursday, so it's like being sprung from prison. And I've got some really good stories going."

"That's great. By the way, I did have a pension expert look at those documents and he couldn't find a thing wrong with them."

I wanted to tell him I was about to break that story, that all his experts were wrong, that he was wrong, but I figured, why make the guy feel bad? "Well, thanks for trying." Besides, he'd be surprised enough tomorrow night when he saw my story.

"But I'm not giving up yet. I've got another guy who's a whiz with that stuff. Smartest guy I know. He's looking at it now and said he should be able to get back to me on Wednesday."

Okay, enough with my story. I'd waited through soup, salad, been through a veritable armada of forks. It was time. "You said you had something important to tell me. Something that I'd like?" I raised both eyebrows.

"Well, actually two things. First..." He reached into his pocket, pulled out a large flat black jewelry box and slid it across the table to me. "I spotted this on my last trip and thought it would look great on you. Just a little something. I figure I know you well enough that you're not going to think it's too forward of me and go running away."

The box was too big for an engagement ring, but hey, I wasn't complaining. I lifted the box, opened it, and my jaw dropped as I saw a huge deep-green emerald surrounded by diamonds on the end of a heavy gold chain. "Oh, Scott, it's gorgeous."

"It matches your eyes."

Now I'm not an expert on this stuff, but the thing had to be four carats at least. "I'm certainly not going to run, but it's too much, really."

"Not for someone like you. You're worth it. Besides, one of my clients owns a jewelry company and he gave me a good deal on it. Please, Belinda, I want you to have it."

"Oh, what the hell!" I pulled it out of the box and handed it to him. "Put it on for me, will you?"

He took the necklace, got up, and moved behind me. I couldn't contain my smile as I held up my hair and he clasped the necklace behind my neck. A few older couples sitting across from me stopped to watch and smiled, obviously impressed with the way I was being treated in such a classic, old-fashioned manner. I felt the emerald land just north of my cleavage and looked down. "God, this thing is gorgeous. Thank you so much." Playing hard to get seemed to have its benefits. Thank you, Mrs. Baymont.

"You're welcome," he said, sitting down. "You've been so patient putting up with my travel schedule."

"And you've been patient with me when I need alone time."

"I think every woman needs that from time to time."

"Well, this is a wonderful surprise. You thought I'd like it, ha! What woman wouldn't like it?"

"That wasn't the surprise I was referring to."

But wait, there's more. And behind door number two...

"I've been thinking a while about this, and I've made a decision regarding my religious beliefs."

It was all I could do to stop myself from leaping across the table and taking him right there on the restaurant floor.

A sheepish grin grew on his face. "I think it's time. For, you know."

"Really?"

He nodded. "Look, the way this relationship is going I know it's an awful lot to ask a woman to take such a big leap. And I want you to be sure. Because... I'm already sure about you."

"Scott... I don't know what to say. When—"

"Well, if you don't mind skipping the movie, I was thinking you'd look great right after dinner in nothing but that necklace."

***

As far as I was concerned, the Town Car couldn't move fast enough as it headed for my apartment. My heart raced like a trip hammer as everything around me disappeared.

Except for Scott.

I'd role-played this in my mind dozens of times. What I'd wear (though apparently now it would be nothing), how I'd try to be patient and lead him since it would be his first time. How I'd ravish him the second time. Wondering if he'd mind being tied to the bedposts the third time.

And I remembered his exact words from moments ago. "*It's an awful lot to ask a woman to take such a big leap...*" Such a big leap could only mean one thing.

I mentally started a wedding guest list—

The ringing of his cell phone interrupted me.

He answered it, listened a moment and his face dropped.

"What's wrong?" I asked.

He put up a finger, listened for about thirty seconds, nodded and said, "Okay. I'll get there as soon as I can."

Oh, shit. You gotta be kidding me.

He ended the call. "That was my sister. It's my father..." His voice cracked. "He, uh, had a heart attack and it doesn't look good."

"Oh, Scott, I'm so sorry. Where is he?"

"Upstate. It's about a four-hour drive unless I can catch a flight. Belinda, I'm so sorry—"

"Don't be ridiculous. Drop me off and go. I'll be waiting when you get back. I'm not going anywhere."

He kissed me on the cheek. "This is why you're so special." He leaned forward, told the driver he might be in for a long night and sat back as we pulled up to my apartment.

I leaned over and hugged him. "Hang in there. Call me when you know anything."

"Okay," he said. His eyes were moist. I opened the door myself, got out, shut it, then watched the car and my perfect night speed away.

CHAPTER TWENTY ONE

The stakeouts you see in the movies and on TV are nothing like real life. In Hollywood, cops sit in a car for two minutes and the bad guy emerges. In real life, you can sit for hours, drink gallons of coffee and have your joints stiffen to the point you feel like you've slept on the floor. All this until your target appears... if he ever does. In my experience, stakeouts are a total bust half the time.

I personally hate them. Stuck in a news car for hours on end, often with no decent food or bathrooms nearby, and no room to stretch, is not my idea of fun. It's like spending a day in the middle seat on a cross-country flight. However, we were reasonably sure our thief would appear shortly after the mail was delivered. And if I was gonna be stuck on a stakeout, the FBI surveillance unit was a lot more appealing than a news car.

It was outfitted like a television satellite truck, a long trailer equipped with monitors, wireless microphones, phone-tapping equipment, and other stuff you see in James Bond movies. Some legal, some not. I could look the other way as well as anyone when it comes to catching the bad guys. They've also got comfortable chairs and Agent Willis is known for having good coffee and decent food on hand for his crew.

There were two other agents besides Willis in the truck, one monitoring audio and another techie manning the video equipment that was keeping everyone connected. Frank had recording decks plugged directly into the feed coming from the post office, so he could jump out of the truck with his camera when the agents brought the bad guy out. I was in a swivel chair next to Agent Willis in front of the bank of monitors as we were both locked on the video feed. As you can imagine, watching static shots of post office boxes for a couple of hours was riveting.

By eleven I was getting frustrated and stood up to stretch. The mail had been out since nine, a little earlier than usual according to the postmaster. There had been a few close calls with patrons visiting boxes next to 504, one of the largest boxes, which was at the end of a long hallway, but so far the mountain of envelopes remained inside. At one point a little old lady with a huge shopping bag and a walker headed toward 504. Willis gave everyone a standby with "possible suspect", which gave all the agents a good laugh as she ended up at 502.

Suddenly Willis sat up straight. "Hey, check it out. This guy's got a duffel bag," he said, pointing to the monitor. We'd been keeping an eye out for anyone like that, since you wouldn't carry six hundred envelopes in your arms. A slender, dark-haired man was heading toward the envelope-filled box carrying a large black bag. We could only see him from the back, as the camera was trained right on the box.

"C'mon, five-oh-four," I said, blowing on my fist like I was about to shoot craps. "Mama needs a new exclusive." Frank crouched down next to his camera and grabbed the handle.

Willis got on the two-way radio to all the agents outside. "Possible suspect in sight. Stand by for confirmation."

The man continued down the hall, heading directly for our box. My heart pounded, the adrenaline kicking in big time.

Frank picked up his camera and turned it on. "Get ready," he said to me, as he handed me a wireless microphone. I flicked the switch on the bottom to turn it on. The little red button lit up to confirm it was working. I heard the tape engage in Frank's camera.

We were ready to roll.

Number 504 was on the bottom of the bank of boxes. The man reached the end of the hall, dropped the duffle bag, and kneeled down.

We heard a whisper over the radio from the agent on the other side of the boxes. "Box is being opened."

Willis keyed the two-way. "Target confirmed. White male, slight build, five-eleven. Jeans and black long-sleeved shirt. Carrying a black duffel bag. Stand by." Then he said to himself, "Geez, this guy's pretty ballsy. Not even a hat and sunglasses."

Frank stood up and headed to the door, ready to jump out. I was right behind him as I kept an eye on the monitor. The man opened the box and started sliding the bundles of envelopes into the bag. A beeping noise came from the console, which told me the GPS had been activated by the tech guy. The suspect closed the box, locked it, zipped the bag, stood up, and headed toward the door.

We had a clear shot of his face.

"No!" I yelled. I dropped my microphone, which hit the floor with a thud. "No, no, no!"

"What?" said Frank as he opened the door. "C'mon, we gotta move!"

"No!"

"Waddaya mean, no?" He picked up the microphone, put it in my hand and grabbed my arm. "Let's go! Now!"

I barely had enough energy to speak, as the adrenaline all but drained from my body. "No." The word came out softly. I was paralyzed, unable to move. My eyes were locked on the monitor as Scott's face filled the screen.

***

Frank had practically dragged me out to the car which was

waiting to transport the thief back to the FBI office. The microphone was at my side, not in front of me, as Scott was escorted to the car by two agents, one holding each arm, his hands zip-tied behind his back. Another agent followed with the duffel bag and tossed it in the trunk.

Frank trained his lens on Scott as he approached the car. Scott spotted me and our eyes connected.

I said nothing as Scott grew closer. Frank noticed. "Ask a question!" he whispered.

My mouth hung open, but nothing came out. And suddenly I wasn't a reporter any more. The FBI, Frank, the camera, none of it was there. I tried my best to look deep into Scott's soul, to ask the questions with my eyes that had nothing to do with stealing money. But his eyes were lifeless, vacant, and showed no emotion. He looked at me as if I were a stranger.

Finally Frank shouted at him, "Why did you steal the money?"

No response as he grew closer to the car.

"How many millions did you take?"

Scott said nothing as an agent pushed his head down and he got into back seat of the car, which immediately drove off. Frank followed the car with his camera until it was out of sight, then turned it off, put it on his hip and glared at me. "Seriously, you go into vapor lock on a story like this?"

I kept staring at the empty spot vacated by the car and said nothing as Agent Willis came up to us. "Guys, let's head back—" he noticed the vacant look in my eyes. "Belinda, you okay?"

Frank put his camera on the ground, took my shoulders and turned me so I was facing him. "Cupcake, what's wrong?"

I bit my lower lip as my eyes welled up, then forced out the words. "I... I know him."

"Really?" said Willis. "Who is he?"

The tears rolled down my face. "His name is Scott. Scott Shepard."

Frank's eyes grew wide. "Holy shit." My head dropped.

"What?" asked Willis.

Frank tilted my head up so I was looking at him. "Is this the guy you've been dating?"

I nodded and the dam holding my emotions broke. I began to sob, Frank pulled me close and I buried my face in his chest.

As it turns out, there *is* crying in news.

***

The sound of a soda can popping behind me and the fizz that followed broke me out of my trance. Agent Willis placed the can on the corner of his desk, then sat down behind it. "Drink," he said. "You look like a rookie who's seen his first dead body. You need some sugar before you crash."

"Thank you." I grabbed the cold can and took a long swig of what turned out to be an ice-cold Dr. Brown's root beer. I savored the sharp taste as the bubbles bounced around in my mouth like pinballs.

"From my own personal stash," said Willis. He was as kind a federal agent as you could find. I'd briefed him on my relationship with Scott and he assured me I wasn't in any kind of trouble, not that I had any doubt. Of course, that was the farthest thing from my mind as I wanted to a: get an explanation from Scott about our relationship, and b: wring the sonofabitch's neck. Willis adjusted his chair, then looked up at me and Frank, sitting on the other side of his desk. "He's declined an interview with you."

"What a surprise." I said.

"But he's ready to cut a deal as soon as his attorney gets here."

"When will that be?" asked Frank.

"About an hour. Oh, by the way, thanks to you we got him just in time. He had two tickets to Switzerland in his bag. He was flying out tonight."

The dagger already in my heart twisted. Not that I had much

207

of a heart left at this point. "Let me talk to him."

Willis shook his head and put up his hands. "He said no interview. Nothing I can do."

"Let me talk to him without a camera. This isn't about the story. Please, Agent Willis. I have to know..." My eyes silently begged for a favor.

He nodded slowly. "I, uh, understand where you're coming from. I have to admit this is a unique situation." He exhaled deeply and looked to the side, then back at me. "Okay."

"And no cameras of yours either, no one-way glass, no one else in the room. No one can know about my personal involvement with this guy. It would kill my career if this got out. It would be a scandal—"

"Understood. I'll put you two in an empty office. I've got one with no windows at all. But I'm putting him in shackles and bolting him to the chair."

"Not necessary, Agent Willis. The way I feel right now I could kick his ass, and I wouldn't fight fair."

***

"I'll be right outside," said Frank, who then gave me a soft pat on the back.

"Thanks. This won't take long." I nodded at Agent Willis, who opened the door for me.

"I'll be right here, Ms. Carson," he said, loud enough for Scott to hear.

I took a deep breath, tried to summon my "prosecutor from hell" mood and it occurred to me this might be the hardest "interview" I'd ever done. I moved through the door. The sight took me aback for a moment. Scott was in an orange jumpsuit, handcuffed to the arms of a metal chair, ankles in irons that were attached to the chair legs. He sat next to the only other pieces of furniture in the room, a small steel table with an empty chair on the other side. Twelve hours ago this was the man I thought I loved, the man who was about to prove his love for me. Now he was a common criminal. He looked up at me, then turned away. "I told them no interviews."

I closed the door behind me, sat down opposite him and pulled the chair close to the table. We were as close as we'd been eating dinner last night. My knees slightly brushed his and I slid back a touch. I tried my best to remain calm, though my heart raced. He still wasn't looking at me. "This isn't about my story. There are no hidden cameras or microphones in here, so you're going to talk to me, you sonofabitch. You owe me that." He continued to look down. I slammed my hands on the table. "Look at me, goddamit!"

Well, so much for calm.

He lifted his head and looked at me with dead eyes, like he didn't even care. "What?"

"Is Scott Shepard even your real name?"

He nodded. "Yeah. That part's real."

"Wow, a bit of truth." I folded my hands and rested them on the table. "Explain yourself."

"What do you want to know? How I stole the money?"

I shook my head. "I already know that, down to the smallest detail. I want to know why."

"Why I stole money? You're kidding, right?" He shook his head and laughed a bit. "Because I'm a thief and I wanted to be rich. I wanted to live a life of luxury on a secluded island and never work a day in my life after I was done with this."

"That part I get. I want to know *the other why*. Why you led me on, why you talked about love, why we had a relationship that I thought was leading... I want to know all of it. Tell me *why*."

Scott shook his head and exhaled. "Ah, what the hell, I'm going to prison anyway." He paused a moment, looked at the ceiling, then back at me. "You were necessary for the scam to keep working a while longer."

"I was *necessary*?"

He nodded. "We've had Jagger's office and phone bugged for the past two years. Things were rolling along without a hitch until the Councilman somehow noticed money was missing. And when we heard him talking to his secretary about calling you, I knew our days were numbered. But I wanted to get a few more paydays. I needed a little more to make my future totally secure. You can argue I got greedy and you'd be right. Anyway, in order to do that I needed a relationship with you. I found out you volunteered at the cat shelter, so I figured that was a good way to meet you without using the obvious tactic of hitting on you in a bar or something like that."

"But you were there at the shelter *before* Jagger called me."

He nodded. "Right. As I said, we heard him talking about calling you before he actually did, so it was a preventive measure. The worst that could happen is that I'd be out a few Sunday mornings. And then when he really did call you, I was already in place."

"Do you even *like* cats?"

"Actually, I do. I have one of my own."

"How nice of you to be truthful about something. You still haven't explained why I was *necessary*."

"Once Jagger called you I needed you to either back off the story or look in the wrong direction. I knew your reputation as a reporter and figured you weren't going to give up on it, that eventually you'd crack the case if left alone. So when you asked me to look at the books, I told you nothing was there and continued to string you along, telling you I was going to have other people look at it. I had to stall you. We needed to pick up this month's checks and then we were going to end the thing."

"And then you were leaving the country for good."

He nodded. "Yep. Never to return."

"With no goodbye."

"Like I said, you were simply necessary. I never felt anything for you."

My head snapped back as that hit me like a shot to the heart. The words suddenly grew thick in my throat as my anger morphed into hurt. "*None* of it was real? What about our dates, the weekend in Connecticut?" My voice was cracking with emotion. "We got along so well and had everything in common."

He rolled his eyes. "Oh, please. We had nothing in common." He shook his head, not reacting to my emotion, showing none of his own. "You know, for such a supposedly smart reporter I was surprised you were such an easy mark. You never connected the dots. You never noticed I feel asleep during that science fiction movie, never questioned all my trips out of town, never wanted to see where I lived. It was all I could do not to crack up when I met you at the airport. I thought I'd really screwed up that time. I mean, I told you I was away for two weeks and all I had was a carry-on bag. Talk about missing the obvious."

"You never traveled to all those places?"

"I've hardly left town since I met you. That particular time was a same-day trip. You know, for someone who asks questions for a living you simply took everything I said as gospel. I was frankly amazed at some of the stuff you said on the phone."

I sat up straight and leaned forward. "Excuse me?"

"Oh, yeah, I cloned your cell phone. Remember that night at dinner when I borrowed your phone and went outside to make a call? My accomplice was waiting and cloned your phone. Which really came in handy when Jagger bought a burner phone and stopped using the one in his office."

I felt violated and the anger rushed back, though it was quickly approaching hate status. "You heard everything I said? My personal calls—"

"Yeah. Man, I knew you were falling for me, but you were head over heels like a teenager. I particularly enjoyed your *playing hard to get* strategy."

"I'm guessing the thing about you being a virgin was a lie."

He nodded. "Hard to believe you bought that one, but you did."

"You seemed to enjoy things when we got physical. Considering you're such a scumbag, I'm surprised you didn't screw me that way as well."

"That was part of the plan my wife didn't agree to."

My eyes widened. "Your *wife?*"

"I'm guilty of many things, including loving my wife. The one thing I could never do is cheat on her."

"How very noble of you. So our dinner last night—"

"Just had to keep you on the edge till Wednesday, since I was going to fly outta here tonight. Oh, by the way, don't bother getting that necklace insured. It's a fake."

"Sort of like the person who gave it to me." I felt the Brass Cupcake returning, pushing my feelings for him out of the way, starting to look at him like a story instead of a boyfriend. I paused a moment, trying to sort all of it out. He sat there, with a sick grin on his face. Like he'd won. He was sitting there in irons and acting like a winner. "You trying to tell me you never felt anything? Nothing at all?"

"Sorry, Belinda. You were so easy, so... desperate. But I didn't feel a thing. I may as well have been kissing a prostitute."

My anger boiled over as I stood up, reached across the table and slugged him so hard on the chin his chair went backwards and landed with a loud bang. The door flew open as Frank and Agent Willis ran into the room.

"You all right?" asked Frank.

"Fine," I said, as I shook my hand, which was already hurting.

"Geez, Belinda, you can't assault my suspect," said Willis, who moved behind Scott and lifted his chair into the sitting position.

"She didn't," said Scott, stretching his jaw. "I leaned back too far and fell over. My face broke my fall."

I looked at him and our eyes connected for the last time. He gave me a sly wink.

"And even if she did," said Scott, "I would have had it coming. I was trying to provoke her."

"We're done here," said Willis, not looking terribly pleased as he led me out of the room.

"Hey, Belinda," said Scott.

I turned to look at him. "What?"

"I've got one question for you."

"What?"

"I gotta know. How did you ever figure out how I was stealing the money?"

"Simple, Scott. I'm smarter than you."

"But how did you figure out *how* I did it?"

Finally, I had a chance to smile and did my best to copy his. "Well, Scott, from what I hear you'll have about twenty-five years to solve that riddle."

***

Frank followed me into Harry's office and closed the door. We both took a seat as Harry finished up a phone call.

"So, get him?"

I nodded, not looking at him. "Yeah." My voice was without emotion and barely above a whisper.

"Great!" Harry smiled until he obviously noticed the shell-shocked look I was wearing. "You okay, Cupcake?"

"Harry, there's a slight problem," said Frank. "Well, more than slight."

Harry furrowed his brow. "You got the story, right?"

Frank looked at me and since I didn't say anything he picked up the ball. "We got the story and it's solid. Exclusive. But there's a, well, there's what you might call a conflict of interest."

"I can't be associated with the story," I said, staring vacantly at the stack of business cards on Harry's desk.

"What's the conflict?" asked Harry.

"The guy who was caught stealing," I said. "I've, uh... been dating him."

"You were dating an embezzler?" asked Harry.

"She obviously didn't know that," said Frank. "He was using her. He found out Jagger had her investigating the story and was trying to send her down dead ends. She's not implicated in any way, but obviously her name can't be associated with the story."

I felt Harry looking at me and raised my eyes to meet his. "I'm so sorry, Harry."

"Sorry for what?"

"I screwed up—"

"Stop it," said Frank. "You don't need to beat yourself up over this. You had no way of knowing and you didn't screw up." He turned toward Harry. "I can turn this into an anchor package for Jenna to voice-over. Treat it as a regular news story. It's still an exclusive and a damn good one."

"That'll work," said Harry, looking at me. "And Frank's right, you didn't screw up. I'm sorry you're losing a good story."

I shrugged. "I've had plenty of big stories, Harry. And I'll have a lot more, but I won't if this ends up in the tabloids. If it got out I was dating a criminal and he was using me, my credibility would be shot and I'd be the town joke. No one would ever trust me again. Talk about sleeping with the enemy." Harry's eyes widened a bit. "Figure of speech, Harry. I never had sex with the guy."

"Thank God for that." Harry leaned back in his chair. "First, I don't want you to worry, because it will never leave this room." He studied my face for a moment. "Second, you take the rest of the week off."

"That's not necessary, Harry."

"Yes it is. I've never seen you look like this. It's obvious you're not yourself and you're not thinking clearly. You're hurt, kiddo. As far as I'm concerned, you still have the flu."

"But I don't."

"That's the only way to send you home without everyone wondering why the hell you broke a big story and aren't here to front it."

Why didn't I think of that? Because Harry's right, I'm not thinking clearly.

It made sense. And to be quite honest, I was a basket case and probably wouldn't be worth much to the newsroom anyway.

"You're right, Harry. I'll go."

"Take her home, Frank."

"I can grab a cab—"

"No," said Harry. "Frank will take you."

Frank got up and extended his hand. "C'mon, Cupcake. Lemme run you home and then I gotta get back and edit this."

"Okay. Thank you, Harry. I really appreciate this." Frank opened the door and I headed out into the newsroom. Frank and Harry followed. There weren't too many people around at that hour, most being out on stories, but Harry took care of those who were in a loud voice as I headed for the door.

"Cupcake, you go home and get well. And don't come back until the doctor says you're done with this flu thing."

I looked back at him and gave him a soulful look that only a daughter can give a father, thanking the broadcasting gods for giving me such an understanding softie as a boss.

Old school, my ass.

CHAPTER TWENTY TWO

I was in hour two of what passed for a full-scale Brass Cupcake booze-and-chocolate bender and had just cracked my second bottle of wine as I crumpled up the foil from a demolished Cadbury bar. I hadn't even called Ariel, Serena or Roxanne yet to let them know what happened. I knew Roxanne would be thinking about her bullshit detector and kicking herself that she should have given me a stronger warning, but she cared about me too much to say *I told you so* and she'd be the first to comfort me. Since the story had already aired it was only a matter of time before they knew and showed up at the door.

The television wasn't even on. I didn't have the heart to watch it and the last thing I wanted to see was Scott's face, which would be plastered over every front page in town tomorrow. All I could see was that sickening grin of his, hear that comment comparing me to a prostitute. Ten minutes with him wiped out the good memories of our time together. Ten minutes that killed my dreams.

I never felt anything for you.

I thought I was finally all cried out with no tears left when the intercom buzzer from the doorman rang. I pushed the button and talked into the speaker. "Yes?"

"Ms. Carson, you have a soup delivery here from Martino's. Shall I send him up?"

I released the button for a moment.

And then it dawned on me that Vincent had dropped by with the leftover soup I left in his apartment. I hit the intercom button. "Sure, send him up."

I wasn't sure I wanted to see Vincent, or anyone for that matter. But the idea of comfort food did sound appealing, and I needed to put something in my stomach besides alcohol and chocolate. At that point if a serial killer had shown up with meatball soup I would have let him in.

Two minutes later there was a gentle knock on my door. "You decent?"

That brought a slight smile for the first time in hours. I opened the door and found Vincent standing there, holding a large plastic container filled with soup.

"C'mon in, Vincent," I said, with very little life in my voice.

"What, no snappy comeback?"

"Sorry. Not today."

"Aw, I love those." He held up the soup container in front of me. "You should know you have to finish the whole prescription if you're gonna get well," he said, smiling. He stepped in and looked around, spotted the kitchen to the right. "I didn't notice you'd forgotten this until an hour ago." He walked to the kitchen and placed the container in the refrigerator, then turned to look at me. "Hey, I just saw your story and you weren't in it—" He stopped, as he studied my face. "Belinda, are you sick again?"

I shook my head. "No. It's... it's kind of a long story, Vincent. But here's the short version because I don't feel like telling it and it's too embarrassing. That guy you saw in my story who was stealing all the money..."

"Yeah?"

"He's the guy I've been dating for a few months." I slumped into a chair and grabbed my glass. "You want some wine, help yourself. But you might have to hurry to catch up with me." Vincent bypassed the wine and sat down across from me, then looked into my eyes, his filled with concern. And for some reason I knew I could tell him, I knew he'd understand. "He used me, Vincent. He tapped my phone, tried to keep me from pursuing the story. He was so nice to me, took me everywhere." My voice was quivering badly now, the emotion spilling into it, and I was unable to control it. "We seemed to have everything in common, though that turned out to be a complete lie. I was falling..." I bit my lower lip as my eyes welled up again. And I had thought I was all out of tears.

"Geez, Belinda, I don't know what to say. That must have been horrible for you to find out, especially while you were in the middle of a story."

I nodded and looked down at the floor. My body began to tremble as I felt the waterworks about to blow. I was actually losing it. For the first time in my life.

Vincent took the wine glass out of my hand, put it on the end table, got up and extended his hand. "C'mon. Get your coat."

"Where are we going?"

"Out to get something to eat."

I looked up at him through my tears and shook my head. "Vincent, I appreciate the thought, but I'm in no condition—"

"You're in no condition to be alone." He took my hands and pulled me up out of the chair. "I'm not letting you sit at home by yourself like this. What you need when you're depressed is good food, good company, and something to make you smile. We're going out to dinner and a movie. And don't argue with me." He picked up my coat, which was draped over a chair, and handed it to me.

I didn't take the coat. "Vincent, you're very sweet, and I know you mean well, but—"

"Take it. You're a damsel in major distress. So shut up and put your coat on. I'm rescuing you."

***

As it turned out, comfort food was much more comforting than wine. Though the combination of the two had definitely improved my mood.

The Italian restaurant was an old-fashioned mom-and-pop in Little Italy, complete with the requisite red-and-white checkered tablecloths. An empty Chianti bottle, the old kind with the bottom wrapped in wicker, sat in the center of each table topped by an unlit candle. A full bottle of olive oil was next to it. The place was fragrant with spices and freshly baked bread, loud with laughter and Sinatra tunes actually recorded by Ol' Blue Eyes and not some *American Idol* copycat wannabe.

Ariel and Serena called, having seen my story. Both wanted to get together immediately, but I told them I was in good hands for the time being and would call when I got home. It was Roxanne's day to take care of Vincent's mother, so I planned to talk to her later. Vincent did his best to calm me down, and it was working. He hadn't asked about what happened, hadn't brought up my job, kept the conversation locked on baseball and science fiction, while tossing in some hilarious stories about bizarre goings-on in his cab over the years. The events of this morning were fading into the background, my hurt was slowly melting away.

You might think a girl can't get over something so traumatic this fast, but let's be honest here. The guy I thought I was falling in love with didn't really exist. He was simply a creation, woven from my desire for a relationship and Scott's quest for money. Remember, I'm a girl who sees things in black and white, and Scott was simply a criminal who toyed with my emotions. The way he looked at me in the FBI office was the way I now thought of him. Like a stranger.

Meanwhile, by now you've realized the other route to my heart that does not require a GPS is through my stomach. And as comfort food goes, fettuccine Alfredo was hard to beat, with all

219

that cream and butter and parmesan cheese, but this version was topped with huge shrimp and hunks of crabmeat, which took it to another level.

Vincent had ordered the linguine with clam sauce, so heavy with garlic that I could smell it across the table.

The hot bread dipped in olive oil and spices was wonderful. Meanwhile, I was trying my best to get the fettuccine in my mouth without dripping the wonderful sauce in my lap, but I wasn't having much luck. Thank goodness for the large napkins. I was getting jealous watching Vincent, who was expertly twirling his pasta and popping forkful after forkful into his mouth without so much as a drop on his starched white oxford shirt.

Finally, I put my fork down with half my plate empty.

He noticed. "Full?"

"You've seen me eat. What do you think?"

"Nah, you're taking a breather. It's just halftime. You've got a hollow leg or something. I don't know where a little thing like you puts it all."

"Teach me to twirl, Vincent."

"Huh?"

"To twirl. Pasta. The way you do it with your fork and never get a spot of sauce on that white shirt. I can't figure out how the hell you can do it. Teach me."

"Oh, sure. Italian life skill. It's easy. Grab your fork and spoon."

I picked up both, poised and ready. (By the way, I found it refreshing that you only got one fork in this restaurant.) "Okay."

"Now, watch." He took his fork and spoon and demonstrated. "You line up a few strands of the pasta with your fork, lift them, place the fork into the middle of the spoon, and twirl the fork around until all the pasta is nice and neat in a little ball. You try."

And here we go again, as Wing Girl learns to feed herself.

I carefully zeroed in on three strands of pasta, lifted it with the fork, placed the fork in the spoon and twirled it. "Am I doing it right?"

"You got it. Now pull the fork away."

I did and looked at a perfect little nest of fettuccine. "I did it!" I smiled as I popped it in my mouth.

He looked right into my soul for the first time. "It's good to see that beautiful smile again."

I finally knew what warm and fuzzy meant.

***

I patted my full belly and wished I was wearing my old stretch pants as we headed across the street to the multiplex. "You proud of me?" I asked.

"Huh?"

"I cleaned my plate. You didn't think I could do it, did you?"

"I'm beginning to think we need to trace your ancestry and find the Italian somewhere in your past. What nationality are you, anyway?"

I held up my red hair. "I'll give you one guess."

"Uh, I'll take a wild stab and say Irish."

"Very perceptive, sir." We reached the back of the line for the theater ticket booth and scanned the list of eighteen movies currently playing. A few blockbusters, some sci-fi, the ubiquitous vampire and zombie flicks, and some other stuff I hadn't heard about. "So, what are we seeing?"

"A movie."

"Ah, so you're the smartass tonight. Which one?"

"You'll find out shortly."

"Don't I get to pick?"

He shook his head. "What did I tell you when I handed you your coat?"

"I know, I know. Shut up, you're rescuing me."

The romantic comedy had been a perfect choice. Hilarious with a happy ending, it was just what I needed.

We headed out into the chilly night air and I pulled my coat collar tighter around my neck. The movie had been a short one, maybe an hour and a half, so it was only quarter to nine. "I can't thank you enough for tonight, Vincent. You really cheered me up."

"Don't thank me yet. Night's not over."

"I though we were just going for dinner and a movie."

"We didn't have dessert at the restaurant, remember? And I know damn well you have a sweet tooth and won't turn down dessert."

"Hey, bring it on. Still got some room in my hollow leg. Where are we going?"

"Nick's pastry shop. You know, about four blocks from your place."

"Not sure I've ever been there."

"Really? Wow, you're in for a treat. It's right next to my garage so we can drive over there, ditch my cab, and I can walk you home."

***

Nick's pastry shop was a beehive of activity considering the late hour. A long, narrow place lined on one side with glassed-in cases of goodies, while the other side was filled with a dozen or so bistro tables lined up single file on old cracked black and white tile. The high chairs were black wrought-iron with candy-apple red upholstered seats, like something out of a fifties malt shop. Several other couples were sharing dessert and coffee while a few customers picked out cookies, pastries and other Italian delicacies I'd never seen. The walls were covered with autographed photos of celebrities, all shown eating something in the shop.

Vincent apparently was on good terms with the owner, Nick, a short pudgy fiftyish guy with thick white hair and black horn-rimmed glasses. He waved as we came in, took off our coats, slung them over the backs of two chairs and grabbed a table. The air was thick with the smell of sugar and freshly brewed coffee.

"Cute place," I said. "Like stepping into the past."

"Yeah, it's been here about sixty years. Nick's grandfather started the place. They do a helluva business here," said Vincent. "People come from miles around for the Italian cookies."

I surveyed the glassed-in case across from our table. "Everything looks wonderful. And very fattening."

"Like you need to worry. By the way, the coffee here is to die for, if you like coffee."

"I love it. You know, I drink the stuff all day, but I don't even own a coffee-maker. The newsroom has free coffee and I buy it on the weekends. Kind of a waste of money at five bucks a cup when I could make my own. I'm just too lazy."

"Well, maybe Santa will bring you one for Christmas."

I heard the old brass cash register ring and saw the owner head around the corner of the case toward us. "Hey, Vincent," he yelled, "who's this pretty girl?"

"This is Belinda," he said, as Nick arrived at our table.

"Nice to meet you, Nick," I said. He extended his hand and I shook it.

"Sure, I know you from television. What're you doin' hangin' out with this guy?" He slapped Nick on the shoulder.

"She wants me for my food," said Vincent, who then looked at me. "You wanna split some tiramisu, or you want your own? I'm guessing it's the latter."

"I want my own." Hey, the FBI agent said I needed sugar.

"Okay," said Nick. "The usual times two. Coffee?"

"Two cappuccinos," said Vincent, who then looked at me. "Oh, sorry. Is that okay?"

"Sounds great."

"Be out in a minute," said Nick.

Nick turned and headed back toward the counter. "So, tiramisu is your *usual*?" I asked.

"I'm hooked on the stuff. Sometimes I have 'dessert for dinner night', and just come here and eat two pieces."

"That sounds adventurous. I may have to try that sometime when I don't feel like cooking, which is every day."

I heard hissing coming from a coffee machine, and knew our cappuccinos were already being made. Then I saw Nick heading back to our table with a small plate in one hand and a camera in the other.

He slid the simple white plate in front of me, which held a single cupcake. "I was hoping I could get a photo of the Brass Cupcake eating an actual cupcake for my wall. It would be a unique picture."

"Ah, you know my nickname." I couldn't help but smile. "I'd be honored."

"Okay. Hold on." He backed up a bit, crouched down, aimed the camera, and then gave me a thumbs up. "Any time. And if you could smile while you taste it."

"I'm sure that won't be a problem." I looked at the camera, gave my face a shot of animation like I do for television, and took a bite of the cupcake. He snapped the photo as the butter cream icing atop the red velvet cupcake sent me into a sugar rush. "Oh my God, that is sinful."

"No calories, either," said Nick. He took one more picture as I licked the icing off my lips. "Thank you. I'll have you sign it next time you're in."

"That means I've got to bring you back here," said Vincent.

"It's a date," I said, so fast I didn't realize it.

***

We took our time walking back to my apartment. The night

224

was chilly but pleasant, a far cry from the rain and cold of the previous week.

My mind was filled with unanswered questions. How had I ended up here, when twenty-four hours ago my life was going in a totally different direction? How did I go from expecting a roll in the hay with Scott to seeing him in leg irons, to nearly breaking down on the job, to having a wonderful evening with Vincent? How had I moved on so quickly when I had been devastated a few hours ago?

It didn't matter. The past, as we say in television, had "gone to Pluto". Like television signals beaming out into deep space, never to return, my memories of Scott had faded fast. The sheer realization that he was a thief sent them at warp speed out of my life. It would have hurt more if he'd dumped me for another woman, but discovering his true nature turned the hurt quickly to anger, which didn't seem to linger as much. Besides, Karma was about to have a field day with him in a federal prison. And much as you're not supposed to take pleasure in getting even, the bastard deserved it. I hoped they'd throw the book at him.

I looked at Vincent as he walked along, hands in his pockets. He and Scott had started the day as good guys; in a few hours they had become opposites. One was headed to jail for decades, the other an embodiment of all that was right with the world. Vincent had a seemingly bottomless reserve of decency. After taking care of a woman who wouldn't give him the time of day for a long weekend, he'd come to the rescue of that same woman, who was about to lose it. Because of her relationship with another guy.

What would possess a man who thought he had no shot with a woman to treat her with such kindness?

For a girl whose career was based on gathering facts, I had a lot of problems dealing with intangibles. Love was too much of a gray area for a journalist. But if this was part of the education of Wing Girl, I needed to find out.

"Nice night," he said, looking up at the fingernail moon. The

Manhattan sky was crystal clear, the rain and strong wind of the weekend having blown all the smog out to the Atlantic ocean.

"Very," I said. I'm not sure why I did this, but I looped one arm through his, letting my hand rest on his forearm. He looked at me and smiled.

"Hope all the sugar and coffee doesn't keep you up all night."

"Nah, I think all that wine cancels it out. I'll sleep great; fat and happy."

"I'm glad about the happy part."

I squeezed his arm a bit. "I have you to thank for that."

I moved my stride to the right a bit, closer to his.

We turned a corner and had almost reached my building. I had a flashback to yesterday morning, wondering what to do. Another kiss on the cheek? Invite him up? I had maybe thirty seconds to decide when his cell phone rang.

Again with the cell phone. But was I saved by the bell, or merely interrupted?

He pulled the phone from his pocket and looked at the screen. "It's Roxanne." He answered the call. "Hi, Rox, what's up?"

He listened for a few seconds and his smile vanished, much like Scott's had the previous night. Only this time it was real. And I had a pretty good idea why.

He stopped walking. "Okay, I'll be right there." He ended the call and turned to face me. "Belinda, it's my mother. Doctor says she could go at any time."

"Vincent, I'm so sorry."

"I'm going to have to say goodnight. I need to get home."

"She's not in a hospital?"

"No, she didn't want to die there. She wanted to spend her last days in her house. Anyway, I have to go." He started to pull away, but I didn't let go.

"I'm going with you."

CHAPTER TWENTY THREE

I heard Roxanne's voice as we entered through the back door of the house. It was dimly lit as Vincent quickly made his way to his mother's bedroom while I followed.

Roxanne was sitting on the side of one of those adjustable hospital beds, holding his mother's hand. A beautiful gold-framed oil painting of the Virgin Mary hung on the wall behind the bed, while the nightstand was cluttered with countless prescription bottles. Roxanne looked up and spotted us. "Hey, Grace, look who's here."

The old woman looked like a ghost, but managed a slight smile and raised her free hand. Vincent hugged Roxanne and kissed her on the cheek, swapped places and took his mother's hand. "Hi, ma, how you doing?"

"Eh, not so good." She noticed me as I slowly walked to the other side of the bed. "Oh, you brought your beautiful friend."

I took her other hand, which was already wrapped in a set of old mother-of-pearl rosary beads. Her skin was nearly translucent, the veins easily visible. "Hi, Mrs. Martino."

"Oh, I interrupted you kids."

"No, not at all," I said.

Vincent patted her hand. "You need anything ma?"

She turned to face him, with *that look*. "Nah, I got everything

I need right here." She squeezed his hand, which told me what "everything" meant. Her breathing was labored as she turned to me. "Honey, you think I could talk to my son for a minute?"

"Sure, Mrs. Martino. I'll be outside with Roxanne."

"Thank you, honey. At least I can go knowing my Vincent finally found a nice girl."

This time my tears were of a different variety.

***

Roxanne was sitting on the couch, sipping a can of diet soda. I sat next to her and wrapped one arm around her shoulder. "How you doing, Rox?"

She wiped away a tear. "It's been a tough day. I'm gonna miss her." Her voice cracked with emotion. "She's been like a second mother to me."

I took her hand. "At least she's at home and not in a hospital or some nursing home hooked up to machines and tubes."

"Yeah. This is the best way to go."

"I agree."

"Oh, I saw your story and didn't have a chance to call you. I'm so sorry—"

"Don't be. It's not important."

"Wow, you're taking this well."

"You can't miss someone who never existed. That's how I'm looking at it. That's how I have to look at it if I'm gonna move on."

"Yeah, I guess you're right."

"Your bullshit detector was spot on."

"Well, I didn't want to say anything. So how did you end up out here with Vincent tonight?"

"He dropped by with some of that soup he'd made for me which I'd forgotten in his apartment and I was a total wreck. He took me out and cheered me up. We were walking home when you called."

"He's nice like that. Vincent's always had a sixth sense about knowing when people need something."

"Yeah. He also seems to be around when I need him."

"So you two had a good time?"

"Yeah, Rox, we really did. Took me out to a nice dinner and a funny movie. It really turned things around for me. What he did tonight was very special. I was so hurt and so angry and so filled with hatred of Scott. He made it all go away. The guy keeps rescuing me. Sometimes I think he's lurking in the shadows like some superhero waiting for me to need help."

"Hell, waddaya expect? He's crazy about you."

"Yeah, I'm finally starting to get that. And I'm—"

I was interrupted as Vincent walked into the room, tears streaming down his face.

Roxanne and I stood up. She looked at him and said, "Is she..."

He nodded.

Then Roxanne did something I didn't expect. She put her hand behind my back and gently pushed me toward him. "Your turn," she whispered.

***

In recent years, the term "celebration of life" has become cliché when describing a funeral.

In the case of the service for Vincent's mother, it was spot on.

As I made my way through a house full of people, I was still amazed at how uplifting the funeral had been. Once we got through the Catholic funeral obligatory rendition of Ave Maria (by Roxanne, of all people), which got the tears out of everyone's system, it was a celebration. Vincent's beautifully written eulogy had focused on how she lived, not how she died. It had been filled with humorous and touching anecdotes about his mother, stories about her favorite things, and even a tale about her one brush with the Mafia. By the time the service was over, the people weren't mourners but friends who had been refreshed by happy memories.

Then we headed back to his mother's house for food, and there was a ton of it.

And when I walked by a doorway and took a glimpse into the kitchen, I saw a disaster.

The counters and center island were cluttered with empty plates, bowls, casserole dishes, pots, you name it.

And I knew it was time for me to pay Vincent back a little.

I headed into the kitchen, found an apron hanging behind the door, and threw it on over my simple black dress. The kitchen was dated, with an avocado-green fridge that sounded like it needed a carburetor and Formica countertops to match. I tackled the easy stuff first, loading the dishwasher with plates and silverware, then turned it on. Then I faced the mountainous task of washing everything else. There was an old-fashioned dishpan in the sink, so I filled it with soapy water and began soaking the first few baking dishes that were crusted with dried tomato sauce.

Twenty minutes later I had made a small dent, but I knew I'd be here a while. Still it was nothing compared to what Vincent had done for me, so I pressed onward.

I heard footsteps and turned around to see an attractive thirty-something woman enter the kitchen. I said, "Hi," while I continued to scrub a large pot.

"Hi, I don't think we've met. I'm Stephanie, Vincent's cousin." She was raven haired like everyone else in his family, with gorgeous huge dark-brown eyes and a winning smile. Petite with an oval face and classic high cheekbones, she filled out her own black dress perfectly.

"Forgive me for not shaking your hand. I'm Belinda."

"I'm guessing from the hair color and freckles you're not related."

"Yeah, I kind of stick out here with the red. I'm a good friend of Roxanne's – that's how I know Vincent."

Suddenly she smiled and raised her eyebrows. "Oh, you're the girl with the flu!"

Oh, geez. What the hell was this? "Yeah. How'd you know about that?"

"Oh, he was telling some of us a funny story about a girl he took care of last week who was sick and how every time he asked if you were decent, you had some hilarious comeback."

"It was kind of a running gag, and I'm kind of a smartass."

"Well, I loved your warped sense of humor, and the way he told the story was priceless. And if you're friends with Roxanne, you know that smartass fits right in with this family." She surveyed the wreckage of the kitchen. "Oh my God, have you been cleaning all of this up by yourself?"

"Giving it my best shot. Unfortunately the dishwasher is already full and I think it needs a new transmission."

"Are there any more aprons?"

"Hanging behind the door. But, really, I can manage—"

"Yeah, and you'll be here till midnight." She grabbed an apron, put it on and tied it behind her back. "You wanna wash or dry?"

"I'm already wet, so I'll stick with the washing."

"Okay." She grabbed a dark-green dishtowel and grabbed the pan I handed to her. "You live in the city?"

"Yeah, couple of blocks from Vincent. You?"

"Upstate, near Albany. I gotta move, it's too friggin' cold up there and winter lasts forever. The joke is that we have four seasons: almost winter, winter, still winter, and construction."

"That's funny."

"Not when you're shoveling the walk in April or digging the pumpkin out of a snowdrift in October. So, Belinda, what do you do for a living?"

"I'm a television reporter."

"Oooh, glamor job."

"Not always, but it does have its perks. And I love what I do. How about you?"

"Travel agent. I love what I do too, but after sending so many people to warm exotic places, I want to live in one."

"I can imagine."

She finished drying a large pot, then handed me a chafing dish that smelled strongly of garlic. "That shrimp scampi was awesome, wish I knew who made it. So, how long have you known Vincent?"

"Oh, I don't know. A few months."

"Are you two... you know?"

How the hell do I answer that? Because I don't know what we are. "I, uh, just got out of a relationship."

"Ah, so your dance card is free."

"Nice way of putting it, but yeah."

"Well, if I were in your shoes, and I shouldn't be saying this about a relative, I'd be beating a path to his door. Frankly, I'm amazed some girl hasn't snatched him up yet."

Hmmm. My chance to get a little background. The reporter's hat goes on. "So, he's never been close to heading down the aisle?"

She grabbed another stack of dishes and handed them to me. "Eh, he's had girlfriends, but you could always tell they weren't quite right for him. Problem is, he's soooo particular. Has such high standards."

"Yeah, I know the type." And I see her in the mirror every day.

"He's always wanted someone who's really smart and can take care of herself, but who doesn't have a problem being put on a pedestal by an old-fashioned guy. I know, that's a contradiction, a kick-ass chick who doesn't mind being a girl, if you know what I mean."

Again, mirror.

An hour later we were nearly done. I heard Vincent saying goodbyes at the front door and noticed the level of conversation had thinned out. "Sounds like the crowd's about gone."

"Yeah," said Stephanie, just as the dishwasher stopped running and beeped. "And so are the dirty dishes. We make a good team."

"It reminds me of when I was a kid. We lived in an old house without a dishwasher. I'd forgotten what it feels like to get your fingertips looking like prunes."

Footsteps were followed by Vincent's voice. "What are you two doing in here? I was gonna clean this up."

"Bullshit," said Stephanie. "You've had enough on your plate today without washing them too."

"Yeah," I said, as I handed Stephanie the last pot and rinsed off my hands, then dried them with a dish towel. "This was no big deal."

He looked at the stack of clean dishes and pans. "Like hell, you guys did a mountain of stuff here." He exhaled, looking like he'd hit the emotional wall. "But thank you. I really appreciate it. I'm dead tired."

Roxanne entered the kitchen and spotted me. "There you are, I've been looking all over for you. And here you are playing Suzy Homemaker."

"She and Steph did all the dishes," said Vincent.

"Very nice," said Roxanne. "Your carriage awaits, if you wanna ride home."

I folded the dish towel and put it next to the sink. "Yeah, I'm ready to roll." I turned to Vincent and took his hands. "Really beautiful service today, Vincent. I'm sure your mom loved it. I hope I get a sendoff that nice."

"Thanks," he said.

"So I'll see you around the neighborhood. Hey, remember, you've gotta take me back to the pastry shop to sign my picture."

***

So once again, I was cruising home in Roxanne's land yacht and we were maybe five minutes from home. The radio was tuned into a classic eighties station, filling the air with an old Paula Abdul song, when suddenly she reached out and turned the thing off.

"So, Vincent's not a monster, huh?"

"What is this, groundhog day?" I grabbed the back of my head and backed against the passenger-side window. "And don't hit me. It hurts when you do that."

"I'm just yankin' your chain. And relax, I only hit you when you're bein' a *stunad*."

"Good to know. I'll wear a football helmet next time I'm acting like an idiot."

"Sooooo..."

"Sooooo... what?"

"You look good in that kitchen."

Okay. Where was she going with this? The avocado fridge matches my eyes?

"Vincent's gonna eventually move back into his mother's house, you know."

Oh, that's where she's going.

"It's a great house," I said.

"Andddddd...?"

"Terrific view from the back yard."

Sideways glare. "That all?"

"Fine! You win! He's not a *monstuh*. (I'm imitating her accent.) He's a really good guy! And I like him! There, I said it! Happy?"

"Andddddd?"

"And... I don't know, Rox. I'm confused."

"Too soon since you broke up with he who must not be named?"

"Maybe. I don't know. This is all new to me." I was staring straight ahead, as if the road signs were going to magically offer an answer, and I started waving my hands. "I mean, look at everything that's happened in the last two weeks. I get the flu and break my shoe with the damn red sole and Vincent plays nursemaid for four days, he helps me break a big story, my big story reveals my boyfriend, who I think is about to have sex and lose his virginity is actually married and has been committing federal crimes and screwing the city of New York instead of me and never felt anything for me and likened me to a prostitute, Vincent shows up to rescue me again, his mother dies just when I'm about to… I end up washing dishes in his house and you say I look good in that kitchen and it's all too much to process because my life is one long run-on sentence with tangents all over the place and I don't have any damn emotional punctuation marks left to make it stop so I can figure it all out!"

Roxanne looked at me with wide eyes, then pointed at the coffee shop straight ahead. "You wanna stop at Starbucks for some decaf?"

"I'm sorry. I just can't process all of this. It's happening too fast."

"Whoa, hang on a minute!" Roxanne pulled over about three blocks from my apartment.

"Why are you stopping here? I live on eighty-second. This is seventy-ninth."

"I know. But let's back up to that part of your little monologue on speed when you said *just when I'm about to*. You were just about to *what?*"

Damn, the woman doesn't miss a trick. "I don't know that either! He was walking me home, we'd had a great time, I couldn't decide if I wanted to invite him up for a while, if I'd be leading him on, if I did that and might eventually break his heart, if I should just thank him and go home. And I never had to make the decision because of your phone call."

"What do you think you would have done?"

"That's the point. I still don't know."

"I see." She slowly nodded as she turned off the car and put one hand on my shoulder. "But you think about it, yes?"

I folded my arms in my lap. Dammit, I hate it when she's right. "Yeah," I said softly. "I think about it. A lot. It's like a damn videotape on an infinite loop in my head."

"So, what are you gonna do?"

"Think about it some more."

"Well, you'd better—"

A tap on the driver's-side window interrupted her and I saw

a cop make a motion to roll down the window. She complied.

"You can't park here, Miss," he said.

"Officer, it'll just be a minute. I got a woman having a bit of an emotional crisis here."

"Well, take your crisis somewhere else. Move the car. Now."

Roxanne rolled her eyes. "Oh, for God's sake. Will you give me *one minute?*"

The cop crouched down and for the first time I got a good look at his face, which was lit up by the streetlight. Black hair, dark eyes, Roman nose, maybe fifty. He turned on his flashlight and took a closer look. "Roxanne?"

She looked at him and smiled. "Oh, hey Carmine. I didn't know it was you."

"You need help?"

"Nah, my friend here is in a complicated situation and I needed to pull over while we talk this out. It's like the single woman's version of texting while driving; you don't want me behind the wheel when I'm talking about men."

"Then you should never be on the road," he said.

"Smartass. Oh, I'm sorry. Carmine, this is Belinda. Belinda, my Uncle Carmine."

He waved through the window. "Hey, how ya doin'?"

"Nice to meet you, Carmine," I said.

"I've been tryin' to hook her up with Vincent," said Roxanne, cocking her head at me.

"A shame about his mom, huh? But what a beautiful funeral." Suddenly the cop seemed to notice something and aimed his flashlight at me. "Wait a minute. Red hair and freckles. You're the smartass girl with the flu!"

I slammed my head back against the bucket seat as my mouth dropped open. "Geez, does the whole town know about this?"

Thankfully Carmine's two-way radio started barking. "Hey, I gotta take this. You girls park here as long as you like."

"Thanks. See ya, Carmine," said Roxanne, as she rolled up the window.

"Is there anyone in this town you're *not* connected to?" I asked.

"Nah, not really. The Mayor's probably still up, if you wanna drop by and say hello."

"Can we go home now?"

"Sure." She cranked up the car and looked at me. "You gonna be okay?"

"I don't know. I need time to think."

She pulled out into traffic. "Look, here's the bottom line. Vincent just got his life back and he really earned the right to have some fun. He's not gonna sit home watching television. A lot of women would love a guy like him. Let me put it this way: if you at least give him a shot, you'll know one way or the other. If you don't, you've lost any chance you might have had at a man who could be your soulmate. And don't gimme this bullshit about worrying if you'll hurt him. He's a big boy and he can take it if that should happen. And I can tell you this: he'd be happy to risk that for a shot at you. So think fast, my friend, or he might be off the market by the time you come to a decision. You do realize he no longer has the obligation that took all his free time."

No, for whatever reason I didn't realize that incredibly obvious fact. But thank you for pointing it out.

And now I had to think faster.

CHAPTER TWENTY FOUR

I'm not a morning person at all, and hate working the vampire shift when I have to. It's bad enough getting jolted out of a deep sleep by an alarm, but having to see the perky morning show staff makes me physically ill. Harry once said I had no future as a morning anchor because I'd begin the show with, "I'm Belinda Carson. What the hell are you doing up at this ungodly hour? Go back to bed!" Anyway, I needed some video for a story that only took place at the crack of dawn, so after coming in at five this morning I was already off the clock by one.

I had a rare afternoon off, an early start to the weekend.

What to do, what to do?

And I know what *you're* thinking. Yes, *I've* been thinking. Fast.

It had been three days since the funeral, and a source whose identity I absolutely cannot reveal tipped me off that Vincent was back at work.

It was time to say thank you for all he'd done. If that was even possible.

I had already picked up a gift certificate for a special treat and stopped at Nick's pastry shop for a big box of those freshly baked Italian cookies, the smell of which was driving me nuts as I walked toward Vincent's taxicab garage. I had no idea if he would be there, but I was willing to wait if he wasn't.

The huge steel door to the garage was open, so I turned off the sidewalk and headed inside. I was wearing jeans and stacked-heel boots, with a cropped suede jacket. I figured a dress or skirt was a bit much for a garage, though this simple outfit still stopped traffic.

The place was huge, big enough to hold twenty cabs. One guy in mechanic overalls had a cab on a lift and was changing the oil. He stopped to check me out and smiled as I passed. I noticed another man was busy putting a coat of wax on the angel cab. The two-way radio chatter echoing off the walls was constant, coming from a beat-up desk manned by an old codger who was obviously the dispatcher as he barked addresses into the microphone. This was apparently the nerve center of the operation, so I headed directly for it.

The dispatcher looked up over his half glasses and smiled. "You lost, young lady?"

"No, not at all. I was hoping Vincent Martino is around, but I don't see him. I have something for him."

He pointed toward the back of the garage. "He's in the office. Go right ahead."

"Oh, great. Thank you."

I headed toward the office, which was basically a corner of the garage with two simple walls added and no window. I knocked on the door and heard his voice. "It's open."

I opened the door and saw him behind a giant metal desk, tapping on an old-fashioned adding machine. "So, you're not driving today."

He flashed a soft smile and I could tell he was still fried from the events of the past week. His eyes were droopy and bloodshot. "Belinda. What a nice surprise. What are you doing down here?"

I moved toward the desk, deposited the cookies and an envelope. "I wanted to thank you for everything you've done lately, and figured you needed some cheering up, so this was a good time." I grabbed a chair and pulled it to the side of his desk.

"Well, I'm not turning down anything from Nick's." He opened a drawer, pulled out a pair of scissors and cut the red and white string that held the box closed. He opened it and raised both eyebrows. "Oh, yeah. Looks like *dessert for dinner night.*" He turned the box toward me. "You've never had these. Try one."

"They're for you, Vincent."

"I'll share. Try one."

I reached out and chose a light-green cookie dipped in chocolate with some sort of red filling and took a bite. The red filling turned out to be raspberry. The tart berries and the sweet chocolate mixed wonderfully in my mouth. "Oh, that's terrific."

He grabbed a cookie and took a bite. "Told you these were the best."

I pointed toward the envelope. "You have another present."

"Oh, there's more?" He slid a letter opener along the edge of the envelope and pulled out a stiff card. "Gift certificate for a one-hour massage. Wow, thank you. I've never had a massage."

"Trust me, you'll get hooked."

"What's this for?"

"For sleeping on your hide-a-bed from hell while I had the flu."

"Roxanne must have told you about that thing. I really need to toss it." He looked at the gift certificate. "But I can really use this, especially after..." His eyes misted.

"So, how you doing?"

He shrugged. "I figured coming back to work would help, but it's hard to concentrate."

"It takes time," I said. "You've been through a lot. So, you're not driving today?"

"I do my own books."

I didn't understand until I spotted a New York City business license hanging on the dark paneled wall behind him that read *Martino Cab Company.* "Wait a minute. You own this place?"

He nodded. "Yeah. I've got two dozen taxis and a few limos."

"Wow, I didn't know. So why are you out driving a cab?"

"Gets me out of the office. That's how I paid for college, driving a cab during the summer. I do it once a week. Keeps me grounded. And sometimes you meet the nicest people."

I leaned back in the chair and looked around the office.

The diploma from Harvard Business School stuck out. "You went to *Harvard*?"

"Yeah. I knew I wanted my own business, and that was the best place to learn, though Roxanne will always argue that Wharton is better."

"Damn, Vincent, I had no idea."

"A blue-collar business is still a business. Same principles apply."

"Yeah, I know that from Roxanne. So, the angel cab was your idea?"

"Uh-huh, but I didn't give it that name."

"Must have been expensive to outfit that thing."

"Eh, no big deal. My mother always said, 'you do well, then you do good'. She believed in giving back, so I'm doing a small part."

"She was very wise. And it *is* a big deal to the sick people you transport. It's not a small part by any means."

He didn't say anything. He picked up another cookie and ate it slowly, his eyes vacant. I could tell his mind was somewhere else.

I pointed to the adding machine. "Do you have to do those books today?"

"Nah, I can do 'em anytime. Why?"

I stood up. "C'mon. Grab your coat."

"What for?"

"We're going out to dinner."

"Belinda, you don't have to—"

"A very smart man once told me that when you're depressed you need good food, good company and something to make you smile." I grabbed his coat from a metal rack near the door and tossed it to him. "So put your coat on and don't argue with me."

"Belinda—"

I reached out toward him, grabbed his hand and pulled. "Shaddup, I'm rescuing you."

"Why am I not surprised you picked an all-you-can-eat place?" said Vincent, as the waitress placed a few more crab legs on his plate with a pair of silver tongs.

"Hey, I like to get my money's worth." I pointed to my plate and the waitress loaded me up as I bounced up and down on my chair like a little kid.

"Something tells me they're losing money on this table. But this is terrific seafood. Good choice."

"Glad you like it." The place was simple, with good food served on paper tablecloths and a roll of paper towels on each table that served as napkins. Steam constantly rose out of the kitchen, which was not separated from the dining area, as seafood was being cooked around the dock. I grabbed a crab leg, broke it at the joint and within seconds I was dipping a big hunk of meat into hot, melted butter.

"You're really good at that," he said, as he struggled to open a crab leg with a nutcracker.

"My family loved the fish-on-Friday thing. And crab was our favorite."

He watched me intently as I snapped another leg and dipped the succulent meat. "Teach me to do that, Belinda."

"What?"

"That thing you do without a nutcracker. How you pop the meat out so easily."

"Let me get this straight. An Italian is asking an Irish girl something about food?"

"Yeah. Call your station, breaking news."

"Okay. Grab a leg."

He picked one up.

"Okay, now bend it at the joint so it breaks, then pull one section. That will pull out the tendon from the other piece."

He followed my instructions, doing quite well. "Now what?"

"Now take the piece without the tendon and snap it in half. The meat should be in one piece and you can dip it in the butter."

He did so and it worked. "Wow, that was pretty easy."

"Irish life skill," I said.

***

The line at the theater was pretty short. Vincent looked at the movies on the marquee, but I had made my choice in advance.

"So, what are we seeing?"

"A movie."

"I'm getting the feeling of *déjà vu* here."

"Yeah, it's kinda like those movies where people switch bodies. I'm suddenly having an incredible desire to drive a cab." The line cleared in front of me and I moved to the gate. "Two for *C-4 Apocalypse*."

"You're kidding, right?"

"No. Don't you like action movies?"

"Yeah, what guy doesn't? But you should pick something you'd like as well."

"Why do you assume girls don't like action movies? Hey, I saw the previews and they blow up a ton of shit in this one and the good guys win. What's not to like?"

***

Nick handed me the photo as we took our seats in the pastry shop. I looked at the color print, which showed me wearing a huge grin while my eyes were wide as saucers as I was about to devour a cupcake. Not sure Mrs. Baymont would approve, but what the hell? "So that's what I look like when I eat sweets, huh?"

"The camera doesn't lie," said Vincent. "It's what you look like when you eat *anything*."

I autographed the photo for Nick and handed it back to him. "Here you go, and I'm honored to be on your wall."

"I'll have it up tomorrow morning," said Nick. "And I'll be right back with your usual, unless you two want something else."

"The usual," we said in unison. That got a small laugh from Vincent.

"Good to see you smile," I said.

Vincent looked around, as if looking for something. "Is there a teleprompter in here? Because I swear you're following a script that I've read before."

"Just hitting you with your own logic."

***

My fast thinking was all done as we walked back to my apartment. Same deal as last time: nice night, his hands in his pockets, my arm hooked around his elbow.

And my cell phone was turned off. In fact, he didn't remember to turn his back on when we left the theater.

Unless we got hit by a meteor, we wouldn't get interrupted.

We reached the front of my building, and he turned to face me. "Belinda, I can't thank you enough for tonight. You really cheered me up."

"Like I said, just taking advice from someone I trust."

"Well, this was all terrific, from the cookies to the massage to dinner and everything else."

"Speaking of everything else..." I took one deep breath in an attempt to slow down my heart. "Vincent, would you like to come up for coffee?"

He furrowed his brow. "I thought you didn't have a coffee pot."

"I don't."

"Instant?"

"Nope. Don't even have cream and sugar."

"Then what—"

I put one finger on his lips to interrupt him. "You know, for a guy who went to an Ivy League school, you're being a real *stunad* right now."

He chuckled a bit. "Let me guess, you learned that term from Rox."

"Yeah. Actually, she's taught me a lot lately. Stuff that goes beyond Italian slang. She's very wise, you know. Very perceptive about people, and what they need."

He moved a little closer and looked deeply into my eyes. "This isn't about coffee at all, is it?"

"You catch on quick, Harvard."

"So... what *is* this about? You've been dancing around something the last two weeks."

"I haven't been dancing. Bad ankle, remember? That's how all this started."

"That's what I'm talking about, Belinda. What exactly is *all this*?"

I moved closer and wrapped my arms loosely around his neck, dipped my head a bit and looked up at him through my long eyelashes. "*All this* is about a damsel who happens to be in major, serious distress. And you seem to be a guy who, shall we say, specializes in rescues."

He gulped, his breathing getting short. "So, uh...what sort of distress would, uh, this fair damsel be in?"

"Well, this particular damsel needs to be held. She needs many, many hugs, the kind where she can rest her head on a strong shoulder. She desperately needs to be kissed, which, I might add, needs to take place over an extended period of time. But most of all, she needs to be loved. That is perhaps her greatest need, but she will only accept it from someone who is kind and funny and sweet and strong, someone who can accept the fact that she can take care of herself but loves it when he takes care of her, if that makes any sense. And most of all, he has to be a decent guy. So, are you decent?"

He shook his head and smiled. "Nah, I'm a shallow gigolo." He put his hands on my waist and slid them toward the small of my back. His touch sent a shot of electricity through my body like none I'd ever felt. Now *my* breathing was getting short.

"Good one. Oh, one more thing. This particular damsel has been walking a lot, so she isn't sure if she should rest her ankle. And if I remember correctly, you *are* in the transportation business."

"Sounds like she needs a lift." He scooped me up easily as I tightened my arms around his neck. "This damsel of whom you speak... does she always talk about herself in the third person?"

"She does because she's sometimes been scared to admit her true feelings, so she pretends she's talking about someone else. But at this point in her life, she's not afraid any more."

"How would one discover these true feelings?"

"Why don't you come up for coffee and find out?"

Vincent lifted me a little higher and kissed me, long and soft, holding the kiss right there in the middle of the sidewalk. He cradled me like a groom carrying a bride, while pedestrians walked by and cars honked their horns. And as is always the case in New York City, this magical moment was doused by a bucket of ice water delivered via a wicked accent.

"Why don't youse two get a room?" asked a middle-aged hardhat who walked by.

We broke the lip lock and laughed. "What an excellent idea," said Vincent, who then carried me toward the building with my head resting on his shoulder. "By the way, about that coffee?"

"Yes?"

"You'd better make a large pot. We might be up a while."

***

I was already set to meet the girls for lunch on Saturday and wasn't really sure what I should tell them about the previous night or even if I should tell them anything. This stuff should remain private, right?

Well, that was sensible girl talking. Happy girl could not wait to share her experiences with the world. What the hell, call *The Post* and get it on *Page Six*. Call the station and break into programming. *This just in... Belinda Carson might have found her soul mate. Film at eleven.* Happy girl didn't care. Happy girl was too damn excited about what the future might hold. But sensible girl was telling happy girl to tone it down, that one great night doesn't necessarily mean happily ever after.

I was the last to arrive at the restaurant, an old-fashioned Greek diner with a hundred things on the menu, all of them good. Burgers or salads or pasta, you couldn't go wrong. It looked like a silver train car on the outside, while the inside was filled with old beige Naugahyde booths and a long counter, which was always packed with customers, mostly of the blue-collar variety. Those old-fashioned jukebox selectors sat on each table, offering nothing recorded after 1963. We all loved the place because it was a throwback to a happier time.

I tried to keep my smile casual as I reached one of the round tables in the back, not wanting to tip my hand. "Hey guys." There was already a menu in front of my seat so I picked it up as I sat down.

"So, how was your week?" asked Serena.

"Not bad," I said. "Couple of good stories. Nothing Emmy-worthy, but okay. You?"

She shrugged. "Boring week. Plain old civil lawsuit. I got an itch for another good sexual harassment case."

"You would," said Ariel.

"So many sleazy men, so little time," said Serena. "And I've got a new outfit that's crying out for a male jury."

"In your case, you'd want a *hung* jury," cracked Roxanne.

"Speaking of which, I have to write some copy for an erectile dysfunction commercial," said Ariel, with a gleam in her eye.

"Sounds like a hard assignment," I said, which made her laugh.

Roxanne had thus far said nothing and was studying my face. "You go see Vincent yesterday?"

I nodded. "Yeah, I brought him a box of Italian cookies from Nick's pastry shop and got him a gift certificate for a massage, since he slept on that hide-a-bed while I was sick."

"That's nice," said Ariel. "He's done a lot for you lately."

"Really," said Serena. "Man is a saint. I'm surprised he hasn't been canonized by the Catholic Church after taking care of you for four days."

Roxanne was still staring at me when suddenly her eyes grew wide. "Aha!"

"Aha *what*?"

She pointed at me and lowered her voice to a sultry tone. "You had sex!"

I played dumb. "What are you talking about?"

"You got the glow." She turned to Serena and Ariel. "She's got the glow."

I waved it away. "Pffft. You and your glow. That's a bunch of bullshit."

"No, no," said Serena, "there might be something to it. You did have a little bounce in your step when you walked in. And your skirt was on backwards."

I snapped my neck down, horrified.

"Made you look," said Serena.

"So there *is* something there," said Ariel.

"There's nothing there. And stop trying reporter's tricks on me. I'm happy because it's Saturday. I enjoy the weekend."

"Enjoy the weekend, my ass," said Roxanne.

"C'mon, dish," said Ariel. "Your left eyelid is starting to twitch like it always does when you're hiding something. It's your *tell*."

"I have a tell? You never told me I have a tell."

"You don't tell someone they have a tell because if you told them they wouldn't have a tell anymore," said Serena. "Law school 101." Now all three of them were staring at me and I was cornered at a round table. "Cough it up, Wing Girl, lest your left eyelid go into convulsions."

"Fine! I had..." I dropped my voice, realizing I was in a public place. "What you said I had."

"Aha!" said Roxanne.

"Will you stop with the *aha!* already?"

"C'mon, details," said Serena. "Rebound sex after you know who, one-nighter, guy you found on Craigslist, what's the story here?"

"Yeah, we're supposed to have approval," said Ariel. "You sneaked one by us. So who is it?"

"Just a guy," I said.

"What a steaming pile of horseshit," said Roxanne. "You don't do one-nighters because of the guilt factor. You'd be too afraid you'd get hit by a bus before you made it to confession." Suddenly a huge smile grew on her face. "I know who's been sleeping in *your* bed," she said, like she was reading a bedtime story.

My face flushed, with no way to stop it. "Can we please change the subject?"

"No!" They all responded in unison.

"So who is it, Rox?" asked Ariel.

"Yeah," said Serena, "Tell us before we have to waterboard her."

"She can tell you," said Roxanne, looking in my direction.

"Fine," I said. I looked around to make sure no one was listening before lowering my head and my voice. "It's... Vincent."

To say the mouths of Ariel and Serena hit the table would be an understatement. Roxanne sat up straight and put her nose in the air. "And you're very welcome," she said.

A college-age waiter showed up a nanosecond later. "You girls ready to order?"

"No!" from all four of us.

He backed up a bit. "Okay then. I'll, uh, give you a few minutes." Then he walked away.

"Soooo..." said Serena.

"What?" I asked.

"Details," said Ariel.

"Hey, that's my cousin!" said Roxanne, who slapped Ariel on the back of the head.

"Ow! Will you please stop doing that?" said Ariel, holding her head.

"That's why I always sit directly across from her and that damn Sicilian head slap," said Serena. "C'mon, Wing Girl, we just want one little detail."

"How about one *very big* detail," I said with a devilish smile while I raised my eyebrows.

Roxanne slapped me across the back of the head.

"Ow!" I rubbed my head. "C'mon, Rox, it was a hanging curveball over the middle of the plate. I had to swing at it."

"No," said Roxanne, who folded her arms. "What happens in the bedroom stays in the bedroom when it comes to my family."

"Fine," I said. "I'll just say—"

She glared at me and pulled her arm back, ready to strike.

"He was a real gentleman." She dropped her arm and smiled like the cat who ate the canary.

"So," said Ariel, sliding her chair closer to Serena and turning it to protect the back of her head, "what's next?"

"We're going out tonight. It's our first date."

"I think you've got it backwards," said Serena. "You're supposed to have sex *after* the first date."

"We've been out twice," I said, "but both times one of us was trying to cheer up the other and it was an impromptu thing. We've never really been on a traditional date. So it's dinner and a show tonight. And then tomorrow he's taking me to the Giants game."

"Wow, Wing Girl, you've moving at warp speed. Already spending the whole weekend together," said Ariel.

"We already did that when I had the flu," I said.

"Well, you have my approval to proceed," said Serena.

Ariel nodded. "Mine too."

I looked at Roxanne, half expecting some smartass comment. Instead she said, actually tearing up, "I'm sorry I ever called you a *stunad.*"

"Fuhgeddaboudit," I said in her accent.

"So, guys," said Ariel, "where do we go from here? Is charm school over?"

"Wing Girl still needs you guys for advice," I said, back in third-person mode.

"Uh-oh," said Serena. "What now?"

I shrugged. "I don't know. I'm just a little worried."

"You just had a great night and you're spending the whole weekend together. What the hell are you worried about?" asked Roxanne.

"That I'll do something that will hurt him. I mean, he's such a good man... what if this doesn't work out? He'd be devastated."

"Did it ever occur to you," said Ariel, "that if you lost him, *you* might be the one who's devastated?"

***

I got a present on Monday from an unexpected source when I picked up the tip line.

"Hi Belinda, it's Special Agent Willis."

"Agent Willis, nice to hear from you. How are you?"

"I'm fine. The more important question is, how are you?"

"I'm over it and have moved on, but thank you for your concern. I, uh, never got the chance to apologize—"

"Apologize for what? I have no idea what you're talking about."

"You're a good man, Willis. I owe you one. So what can I do for you?"

"Well, I have a little news about that person who stole all the money from the pension fund. I thought you'd like to know we recovered almost all of it. Forty-seven million dollars."

I whistled, not believing the amount. "Good God. And they needed one more payday?"

"Greed has no limit, as you quickly discover in the white collar division. Anyway, he sang like a canary, giving up his two accomplices. One of whom was his wife."

"You're kidding me! He wouldn't cheat on her, but he sold her down the river?"

"Yep, in return for three fewer years on his sentence."

"So how was she involved?"

"She was Jagger's executive assistant, if you can believe it. The third person involved was a bank president, who had no trouble cashing all those checks and wiring the money overseas without anyone knowing about it."

"Incredible."

"Anyway, they all plead guilty and were sentenced immediately. Shepard got twenty-seven years, his wife got thirty, as did the bank president."

"Good. I was hoping someone would throw the book at him."

"By the way, Belinda, I know you were very angry when you asked me to send him to a prison in a miserable place, but you know I have no input on that."

"Yeah, I know. I was pretty pissed off. You know, the proverbial woman scorned."

"Anyway, I thought you'd like to know that Mister Shepard will be spending the next twenty-seven years in a federal penitentiary in North Dakota. I hear it's lovely this time of year."

"Agent Willis, you have a wicked streak in you. Thank you."

"Belinda, again, I have no idea what you're talking about, but have a good holiday."

"You too, Agent Willis. Bye."

In the news business, we often use the term "closure" to wrap up a story.

I finally knew what it meant.

CHAPTER TWENTY FIVE

The Fourth of July

The house had undergone a significant makeover since Vincent's mother passed away. Gone were all the pieces of medical equipment: the motorized wheelchair, walker, special adjustable bed, and stair climber, which had transported Mrs. Martino to the second floor. Vincent ripped up the old stained carpet (which he had left in place as a cushion since his mother was prone to falling) and had hardwood floors installed, but not before I helped him put a fresh coat of paint indoors. I even discovered I was pretty good with wallpaper. The avocado-green kitchen appliances, outta here. He kept the things important to his mother, little stuff like the religious statues and the prints of Frank Sinatra and the Pope that hung in the hallway, though the plastic-covered velour couch went right to Goodwill. It had been good therapy for him; keeping enough stuff to honor his mother while updating the house to modern standards.

It had brought us closer. Imagine, most couples grow their relationship through a series of dates. We used sprained ankles, the flu, and house painting. Then again, we were not a normal couple.

Yes, after several months we were officially a couple. I can say the "c" word.

Neither of us has dated anyone else since our first night together. I wasn't wired that way and neither was he. I mean, you can't sleep with one person and date another. Well, some people can, but not us. I'm not some wanton harlot or a trashy jezebel.

The relationship was solid. My worry about possibly hurting Vincent had been slowly dissipating, but it was always lurking in the back of my mind and I still could not figure out why. We were comfortable, enjoying both our time together and our own space.

This Fourth of July would be different, obviously, without his mother around. Vincent was relaxing in a deck chair, sipping a beer and talking sports with the guys. I'd been keeping an eye on the grill while stuffing my face with more Italian goodies I never heard of. The weather was perfect again: warm, but not too hot. And more important, there was not a cloud in the sky to ruin the fireworks.

Last year I was a guest. This year everyone was treating me like family.

***

When it was time for charades Roxanne curiously picked me and Vincent out of a hat as a team, which confirmed my year-long suspicion that the fix was in last time. (I was beginning to wonder what other strings she may have been pulling along the way.) Anyway, we were much better at the game this time, knew each other's moves and often what the other was thinking. But we were in second place with only one more round to go, and you know how I hate to lose.

"Velinda, you're up," said Roxanne. (She has combined our names, like Brangelina, though I'm not sure it had the same *cachet* as it does for the two actors.)

"You first," said Vincent. He pushed me toward Roxanne, who already had her fedora out. I reached in and pulled out a slip, then nodded at her.

"Let's rock," I said.

"Anddddd… go!" She clicked the stopwatch and I did the movie pantomime I remembered from last year.

"Movie!" yelled Vincent.

I laid down on my back, started to twitch and used my hands to demonstrate something exploding from my stomach.

"Alien!" he said.

"Aw, c'mon. Too easy!" yelled a member of another team.

"Fifteen seconds," said Roxanne, as Vincent extended a hand and helped me up. "Very impressive. You do the next one in less than twenty-nine seconds, you guys win."

I sat down as Vincent reached into the hat, looked at the paper and nodded at Roxanne.

"Anddddd… go!"

Vincent took his right hand and made a swooping motion around his head and down to his waist, then jabbed his finger in the air.

"A question," I said.

He nodded. He pretended he was writing something on a piece of paper, then his head dropped to the side, he closed his eyes and let his tongue hang out.

"You're writing something… and you're dead. A will!"

He nodded, then pointed at me.

"Will… me?"

He shook his head, then pointed at himself.

"Will… you?"

He smiled and nodded, drew a circle in the air with one hand, then tapped his ring finger.

"Uh, a ring?"

He gave me the "come-on" motion with his hands, which told me I was close.

"Uh, wedding ring?"

He shook his head, made an exaggerated motion and placed

the imaginary ring on his finger.

"Wedding? Marriage? Marry?"

He nodded, then pointed to himself.

"Will... you... marry...you."

He rolled his eyes, then pointed at me.

"Oh! Will you marry me!"

He nodded and clapped.

I turned to Roxanne. "Time?"

She shrugged. "How the hell should I know?"

"Did we beat twenty-nine seconds?"

"I didn't start the watch."

"Why the hell not?"

"Because, it wasn't necessary."

"Belinda?" It was Ariel, who was sitting behind me next to Serena.

I turned around to face her. For some odd reason everyone was wearing this silly grin. "What?"

"Answer the question."

"What the hell are you talking about? I just want to know if we won."

"The witness is directed to *answer the question*," said Serena, who had a huge smile as she pointed behind me.

I turned around and saw Vincent on one knee, hand extended, holding a small jewelry box with a seriously big emerald-cut diamond in it.

The air was knocked from my lungs as my jaw dropped.

"You didn't answer the question, *stunad*," said Roxanne. "Answer the friggin' question. The man is waiting. C'mon, tick-tock."

Everyone laughed, then grew quiet. I locked eyes with Vincent, who looked right into my soul. "Brass Cupcake," he said, "will you do me the great honor of being my wife?"

The adrenaline of a big story couldn't hold a candle to this moment. In the space of a few seconds, I had to make a decision about the direction my life would take, possibly for the rest of my years. I had to decide whether my love of Vincent outweighed my fear of hurting him.

For a girl who works in an industry that deals in black and white, I had to choose a gray area. But then again, love is not a black-and-white issue, never a sure thing. That was the one fact in the equation.

I finally composed myself, realizing the decision was a no-brainer despite the risk. Besides, I knew I'd kick myself till the end of time if I didn't take the shot. "Harvard, you've got it backwards. The real question should come from me, because I'm the reporter here. Will you do *me* the great honor of being my husband?"

***

The fireworks exploded high in the air but all I could do was stare at the huge ring on my left hand. Vincent had one arm tightly wrapped around me as the sound of the Sousa marches washed across the water with the gentle waves.

The facets of the ring caught the light of the fireworks, acting as a prism and creating an intoxicating dancing rainbow of light within the diamond.

I looked up at his face, into his eyes, and saw the same thing.

CHAPTER TWENTY SIX

I heard the key in the lock, put down my cup of hot chocolate and headed for the door. It opened before I got there, revealing Vincent carrying a huge rectangular box.

"Ariel asked me to pick up your wedding dress. And no, I didn't look at it."

"Just drop it on the kitchen table, cause there's no other place to put it," I said.

He set it down. "Damn, that thing weighs a ton."

"Better start working out, Harvard. You're gonna have to carry me and it across the threshold."

He leaned down, wrapped one arm around my waist, lifted me up and gave me a quick kiss. "Oh well, no more trips to Nick's for you." He put me down, looked around the apartment and saw the mountain of other boxes. "Wow, you really cleaned up at the shower. Or was it a bachelorette party?"

"One followed the other," I said.

"Which was more fun?"

"Bachelorette party. Four male strippers."

He folded his arms and gave me a stern look. "I see."

"Yes, they all wanted to have sex with me, but I told them I have my own Chippendale at my beck and call."

"Very good, Cupcake. So, did you get a lot of nice stuff?"

"Most of it is really for you."

He furrowed his brow. Excuse me?"

"Bridal showers are really for the men. You don't expect me to wear thongs and dominatrix boots around the house because they're comfortable."

"Point taken, but I will say your friends are very thoughtful."

"Hey, there's lots of cake left on the kitchen counter. Chocolate, from Nicks."

"Sounds good." He took off his leather jacket and hung it on the back of a chair, then headed for the kitchen and grabbed a plate out of the cupboard. He picked up a knife to cut the cake and stopped. "What the heck does *so long, Wing Girl* mean?"

I realized the half of the cake with the inscription hadn't been cut. "Well, cut a slice, get a glass of milk and I'll explain it to you."

I headed to the couch. He followed me after getting a piece of cake and glass of milk. He sat next to me, put the milk on the coffee table and took a bite of the cake. "Wow, this is rich."

"Yeah, you can get a sugar high off that stuff."

"So what's the deal with the writing on the cake?"

"Vincent, there's something I need to tell you about myself."

He put the fork back on the plate and grew a worried look. "What, you were married before?"

"No, of course not."

"Used to be a nun?"

"Seriously? You're actually considering the possibility that I was Sister Belinda in a previous life?"

"Well, you're such a hellcat in bed. I mean, could be all that pent-up sexual energy from the convent." He flashed a wicked grin. "And you seem to be comfortable on your knees."

I playfully slapped his arm. "God will punish you for that one. No, *Wing Girl* is my nickname."

"What, you like chicken wings? I've never seen you eat those."

"No, it has nothing to do with food. You know what a *wing man* is, right?"

"You mean the guy who helps his friend pick up women? Sure, every man knows that."

"Well, I'm the female version."

"So... let me get this straight. You're called *Wing Girl* because you went out with your friends and chatted up ugly guys?"

"No, the scenario is different for women. Basically I was the lure for my friends. Men came up to me because I'm on television and have a degree of fame. But, as you noticed the first time we met, I had the propensity to turn men off. Roxanne, Serena and Ariel would then swoop in and grab them. So, in a roundabout kind of way, I was taking one for the team, and they named me *Wing Girl*."

"That's it?"

"Yep, that's it."

He picked up his cake and started eating again. "Oh. I like Brass Cupcake a lot better."

"Yeah, me too. And, according to the cake, *Wing Girl* is soon to be permanently retired." The story made me think back to the first night we met. "Vincent, there's something I need to know about you. Actually a few things."

He took a sip of milk, leaving him with a white moustache. "Despite your suspicions, I was never in a seminary."

"Cute. That night we first met in the bar. Before I became... you know..."

"Smoking hot?"

I couldn't help but blush. "Before charm school. Before my makeover. Is there any way you would have asked me out for a date?"

"Absolutely."

"You're saying that to be polite."

"No, I'm being honest."

"But I was rude and awkward. And you said I had bad clothes."

"Well, you were snotty and dressed like a longshoreman, but then I took off your glasses. Oh my God, those eyes. I'd never seen green eyes like that. And they had such fire."

"That's because I was pissed off."

He shook his head. "No, no, you're missing the point. A lot of girls do their eyes with a lot of makeup, and they look like models, but they still have dead eyes. Not much life. Yours were off the charts. I could tell you had great depth of feeling, that you were passionate about everything, and I wanted to know you from that moment."

"Just from my eyes?"

He reached behind my head and started playing with my hair. "Well, you also had the red hair and those cute freckles. If it's one thing Italian men can't resist, it's redheads with freckles."

"Really?"

"Yeah, no matter how old you get, those freckles will always make you look like a little girl. Like they do right now."

I blushed again. "Thank you. I also need to know about those coincidental run-ins we kept having."

Now *he* started to blush. "Oh. That."

"Aha!"

"Now before you go all *aha!* with me, it was just a couple of times. When I picked you up in the cab was one."

"What, were you waiting outside my station all day?"

"No, Rox told me what time you usually got off from work, and if I had the cab I would cruise by there at that time of day. And finally the stars aligned."

"How did you even recognize me? You hadn't seen me since the bar."

He pointed at the large flat-screen TV in the living room. "Well, duh..."

"Oh, right. So after that... the time with the groceries?"

"Pure chance. As it was when you sprained your ankle. And the sci-fi convention. I really do go every year. The only other set-up was when I adopted Gypsy. I had mentioned to Roxanne I was going to get another cat, and she told me you worked at the shelter on Sunday mornings."

"So that's it?"

"Well, Roxanne put us together for charades on the Fourth of July, but I didn't know she was going to do that. And I wished she hadn't after my mother embarrassed the hell out of me earlier."

"You avoided me all day after that. It was pretty funny."

"Yeah, for you. You really had the upper hand after that one."

"You got it back from my photographer at the convention."

Big smile. "True. Now *that* made my day. Kicked your ass in trivia and found out you liked me. Talk about a daily double."

"So, after the meeting in the bar, the cab ride, running into me with groceries, you still wanted to go out with a total bitch?"

He finished the cake, put the plate on the table and leaned back with his glass of milk. "I never saw you that way. Look, I'd been watching your station for a few years and I knew you were this take-no-prisoners chick. And I love girls with a lot of spunk who can take care of themselves, even though I like putting them up on a pedestal. This might sound strange, but the more snarky you got with me, the more I wanted you. I really fell in love with you when you had the flu. You were sick as a dog and cracking me up every day."

"Funny, that's when I realized I liked you. What really amazed me is how kind you were even though I was dating someone else."

"Well, Roxanne had told me that guy would be out of the picture eventually."

"Really? We were getting pretty serious at that point."

"Hey, all I know is that Rox is never wrong about relationships. And even if she turned out to be wrong, I wanted you as a friend."

"Really? Wow."

"Yeah, really."

"Speaking of Roxanne, what's this garbage about you once saying I was out of your league?"

"Hey, I knew you could have any man you wanted."

I took the glass from him, put it on the coffee table, and climbed onto his lap. "Well, if that statement is true, Mr Ivy

League deductive reasoning, what do my actions and the ring on my finger tell you?"

CHAPTER TWENTY SEVEN

In the week before my wedding day, I had been told, "don't be nervous" about a dozen times by various people.

As I stood in the doorway of the massive old stone church, I was amazed that I was not.

That fear I've had about possibly hurting Vincent? Almost gone. (I know, at this point you're saying it should be outta here, but I am a world-class worrier, which you should know by now.)

The girls gathered around for one last hug with Wing Girl before she took the big leap and her nickname was retired into the singles bar Hall of Fame.

"You look amazing," said Serena.

"Thank you. I feel amazing."

Ariel took my hands and looked into my soul. "I can't tell you how happy I am for you. You really deserve this."

"Couldn't have done it without you. Thank you for turning me into a better person."

Roxanne was next. By the way, she was my Maid of Honor, even though Ariel was my best friend. Ariel did an incredibly classy thing and stepped aside, saying this whole relationship would not have happened without Rox. Roxanne was thrilled like you wouldn't believe, as if she'd been chosen for prom queen. She looked at me and for once in her life was at a loss for words.

"Rox, I can't thank you enough."

Her eyes got misty as she hugged me, as neither of us had to say anything else.

We heard the organ crank up and knew the ceremony was about to begin. Oh, I asked Harry to walk me down the aisle because he'd been my father figure since my dad passed away. Despite grumbling about having to wear a "damn monkey suit" I think he was genuinely touched when I asked him. And he actually looked very distinguished in a curmudgeonly sort of way.

"Time to go, girls," said Mrs. Baymont, who thankfully has been the wedding planner, turning herself into Martha Stewart on speed. The church, which is more than one hundred years old, was turned into something out of a fairy tale. Candles everywhere, huge white bows on the end of each pew, enough flowers to stock a florist for a month. The church was the perfect setting, with a three-story ceiling and a beautiful white marble altar. Ariel's mom even figured out the perfect time that the sunlight would be filtering through the massive stained-glass window behind the crucifix, which was blending the sun's rays and candlelight into something ethereal. The photographer for her magazine was doubling as the wedding photographer, so we'd get free wedding photos since they'd end up in print anyway. The bridesmaids, who were actually wearing dresses they could wear again on days other than Halloween, began the procession as the organ music picked up and filled the air.

Harry extended his elbow and I took it. We both stared straight ahead at the bridesmaids as they headed down the aisle. "By the way," he said out of the side of his mouth, not looking at me, "I hope you're not keeping your maiden name."

I responded in the same way. "I'm not, but why do you ask?"

"You're scary enough to politicians and adding a Sicilian last name takes the fear level up a notch."

"You're funny, Harry. But yes, you can tell the art department to make some new billboards with Belinda Martino. And none of that hyphenated bullshit either."

"Watch it, you're in church."

"Like you're an altar boy."

It was almost time to start walking. He took one look at me, smiled and shook his head.

"What?" I asked. "Is there a price tag hanging off me?"

"Cupcake, you're just so damn beautiful. Who knew?"

My eyes grew misty. "Thank you, Harry."

Roxanne took her place in front of me and started walking. The organ segued from the procession music to the beginning notes of *Here Comes the Bride*. We hit the top of the aisle and naturally everyone was looking at me.

I flashed what must have been the biggest smile in my life at our guests. Then I looked past them to the altar, right at Vincent, and everything else went out of focus as if I had tunnel vision. Vincent smiled softly as he locked eyes with me. And all the worry, all the indecision, all the apprehension disappeared in a flash as if I were touched by a higher power. Pure joy rushed through my veins for the first time in my life.

And right then and there, I knew I would never hurt him.

I finally realized there are no gray areas when it comes to true love.

***

The reception was unlike anything I'd ever seen. Half Italians, half news people, all loud and very well lubricated by the time Vincent and I arrived after taking pictures. I actually got the photographer to take a shot of the parking lot, since it was half filled with taxicabs and the other half with news cars and satellite trucks. (I'm sure if the Inhuman Resources troll had been invited, she would have cited everyone who had used a station vehicle for personal use and charged them fifty cents a mile.)

Mrs. Baymont had supervised the decorations here as well,

turning what was previously an old stone armory into a castle out of a fairytale. It was amazing what the woman accomplished by simply draping colorful fabric along the walls and turning the tables into something special, as each one had a different floral centerpiece. A huge fountain sat on one side of the long, rectangular head table while a slowly dripping ice sculpture of a swan was on the other.

The ceremony had been perfect, and I couldn't wait to see the video shot by Frank. (That was his wedding gift to me.) Harry had started things off with a chuckle when the old Priest asked "Who giveth this woman?" Harry responded, "The staff and management of Channel Six." But after that it was all serious and traditional and sentimental and joyful.

The wedding cake was certainly original, from Nick's pastry shop, of course. And while it was traditional all the way up, it was topped by a cupcake.

By the way, I made a pre-emptive strike against the paparazzi and struck a deal with *The Post*: I'd give them one exclusive wedding picture in return for them not crashing the ceremony or reception. I'd kept one wary eye out all day and they'd kept their word.

We reached the point of the toast and though Roxanne was the Maid of Honor, she insisted that Ariel give it. As Roxanne put it, "She's the writer, and if I had to do it you'd have a toast with a bunch of fuhgeddaboudits and friggin' this and that and *stunads*, so let her do the damn thing."

Ariel stood up, and finally all the eyes that had been on me gave me a break and turned to her.

"Belinda has been my best friend since we met in college a little more than ten years ago. First, I must say I'm thrilled she's marrying an Italian who can cook, because the girl can burn a salad." The crowd laughed. "Long story, but unfortunately true. If the way to a man's heart is through his stomach, she must have taken a detour to snag a guy like Vincent. If any of you should suddenly see him losing weight, we know the reason why.

"But what she lacks in kitchen skills she makes up for in her ability to love, to share, to give of herself. If you don't know her, she will become a loyal friend and the spunky sister you never had, as she has been for me. If you already know her, you appreciate the persona known as the Brass Cupcake, and know she's someone who will always have your back.

"She can be funny, incredibly stubborn, passionate, sarcastic as hell and giving. But regardless of her mood, she has the strongest life force of anyone I know.

"So please raise your glasses and toast my best friend, Belinda, and her new husband. Vincent, there's a new sheriff in town, and she's got red hair."

***

Vincent's cousin Stephanie, my partner in dish-washing, was also a bridesmaid. She handed me an ivory-colored silk bag the size of a large purse as we got ready for the receiving line before we wrapped up the reception and left for the hotel.

"What's this?" I asked.

"It's your boost bag," she said.

"A what?"

"Oh, I guess nobody told you about the old traditions of Italian weddings. We don't give gifts, we give money. It gives you a boost when you're starting out… hence the term 'boost bag'. Couples use it for a down payment on a house, a car, whatever they need. Anyway, the bride gets a special bag, and you put the envelopes in there."

"It's a pretty big bag."

"It's a pretty big crowd."

I looked at the receiving line, looped around the reception hall, and everyone had an envelope in one hand and a drink in the other. "All these people are giving me cash?"

"You got it. Beats the hell out of candlesticks and crock pots,

268

if you ask me."

Stephanie waved the first couple in line to come forward. The couple handed me an envelope, then I got a hug and a kiss.

This happened a few hundred times, and I started to laugh as a silly thought popped into my head. I was thinking how glad I was that Scott was in prison as I held all this loot.

***

Despite the weight of my gorgeous dress (which Mrs. Baymont had specially designed for me) Vincent carried me easily over the threshold into the hotel suite. That, of course, was arranged by Roxanne in yet another of her "deals" that I didn't question. We were greeted by a bottle of champagne in a silver ice bucket along with a plate of chocolate dipped strawberries on a nightstand next to the four-poster mahogany canopy bed. A huge antique armoire stood opposite the bed, serving as a well-stocked bar. The red drapes that matched the bed's comforter were pulled back from the huge picture window, and offered a spectacular view of the New York City skyline with the Chrysler Building in the foreground just a few blocks away. And since it was the penthouse on the top floor, it had a vaulted ceiling, something I'd never seen in a Manhattan hotel room. It was nearly midnight, and between the emotion and the dancing and the booze, I was pretty wiped out.

But it *was* my wedding night. And all that implied.

Vincent gently lowered me onto the bed. "You must be exhausted after all this, huh?"

"Nah, I'm fine." (My first lie of the marriage, but hey, what am I gonna say? *Not tonight, honey, I have a headache...*)

"I'm impressed. I figured the bride had all the stress when it came to weddings."

"What could possibly be stressful about marrying you?"

He smiled and sat down next to me, then gave me a soft kiss.

"Have I told you how amazing you look?"

"Yeah, about a dozen times. Let's see how you feel in the morning."

"I've already seen you in the morning, remember?"

"Yes, that fact did pop up during confession. I suppose you can't wait to rip this dress off me."

"Well, that was the original plan, but I had an idea."

"Vincent, I don't think we can have sex while I'm wearing this thing."

"I was thinking that we could be married for fifty years, and I'll never get to see you in this dress again. You look... well, you look so incredible. I was wondering..."

I wasn't sure where he was going with this though the image of Sonny Corleone nailing a bridesmaid against a door popped into my mind. "Yessss...?"

"I was wondering if you wouldn't mind keeping it on a little while longer. The whole day has been such a whirlwind, and this is the first time I've gotten to be with you alone. While you're in that dress. Remember, I didn't see you in it before today, so let me enjoy it since it's just the two of us."

I had never experienced tears of joy in my lifetime, until that moment.

"Only if you keep the tuxedo on. You look pretty incredible yourself."

"Sure, but I'll wear a tux again. This dress is a one-time deal."

Vincent popped the bottle of champagne, poured two glasses and handed one to me as he sat on the other side of the bed. We toasted each other, piled up the pillows and laid back, a bride and groom alone for the first time. We sipped champagne for the next few hours, both propped up on one elbow facing each other and talked about the future.

Eventually we fell asleep. He in his tux; me in my wedding dress.

As traditions go, it wasn't the typical wedding night.

However, breakfast was off the charts.

EPILOGUE

Only two words can describe how the bride feels on her honeymoon. In this case, those two words were, "Who knew?"

Because suddenly, sensible girl had become Mrs. Martino, sentimental girl. I know you're going to find this hard to believe, but she's been working on her signature featuring her new last name like a high-school girl doodling on her math homework. She's been on a massive cruise ship, enjoying ten glorious days in the Caribbean, and she's actually started a scrapbook.

Oh, sorry, I fell back into third-person mode. But yeah, I had become schmaltzy all of a sudden, a poster child for warm and fuzzy in which everything I did could give someone else a cavity. I even said "awwww" a lot and got choked up every time Vincent did something sweet or I read a wedding card. The first page of the scrapbook featured an article from *The Post* as we had picked up a copy at the airport before flying out. The headline fitted perfectly, as the photo I sent them was one of us getting showered with rice as we left the church.

BRASS CUPCAKE GETS HER SPRINKLES

Single men, take note: you can take Belinda Carson out of the oven, because the Brass Cupcake is done.

The Channel Six investigative reporter walked down the aisle with, get this, Harvard-educated cab company owner Vincent Martino. Carson, who underwent an incredible makeover last year which rocketed her to infobabe status, was set up with her hunky hubby by a good friend.

Carson wore a...

Okay, this was the part of the article that lost me, but I guess women are supposed to be fascinated by a detailed description of my wedding dress. I don't know silk organza from terry cloth, so it was all Greek to me. Personally, had I done the write-up, I would have kept it simple. "The bride wore a white dress and due to her previous after-hours escapades with the groom, attended confession shortly before the ceremony. For her penance she received ten Our Fathers, ten Hail Marys, and a stern look from the parish priest."

Anyway, I'd been adding little odds and ends to the scrapbook as we sailed the crystal-clear turquoise waters of the Caribbean. Ticket stubs from historical sites, some paper money from places no one ever heard of, even a luggage tag from the cruise line. I was currently stretched out on our balcony, as Vincent's cousin Stephanie the travel agent took care of booking the cruise and got us a deal like Roxanne. I quickly reached the point that I stopped asking questions of anyone in his family about how stuff magically appeared, often without a price tag.

I was more relaxed than I've ever been as the ship seemed to glide across the waters. The salt air filled my lungs and ran its fingers through my hair as I sipped yet another incredible rum concoction. There was something about the cruise that relaxed me; maybe because the Brass Cupcake couldn't be farther away from journalism. The world could blow up and I'd say, "Eh, whatever. What time is that chocoholic buffet?"

Oh, several loose ends before I get back to the honeymoon.

- Since Vincent so enjoyed seeing me in the wedding dress I've agreed to put it on once each year on our anniversary, as long as he wears the tuxedo. He was thrilled, though he added, "And it better fit." To which I responded, "So should the tuxedo." The way the man can cook, it might be a tall order.

- Ariel just sent me an email as apparently she hooked up with one of Vincent's cab drivers after the reception. In the back seat of a cab, no less, which would be a scandal if news of that dalliance got back to Connecticut, as old-money girls would never think of giving it up in a car any lesser than a Mercedes. Things got so wild one of her heels flew through the little window between the back seat and the front, hit the meter, turned it on and racked up a ninety-dollar fare making it the first "ride" in New York taxi history in which the cab did not move.

- Despite the rules of the "boost bag" Mrs. Baymont went rogue and sent a traditional gift. Well, actually a truckload full of stuff that I apparently "must have" should I aspire to become the Martha Stewart of Brooklyn. (*Youse take da salad fawk and stab some lettuce. Fuhgeddaboudit!*) She sent a full set of china so I can cook dinner for twenty-four people without breaking out the paper plates, along with assorted tablecloths, napkins, serving trays, you name it. Silver place settings with so many forks I'm going to need a refresher course. Again with the forks.

- Serena spotted a guy she liked at the reception and handed him her business card, inviting him to come by her law firm to "make out a living will free of charge." Uh-huh. Right.

- Roxanne had sparks fly with one of Ariel's friends, a prep school type from Beacon Hill in Boston. Talk about opposites attracting. Anyway, she must be head over heels for this guy because she was taking etiquette and diction lessons from Mrs. Baymont. Who wouldn't love to be a fly on the wall for those sessions? She said she can't wait until I get home so that I can hear her say, "Forget about it," sounding like she's a snob from Massachusetts.

Okay, you're all caught up. Back to the cruise. Our suite was on the shady side of the ship in the afternoon, which was good because I sunburn easily. So I could safely sit outside without the sunblock I usually wore that was strong enough to protect me on the planet Mercury.

The cruise was wonderful. Every morning when we woke up we were docked at a different island. We would spend the morning exploring, then return after lunch to enjoy the ship and sip drinks with umbrellas in them by the pool. (Vincent, by the way, has insisted I wear a bikini on these sojourns, as he likes watching "traffic stop" on the deck. Says it makes him feel like the luckiest man on the planet.) Each night we've shared our assigned table with three other honeymoon couples, all from the New York area, so we have a lot in common. After dinner there's always been entertainment: a magician one night, a Broadway review the next.

My sneaky husband also pulled a fast one on me, as he packed some of my bridal shower "gifts" into his suitcase for after-hours entertainment. Being the football fan that he is, he truly enjoyed the Dallas cheerleader outfit. And while I can take it or leave it when it comes to hot pants, I personally got a kick out of the seven-inch platforms Serena had given me, which took me up to an even six feet. Since she was the one who discovered I didn't own heels, she apparently decided to take things to the extreme and turned me into some sort of glamazon.

There was only one drawback to the ship, and that's the way the room's furniture was aligned with the cabin door. Open any door on the ship and you got a perfect view of the bed. We've had a few interesting peeks at our shipmates while walking by cabins as one person opened a door, not realizing the other passengers were getting a view of their naked significant other. In one case Vincent caught a glimpse of a woman who easily tipped the scales at three hundred pounds who was wearing a thong. He quickly retreated to our cabin, saying he had to rip out his eyeballs to wash away the image or he would not be able to eat dinner.

Anyway, whenever one of us is in the cabin and the other is not, we've developed an early warning system to let the other one know a view of the bed is imminent, and one should cover up. Vincent just went up on deck to get us a snack, even though the ship has free room service 24/7. The man loves waiting on me, and I'm not complaining, though I plan to take my Suzy Homemaker duties to the next level when we return. I had just come inside from the balcony, and was trying to decide which "play clothes" I would be wearing tonight when there was a tap on the door. Could have been the cabin steward, so I threw a robe on over my bikini. But it was a false alarm, as I heard Vincent's voice.

"You decent?" he asked.

"No," I said. "I'm your wife!"